The Plague Road

The Plague Road

L. C. Tyler

FELONY & MAYHEM PRESS • NEW YORK

All the characters and events portrayed in this work are fictitious.

THE PLAGUE ROAD

A Felony & Mayhem mystery

PRINTING HISTORY
First UK edition (Constable): 2016

Felony & Mayhem edition: 2022

ISBN: 978-1-63194-262-4 (hardcover)
ISBN: 978-1-63194-263-1 (paperback)

Manufactured in the United States of America

Cataloging-in-Publication information for this book
is available from the Library of Congress.

To Eleri

A LIST OF PERSONS TO BE FOUND IN THIS BOOK

JOHN GREY—*Myself. A lawyer, of sober habits but in no way a Puritan in spite of what you may be told by...*

AMINTA, LADY POLE—*née Clifford, my childhood friend and tormenter, now a writer of plays much admired by...*

MR SAMUEL PEPYS—*frequenter of the theatres, fondler of actresses, and Clerk at the Navy Office, the loyal creature of...*

THE DUKE OF YORK—*Lord High Admiral, almost-secret Papist and brother to...*

HIS MOST GRACIOUS MAJESTY, KING CHARLES II—*lately restored to his rightful place on the throne of England, Scotland, Ireland and (theoretically) France; well served by his Minister...*

HENRY BENNET—*occasionally my employer, newly ennobled as Lord Arlington and appointed Secretary of State, with responsibility for detecting Treason, as is...*

MR JOSEPH WILLIAMSON—*Arlington's assistant and the only person in this narrative, other than myself, to be wholly trusted, the least dependable including...*

SIR SAMUEL MORLAND—*another assistant, formerly an employee of the now disgraced and posthumously beheaded Lord Protector Cromwell, duplicitous beyond any description I can give or you might believe, as is...*

FATHER HORNCASTLE—*purportedly a priest, who uses many aliases, including my own name for reasons which will become apparent, who may be in the pay of the Dutch (our enemies) or the Spanish (our other enemies) and who claims to have information that will bring down both the Duke of York and his father-in-law...*

EDWARD HYDE, LORD CLARENDON—*the Lord Chancellor, long-time companion-in-exile of the King and enemy of...*

THE DUKE OF BUCKINGHAM—*a somewhat fickle favourite of the King and good friend of his mistress...*

BARBARA, LADY CASTLEMAINE—*the chief (but to her great annoyance not the only) mistress of His Majesty, a friend of actors, such as...*

PATRICK CALLINGHAM—*a member of Lady Pole's company, as is...*

CHARLES FINCHAM—*who is unfortunately dead before the story even begins.*

The icon above says you're holding a copy of a book in the Felony & Mayhem "Historical" category, which ranges from the ancient world up through the 1940s. If you enjoy this book, you may well like other "Historical" titles from Felony & Mayhem Press.

———•◦•———

For more about these books, and other Felony & Mayhem titles, or to place an order, please visit our website at:

www.FelonyAndMayhem.com

Other "Historical" titles from

FELONY&MAYHEM

The Plague Road

Prologue

London—Summer 1665

Jem wrapped his scarf more securely round his face and, in the dancing torchlight, surveyed the desolation before him. This wasn't the sort of work he usually did, but it was work. Regular paid work. And there was little enough of that in London at the moment, what with most of the big houses shut up and all of the gentry fled to the country. It wasn't heavy work either—not like ploughing or haymaking. And it was, you might say, a permanent position, in the sense that it would probably keep him in bread and ale until he died. Jem cautiously pulled the scarf down a couple of inches and repeated the invitation that he had been making all night to the citizens of London.

'Bring out your dead!' he called at the top of his voice. 'Bring out your dead!'

The waggon behind him creaked and groaned as it rolled slowly through the grassy streets, its wheels grinding against the cobbles. It was full, but not too smelly, because they were doing regular collections now and usually got the customers loaded before they started to rot or fall apart too much. You wanted to get them into the cart and out of it again in one piece if you could. Of course they couldn't complain about poor service, being as they were in various stages of putrefaction, but it was a matter of professional pride to Jem that head, body, arms and legs should if possible all go into the same pit, to be reunited in whatever manner God ordained on Judgement Day.

The light from the torches cast a hellish red glow over the lower floors of the shuttered houses. The upper storeys merged into the blackness of the night. No living creature stirred at this hour—not so much as a cat or dog. Jem hadn't seen a cat or a dog for weeks, not since the Lord Mayor had wisely ordered a cull. There were plenty of rats, mainly on account of the lack of cats and dogs, but the cull had been necessary to make the city safe from the pestilence that was now in its third or fourth month—it was tricky saying when it had all started because for a long time nobody had wanted to admit that the Plague was in London, less still that it was in their own house, and the first deaths had been attributed quite imaginatively to all manner of causes. Two groats and a glass of ale got you a death certificate saying 'consumption' or 'impostume of the head', as you preferred; and coffin makers knew better than to enquire about why the deceased (cause of death: 'teeth') was quite so spotty. But Plague wasn't something that could be kept secret for very long. When twenty people died of toothache in the same parish in the same week, folk began to smell a rat. Certainly nobody who strayed into London now could be in any doubt at all that things were not quite as they should be. Houses sealed up. Red crosses on the doors. And an all-pervasive smell of rotting flesh from the ones that nobody had found yet. On the plus side, there was plenty of work in new trades such as Searchers of the Dead and pit diggers and, of course, cart attendants.

'Bring out your dead!' Jem repeated, then, remembering the more artistic part of his duties, he rang the large brass bell that he carried.

Clerkenwell, where Jem came from, was reportedly now as bad as here in Westminster. The Plague was everywhere. He sometimes wondered about his family, whether they were still alive. Since he had become a dead-cart attendant, they didn't ask him to visit so much. At the present rate, everyone would be dead soon everywhere. London would be one big pit of festering corpses, and the last man standing would have to shovel earth over his own head.

He gave the horse's reins a tug, not because there was much point in going faster, but because as the captain of this little team he had to assert his authority from time to time, even if it was only with the horse. On either side of the cart, bearing the flickering torches, tramped Bill and Dick, their faces also covered to protect them from the invisible miasma that, everyone knew, spread the disease. Jem had additionally a bag of cloves round his neck, which he'd been sold as an infallible defence. He was also chewing tobacco because somebody had put round a rumour that no tobacconist had died since the Plague had begun. Trade in tobacco had increased ten-fold and Jem suspected he knew where the rumour had started. Well, he might as well spend his money on that than save it for a rainy day. No point in dying with silver in your purse. He'd need to remind Bill and Dick to check the pockets of the customers on the cart, though he suspected that they had already done so privately before they loaded up. Takings had dropped since Dick joined the team, and Jem reckoned he knew why. Lifting money *after* the corpses had been carried out, and Jem was watching, was a sort of tip for good service. Lifting money *inside the house,* when Jem was busy looking after the horse, was simply wrong in every possible way. Then there was that woman they pitted yesterday. Jem was sure that she'd had a ruby brooch at her throat, but Bill and Dick had said they'd seen nothing at all—maybe a spot of blood? Spot of blood! They must think he was born yesterday.

'A couple more over there,' said Jem, halting the horse by an alleyway. 'Fetch 'em onto the cart.'

Dick peered into the shadows. He could just make out two dark shapes. 'We're full, ain't we?'

'Always room for a couple of small ones,' said Jem charitably.

The two bodies were propped against the wall, as if sleeping off the effects of too much ale, but their wide-open eyes gave evidence that they were not slumbering. Closer inspection revealed that one had the pink face and black fingers you often saw in customers. The other seemed untouched, except he was also dead. That was how it went. You never could tell exactly what the Plague would do to you.

The pink-faced man was starting to bloat up a bit and maybe had been there a little longer than the City Ordinances recommended. But the other looked fresh enough. They carried the fresh one first and dumped him face up on the cart, where he lay with his mouth wide open to the stars. They'd discussed a lot whether face up or face down was more respectful, though customers packed better if you did some one way and some the other. Bill looked at Jem, as if hoping he'd let them off the second one, but Jem shook his head.

'I said, both of them. He'll go on nice if you do him face down on top of the shoemaker's wife. Look lively, now.'

'Can't we leave him for the next cart?'

'No. I told you: fetch him over here. He's not going to get better.'

'It's all right for you. You don't have to touch him. The other one felt a bit...damp.'

'Damp? There's been no rain for weeks. Just get on with it. Unless you'd prefer to starve on the street. Plenty of others queuing up for a job like yours. Regular hours. No heavy lifting.'

'He may not be heavy but he'll fall apart if we move him.'

'He'll certainly fall apart if you don't.'

Jem leaned against the cart and watched carefully as the last corpse was loaded. The man balanced corpulently on top of the heap, inflated by gases within but still in one piece. If there was money on either of those two, Jem thought to himself, he was having his share this time. And a share in the price of that ruby if he could prove Bill had taken it.

'Time to go to the pit, lads,' he said. 'We're full now.'

In fact they picked up another three as they trundled onwards to the nearest of the new Plague pits in Tothill Fields, the cool night air on their faces. It wasn't bad work, if you could just keep healthy yourself.

Jem oversaw the unloading, holding both of the torches aloft, watching carefully to see whether the other two found anything worth pocketing.

'Gently now!' he called, from a safe distance. 'These are Christian men and women. Have some respect there.'

Dick nodded as he and Bill tipped the cart, then respectfully prodded the bodies off with long poles, rolling them onwards into the dreadful chasm. One by one they dropped over the edge and joined their fellow citizens in the deep blackness below.

'Wait!' called Jem suddenly.

There was something odd about that last one. Something he couldn't quite put his finger on. Something he had spotted as the body performed its final turn before being flicked on its way to eternal rest. Something that caught the orange light of the burning brands. Something that had impeded the customer's proper rotation. Something, in summary, that should not have been there. All three looked down from the edge of the muddy chasm at one body amongst the hundreds that lay below them in every possible posture.

'What's that thing sticking out of his back?' Jem demanded.

'I'm not going down into that pit just so you can have the knife,' said Dick. 'It can't be worth more than a shilling.'

'That's not my point,' said Jem. 'I mean, *why* is there a knife sticking out of that customer's back?'

'I don't know,' said Dick. 'Could be all sorts of reasons.'

'Get him back up here.'

'Why?'

'He don't belong there.'

'But he's dead, ain't he?'

'Yes.'

'And that's a grave, ain't it?'

'Yes.'

'So, what's wrong with that?'

'That pit,' said Jem, 'is for customers who've died of the Plague. You don't get to be buried there—free and at the City's expense—if you've died of something else. Stands to reason. Everybody would die of the Plague if you allowed that.'

'What if we didn't notice the knife? We didn't see it in the dark—not until he landed on his front. And that's the honest truth.'

'So you say. Well, we have all seen it now, haven't we? More than my job's worth to bury him here.'

'We could just chuck another customer or two on top of him…'

'No.'

'You fetch him out then,' said Dick bravely. 'If you want him so much, you do it.'

'You threw him in. You fetch him out,' said Jem.

The logic was irrefutable. So, with a very bad grace, and trusting in the light cast by two now guttering torches, Dick lowered himself carefully into the pit and began the joyful process of resurrection.

CHAPTER

1

Apart from the Plague, it is a perfect summer's day.

From here, from this high, breezy casement looking out over Lincoln's Inn Fields, the sky is a deep, untroubled blue. The trees have long since passed from their pastel spring green to the rich dark foliage of midsummer. The pale, brittle, sun-scorched grass crackles underfoot. Heat trickles visibly from the stone paths. You can almost feel it from up here, through this wide-open window with its tiny, diamond-shaped leaded panes.

'*Mr Grey?*'

Far below me, a small black figure begins to trudge across the broad expanse of bleached-out grass. He pauses and wipes his brow, but I cannot see his expression. I am curious about that.

'*Mr Grey?*'

The man looks around him, then his legs seem to crumple and he falls to the ground. I wait to see if anyone will go to his aid, but nobody does. But I wasn't expecting anyone to do so. Welcome to London in the summer of 1665.

'*Mr Grey*, I think you might give me a little attention in view of the money I am paying you. Mr Grey, I am *most* displeased.'

I turn from the bright sunshine and let my eyes adjust to the gloomy shade of my room. My displeased visitor is seated by my cold, dusty fireplace in a well-cushioned chair. He is plump and rural and red-faced, and he is still slightly out of breath from his ascent to my chambers. The dust of the Essex road is on his clothes, for he has not tarried at an inn before coming to see me. He wishes to conclude his business and be gone as soon as he reasonably can. I think that the presence of the Plague in London worries him more than a little.

'Mr Grey,' he demands, 'have you been listening to a single word that I have said to you? You appear regrettably distracted. You seem to think that the view through your window is of greater interest than your clients. Clients on whom you depend for your living, sir. Well, let me tell you that I have no intention of paying your outrageous fees if you treat me with such disdain and...'

I hold up my hand.

'What?' he says.

'In 1601,' I say, 'your grandfather, William Ruggles, made a will leaving his estate to the male heirs of his body, named as John, Christopher and Andrew. In 1602 your father, George Ruggles, was born. On the death of your grandfather in 1642, the will was unaltered and John and Andrew held that, being the only named heirs surviving, the estate should be split between them in equal parts. Your father argued that he was nonetheless a male heir, for all that he had not been named, and threatened to take his brothers to court for his rightful share of one third, Christopher having died unmarried, albeit with four bastard children who, being too poor to be able to afford the services of a lawyer, need not detain us further. Am I correct so far?'

'You have a good memory, I grant you...'

'Thank you,' I say. 'I do indeed have a good memory. What else did you tell me? I think you said next that your father was, after much discussion, offered, and may well have accepted, one quarter of the estate as a compromise, while the other two surviving brothers took three eighths each. Without any written record being made of this agreement, your father departed for the wars then afflicting this country and perished at the siege of (I believe you said) Hull, though frankly it would have made no difference in law if it was Bristol or Vienna. He left his entire estate to you, which you argue should, in the absence of any extant agreement to the contrary, be the one third of your grandfather's estate originally claimed. The case is complicated by the sequestration of the estate of John Ruggles by Parliament in 1650 and a counter-claim by him that you promised, in the event that the King should not restore confiscated Cavalier estates, that his losses might be made good from the inheritance of the previously deceased brother, Christopher, less any pittance that might regrettably have to go to the bastards. A charitable offer that does you much credit and that you deny, in the most absolute terms, ever making. That was the point that you had reached in your interesting story. Have I missed anything of any importance?'

I fear that he now realises how much of his earlier sarcasm was wasted. Of course, as you will have worked out from my meticulous reiteration of the case, I am paid by the hour.

'My dead uncle's name was Christian,' he says. 'And he had only three bastards.'

'Thank you. He showed commendable restraint. But have I missed anything of importance?' I ask.

'No,' he says. 'You have missed nothing of importance. I apologise, Mr Grey, for questioning you thus. I had thought you were not listening, that you were finding what I said dull, that you thought me stupid or the case beneath you...'

'I was listening,' I say. I never tire of it.

'So, do you wish me to continue?'

'You are at leave to speak for as long as you wish.'

'Thank you,' he says.

'Not at all,' I say, checking my pocket watch.

Very slowly I turn back to the window. The small black figure has now seated himself beneath one of the elms, possibly because it is hot, or possibly because he feels unwell. I wonder which it is?

'I don't know how you can stand it,' Ruggles says.

I face him again and smile enquiringly. He is mopping his brow with a large and rather dirty kerchief.

'The terrible quiet, I mean,' he adds. 'The hideous silence all around. Listen, sir! When I was last in London, I was deafened by the constant din. I thought the noise alone would drive me home to Essex, even without the casual fraud and extortion that I met at every hand. Now what can you hear?'

I hear the wholly pleasant sound of the wind in the trees, and a gentle squeak as my casement window shifts on its unoiled hinges, but that is not what he means.

'Nothing,' I say. 'I can hear nothing.'

'Precisely. As I was coming here, through the City,' he says, 'the streets were so noiseless and deserted…it was eerie, sir…it was unnatural. It was as if I was passing through some phantom habitation of the dead. I swear I could make out the noise of the water rushing through the arches of London Bridge, half a mile away.'

'You could,' I say. 'When the wind is in the right direction and the tide is running fast between the great buttresses. Since Plague gripped the city, it has been thus. This is the peaceful slumber before London's final death rattle.'

Then, in the distance, to contradict us both, a bell starts to toll. We listen, at my standard hourly rate, to its slow, deep, repetitive song. After a while it stops. I check my pocket watch again.

'Another poor soul gone to his maker,' says Ruggles.

'Hopefully he has left a will that is clearer than your grandfather's,' I say.

'You jest, Mr Grey.'

'Of course I do,' I say. 'Whatever goods he has left will most certainly have been stolen by those who have been nursing him, or will be plundered by thieves during the funeral.'

'The dead are still accorded funerals here?' Ruggles asks. 'Thank God for that.'

'Sometimes,' I say. 'In most City parishes people are still buried as before with some dignity, though mourners are, of course, forbidden. In the outer parishes, however, beyond the walls, men must share their graves as they do a bed at a busy inn on the King's Highway. The old churchyards are so crammed with bodies that the ground is three feet higher than it was last year. New Plague pits are being dug everywhere, but soon even they will be full.'

I see Ruggles shudder. This is all still a novelty to him. In Essex the Plague is no more than a distant rumour, like unicorns and camelopards. 'I was told of the pits...for those who have died of the pestilence. Christian men and women thrown or just tipped in. One naked body promiscuously on top of another. The horror of such a burial... To think of your wife or your daughter thus...'

'The dead themselves are untroubled,' I say. 'And it saves their families much needless expense.'

'You are hardened to it, sir,' he says. 'Have all Londoners become as unfeeling as you are?'

'You should visit a pit while you are here,' I say. 'They are most instructive. Better than a sermon if you wish to contemplate your own mortality. Men come away weeping and repenting of their sins.'

'No, thank you,' he says. 'I already have sufficient reminders that death is imminent for us all. But have you done so, sir? Visited a pit, I mean.'

'I might have done,' I say.

'But surely you wouldn't forget that?'

'No,' I say, 'you wouldn't forget that.'

He's right, of course. You don't forget your first visit to a pit. I remember the hot sun and the stench of rotting flesh, so strong that you might have seized handfuls of it. I remember the dead cart backing up to the pit with great care, inch by inch, then the tail gate being lowered and the bodies pitched out, some in shrouds, some in their day clothes, some stark naked, rolling over each other in a strange race to the edge of the pit and beyond. I remember the wet thud as each body fell six feet or so onto the layer of corpses that was already there. I advanced, purely out of curiosity, as far as the edge of the pit and looked down. A hundred souls at least were already packed into the space. Dozens of blind eyes looked up at me. Then there was a scream behind me and something hurtled past, almost taking me along with it.

'Live one in the pit!' somebody yelled. 'Stop shovelling, lads!'

The carter, who had been watching the last of his load being pushed over the edge, turned to see who had jumped in. He tapped out his pipe on the wheel of the cart and pointed the stem at the man below him. 'I hope you don't mind me asking, but are you planning to stay there, sir?'

The jumper, a middle-aged gentleman in a mulberry-coloured suit, was now kneeling on the last layer of corpses and looking around helplessly. 'Where is she?' he asked.

'Who's that then, sir?' asked the carter politely.

'My wife. She was on the cart. You took her. I gave her up to your care, you bastard. I thought there would be some form of burial—a priest, some prayers—not that you would just tip her in like…like…'

He was rightly lost for words. I also had nothing to compare this to. I have seen dogs buried with greater ceremony, though not recently.

'We have no time to do it in any other way, sir,' said the carter. 'No disrespect intended. It's the same for all. Beggars and harlots and lords and ladies alike, you might say. It is not a lack of respect for your good lady, sir, just a lack of time. And you were strictly instructed not to accompany us. We did warn you. It isn't pleasant here—not if you're not used to it, as we are. Can I help you out of the pit, sir? It can't be comfortable down there. And it's not very respectful to the ladies and gentlemen you're kneeling on.'

'I have no wish to live,' said the man. 'My daughter, my wife… All dead. Bury me with them. Do you hear me? Just shovel the earth on top of me until I suffocate. Entomb me with those I love. Let the worms that consume them consume me.'

'So, just to be clear, you'd like to stay down there, then?'

'Leave me,' said the man. 'Leave me to my grief.'

'As you wish, sir,' said the carter. 'But, if you were to change your mind, I have to point out that they'll be filling in soon.'

'Good,' said the man. 'And I hope you and the rest of your crew rot in Hell.'

'So, what are we to do?' asked one of the men with the shovels. 'We can't bury him alive. It wouldn't be Christian.'

'It's not my affair what you do,' said the carter, who already had hold of the reins of his horse. 'My contract is with the dead. I bring full carts and take away empty ones. Once they hit the ground, they're no concern of mine. Ask the lawyer if you don't believe me.'

The digger looked at me hopefully.

'If you bury him alive it would probably be murder,' I said. 'He may have requested it, but he is not in his right mind. No charge for the advice.'

'Are you sure of that, sir? I mean, that it would be murder?'

'Another lawyer would doubtless give you a completely different opinion. So, do bury him if you wish. It's all the same to me. And in all probability nobody will notice. But if I were you, I'd leave him as he is.'

The digger looked at me resentfully. He'd hoped the law would be slightly less ambivalent and more as he wished. It's something that most of my clients hope for.

'But we'll lose our positions if we don't cover the bodies with soil,' said the man with the spade. 'That's what the Ordinances say. Can't you use legal trickery to make him come out of the hole, sir? It's not fair on us, sir. We shouldn't have to bury the living, sir. They don't pay us enough for that.'

'Shovel earth on the rest of the pit, in accordance with the City Ordinances,' I said. 'Just give the gentleman a light sprinkling, which should serve to protect the public until he is dead or decides to come out. And that's all the free legal advice I'm giving today.'

As I left the field I could hear the sound of earth being thrown about. I had cause to return a couple of days later. The pit was full and the ground levelled. Nobody could remember if the gentleman had chosen to come out or stay in.

'Yes,' I say to Mr Ruggles. 'I have visited a pit. The Plague has not yet reached your own village in Essex, I assume?'

'May it please God, it shall never reach it,' he says with much feeling. 'We pray most earnestly in church every Sunday for deliverance. I pray. My wife prays. The servants pray on our behalf if we can't attend in person. The pestilence has stayed away so far. God watches over Essex.'

'That's what we thought in the City,' I say. 'Nobody could have prayed harder that the Plague should strike any rather than ourselves. For a long time it seemed as if God had heard us and that He would smite only the outlying parishes beyond the city wall. Now, house by house, street by street, the disease is taking over every ward and every parish here too and making the City its own. God is listening to the supplications of others.'

'Lincoln's Inn seems empty.'

'There is little work for lawyers, except for wills and the attendant litigation.'

'They say the doctors have left too.'

'Not all. But they are obliged to go where their patients go, and the rich have fled. There would be little point in their staying in the City if nobody can afford their services—they would simply be idle. The poor can die well enough without their assistance.'

'If the poor are dying, then they have nobody to blame but themselves. An alderman I know has assured me that the Plague has spread entirely because of the filthy habits of the lower-class inhabitants.'

'An alderman told you? Then it must be true,' I say.

Ruggles looks at me suspiciously. 'I think you mock me, Mr Grey,' he says. 'I have no intention of paying you for your sarcasm, sir.'

'Rest assured, I shall not charge you for it,' I say. 'Consider it a gift. My fees are precisely as we have agreed. No more, no less. And I think you have a good case—or a winnable one anyway.'

'My alderman friend said you were the best lawyer in London,' says Ruggles grudgingly.

'I am possibly the only lawyer in London,' I say.

'Why do you remain, Mr Grey? When I reached the gates of the city, I could scarce force my way through, so many carts and carriages were trying to leave. I am told that the River Thames is full of ships, sir, from London Bridge down to Woolwich, to which people have fled, and that they now live on the water to avoid contact with their fellow men. They say a forest of masts fills the river.'

I shake my head. 'You should not believe everything you hear,' I say. 'I have never seen the forest you refer to. But you are right that London will soon be empty.'

'Precisely. You are not a native of London. You have a family elsewhere. Indeed, you come from the same salubrious part of the country that I do. Why not leave here while you are still in good health and can get a certificate to travel?'

I ponder this question. It has also occurred to me from time to time. The small black figure in the street below has now stretched himself out under the shade of the elm. He is very still. One might almost think he is holding his breath. A woman, crossing the field, sees him and changes direction a little, perhaps not wishing to disturb his repose. She hurries off, with her shawl wrapped round her nose and mouth.

'I stay because I want to,' I say. 'You, conversely, I think, wish to be away as soon as you can. I shall not detain you, Mr Ruggles. I'll consult some precedents concerning your case and then write to you in salubrious Essex. The post is still working and there is little to be done anyway while this pestilence rages.

Once it is over, we shall summon your uncles to appear and give an account of themselves before a judge.'

'Is that all?'

'No,' I say, 'you will leave the fee for this consultation with my clerk as you pass his room. He will tell you how much, for I cannot; it is not considered gentlemanly to know how much gold you are about to pocket for your services. My clerk will then unlock the gates of Lincoln's Inn and let you out. And, as you cross Lincoln's Inn Fields, I would advise you to avoid at all costs the man lying under a tree. He is not well.'

'Thank you,' he says.

'I am delighted to be of service,' I say.

After Mr Ruggles has gone, I call my clerk.

'Paid, two guineas, Mr Grey,' he says. 'Genuine gold with the King's head newly stamped on it. None of your old Republican coin with that man Oliver scowling at us. I'm pleased to note that you are demanding cash and no longer leaving the submission of your bills to a month end that many will never live to see.'

'Take both guineas for yourself and go to the country, Will,' I say. 'It's safer outside London and there's little enough work for either of us here.'

'I'll stay as long as you do, Mr Grey,' he replies. 'And thank you for the offer, but I've already put the money in the strongbox and recorded it in the ledger. In any case there is some work for you, I think.'

'Not another case like Mr Ruggles, I hope. If so, I shall die of boredom long before the Plague carries me off.'

'Not at all,' says Will. 'Lord Arlington's man called while you were closeted with Mr Ruggles. My Lord presents his compliments and requests your company as soon as is convenient. He has a dead body that he thinks may amuse you.'

CHAPTER 2

Henry Bennet, Lord Arlington, is pleased with himself. That is his normal state. I have never seen him otherwise. He is not handsome, but happily he does not know this. He does moreover enhance the appearance of his face in an interesting way. He wears, over the bridge of his nose, a black plaster, covering an insignificant wound received at a battle some twenty years ago. The plaster is slender and quite elegantly shaped—on his nose it forms a sort of crescent moon that sheds no light on anything. It cannot possibly be necessary to protect so old an injury, but he is never without it. It is a thing of greater import than the decorative patches that fashionable ladies have taken to wearing all the time. It serves to remind the King, who is forgetful, that Arlington has been of service to two generations of the House of Stuart. He has not merely been wounded, but he has been wounded on the nose. Not on his back. Not merely on his front. Arlington loyally stuck the very foremost part of his anatomy into the King's affairs. That is the meaning of the patch. A simple scar—clean, inconspicuous, well healed—would not suffice. Not at all. Beneath his nose, like a reflection of the plaster, is a small, neat moustache, which I think is trimmed daily.

'I am grateful, Mr Grey, that you were able to free yourself from your extensive legal practice,' he says, gently touching the nose patch with his forefinger.

'My clients are all elsewhere,' I say. 'Well, most of them.'

'What a pity for you. You have gained quite a reputation of late. You should be reaping the just rewards of your labours.'

Flattery of any sort from Arlington puts me on my guard.

'I do well enough,' I say. 'I understand that you have work for me?'

'If it would interest you, Mr Grey.'

'I would have thought that you had enough agents of your own these days. You don't need my help.'

'I am not John Thurloe,' says Arlington. 'Do you know how much Cromwell gave my predecessor to spend each year on running his network of agents? Seventy thousand Pounds! That's what Mr Secretary Thurloe had in order to undertake espionage for the Protectorate. Things have changed, sir. As Secretary of State for the Southern Department I currently share with my colleague in the Northern Department an allocation of fourteen hundred Pounds. Yes, that's right, fourteen *hundred*. His Majesty generously allocates the two of us one-fiftieth part of Thurloe's budget. The King places a very low value on deceit and deception, sir.'

'And how much of that jointly owned fourteen hundred Pounds do you spend?' I ask.

'All of it,' says Arlington smugly. 'Sir William Morrice is a fool. Taking his share is like taking a baby's rattle.'

'And you would not hesitate to take a baby's rattle?'

'Not if I had a better use for it than the baby.'

'Good,' I say, 'because my services, as you know, are not cheap.'

'I saw your last bill. Very nicely itemised.'

'I have a good clerk. He tells me that you have found a body. I would have thought that was a job for the magistrates.'

'The circumstances of discovering this one were unusual. The gentleman concerned had been stabbed in the back and then transferred in an irregular and unauthorised manner onto the dead cart for transportation to the pits. Only the eagle eyes of the carter prevented his burial with many other people.'

'Deplorable deception by somebody. I assume you rewarded the carter?'

'He is already amply remunerated by the parish. The disappointment he expressed was excessive and out of place.'

'His work is doubtless easy and pleasant. But I still don't see why this should concern you as the Secretary of State. Or me. Do you wish me to make enquiries and find out who the gentleman is? I would have thought there were cheaper ways of doing it.'

'We know only too well who it is,' says Arlington.

'Then I certainly don't see why I am needed.'

'Then pay attention, Mr Grey, and you shall. The man's name was Charles Fincham. He was undertaking a mission to the French Ambassador.'

'So, I can see there are diplomatic considerations...'

'Let me finish, please, Mr Grey. He was no ordinary messenger. He was an actor in the Duke of York's Company.'

'A man of many talents.'

'He was formerly a soldier in both the Royalist and the Parliamentary forces.'

'Many men were.'

'He was also one of my agents—or a paid informant, at least.'

'I begin to see the problem,' I say.

'Not yet you don't,' says Arlington with a patronising smile. 'That our informants should have more than one occupation, and indeed name; that they should have much in the past that they properly wish to conceal from us: all of that is perfectly normal. It would not distress me in any way. Our immediate concern is that when last seen by us he was about to convey a letter from His

Royal Highness the Duke of York to His Excellency the French Ambassador. He was supposed to take it first to one of my people so that it could, unknown to either party, be secretly copied. The entire journey, including the detour to our office, should have lasted half an hour. But he never arrived at our office and the letter was never delivered to the French Ambassador. Had the magistrates not been informed of his attempted admission to the Westminster Plague pit, we might never have discovered what had happened to him.'

'But you now have your Mr Fincham back?'

'On a purely temporary basis, until his reburial. I shall not require him any longer than that.'

'So all is well.'

'But we do not have the letter. It was not on his body. We have searched the pit. We have searched the place where his body was apparently loaded onto the cart. It is nowhere to be found. The weather has been dry. The streets are uncrowded. The good folk of London are honest—or, more to the point, the letter will have appeared to have no value. It should have been possible to recover it in good condition. But we have not done so.'

'I can see that it might be inconvenient if the Ambassador failed to receive it, but the Duke could be requested to send it again?'

'That might suggest to the Duke that we were aware he had sent the letter and that we knew his messenger was dead.'

'Which you would prefer he did not know?'

'Not until we discover what was in the letter.'

'You suspect that the contents are not to the Duke's credit?'

'It is possible that is the case.'

'Did the King know that his brother, the Duke, was in correspondence with the French?'

'I imagine it would have surprised him greatly.'

'So you haven't told the King?'

'Not as yet. Until we know what was in the letter, it is a rather delicate matter. Perhaps he would welcome our discovery that his brother was in secret and possibly treasonous correspon-

dence with the French and congratulate us on our diligence…
or perhaps he might think our interest in a member of his own
family impertinent… Kings can be capricious and often know
only with hindsight what their instructions to us were. We, on
the other hand, have to know in advance.'

'Am I now permitted to say that I see the problem?' I enquire.

'I would certainly hope you do,' says Arlington. He touches
the black plaster on his nose again. He does not realise that I
know he does this when he is worried about something, and I
shall not embarrass him by telling him that I know.

'Am I to search the whole of London for the letter? I warn
you that I charge by the hour.'

'I warn you that I shall be paying a fixed rate for the job,
Mr Grey. Those are my terms and they are not negotiable. Return
the letter and you get the fee. And you will not need to search the
whole of London—just make enquiries in two or three places, to
which I shall direct you.'

'Where should I make my enquiries then?' I ask.

'You know Sir Samuel Morland?' he asks.

'I knew him as Mr Morland, in the days when we both
worked for Cromwell. But titles are handed out freely now to any
fool who will make himself serviceable to the King.'

My Lord Arlington, whose own barony is still very new,
gives me a thin smile.

'He now works for me,' he says curtly. 'It was to Morland
that Fincham was to take the letter for copying. He has information that will help you.'

'Then I shall most certainly speak with him. Thank you.'

'You will find him at the General Letter Office in Post
House Yard. That's near—'

'I know where it is,' I say.

'And you should speak to the author of the play that
Fincham was to appear in,' he adds.

'What is his name?' I ask.

'Lady Pole,' says Arlington, smugly correcting me. 'I think
you know her too?'

'A little,' I say.

'You come from the same village in Essex, I think?'

'I have not seen her for many years.'

'But you have attended some of her plays?'

'Out of curiosity.'

'Merely curiosity?'

'Comedy teaches little of value.'

'Perhaps you do not approve of women writing for the theatre?' he says.

'If Aminta Pole wishes to write plays, it would be a brave man who told her not to.'

'He would also be a fool. She has talent. She has, like you, gained a considerable reputation of late. In her own admittedly lesser field.'

'We both labour with our pens,' I say. 'Though her work involves slightly less inventiveness than mine. I concede she writes well.'

'So, you *do* admire her plays?'

'I do not have time to frequent theatres,' I say. 'So, I cannot judge them as you can, my Lord.'

'I never suspected that you did frequent the theatres, Mr Grey. There is nothing in your appearance of the theatre-goer. But you know the lady and that is far more important. Seek her out. Flatter her. Praise her writing. Gain her confidence. See what she will tell you. She may let something slip to you that she would not to me.'

'I have never known Aminta let anything slip that she did not intend to let slip,' I say. 'Least of all to me.'

'Then just ask her about Fincham—what he was in the habit of doing, who she saw him talking to, whether he had any enemies.'

'My fee will be a hundred sovereigns plus expenses,' I say.

I wait for him to offer less. Much less.

'Agreed,' he says.

We shake hands on it.

Arlington laughs. 'I would have paid you two hundred had you asked,' he says. 'It is a pity that we have now shaken on it, but there it is. As a lawyer I would have thought you would have been more cautious.'

'And you have placed no limit on my expenses,' I say. 'As a minister of the King, I would have thought that you might have felt it prudent to do that. But as you point out, my Lord, we have shaken on it and there is now no remedy.'

Arlington's mask of suave diplomacy slips for an instant. 'Report to me as soon as you have some information,' he snaps.

'And you really have no idea what the letter contains?'

'No,' he says.

'Then you are paying a lot when it may be no more than an invitation to dine.'

Arlington reaches into his pocket and takes out a silver snuffbox. He carefully raises the lid, pinches some snuff onto the back of his hand and breathes it in. He stifles a sneeze. Then, refreshed, he turns his attention to me again.

'Just get me the letter, Mr Grey, and bring it back to me. Unopened. Please note that. Unopened. If you want your money.'

'I am, as ever, your servant in all things, my Lord,' I say.

CHAPTER
3

Between Arlington's door and the end of the road I pass only two people—a matched pair of old women in grubby dresses and stained aprons, carrying gleaming white rods prominently before them. These sixpenny wands of office, newly painted, show that they are both 'Searchers of the Dead', appointed by the parish to seek out and report all deaths. Small, insignificant, largely edentate and wholly illiterate, these women are feared almost as much as the Plague itself. They are the eyes and ears of the authorities. It is on their word that a death in your household will be classified as 'Plague'. It is on their word that a red cross will be painted on your door, with the invocation, 'Lord have mercy on our souls' writ beneath. It is on their word that your house, and everyone in it, will be sealed up for forty days with the front door padlocked and an armed guard placed before it to prevent your leaving or any unauthorised person entering. It is they who will cause you to be placed at the mercy of the said guard as to whether you receive food or not during your incarceration and also to be placed at the mercy of a nurse, paid in full by you but thoughtfully appointed by the parish, a person with no medical knowledge and poor personal hygiene, who will watch night and day to see where you have hidden your valuables, in case the hour arrives when you no longer have need of them. These Searchers are all-powerful but they are also wholly bribable and their price is as yet still quite low. For a few shillings a lying report may be obtained, and you and your family may remain at large to infect your neighbours with the Plague or anything else. And why not? If you don't give your neighbours the Plague, somebody else will. I touch my hat to them politely and they give me toothless smiles in return.

'Any dead ones in your street, sir?' asks one. 'Or a bit sickly, maybe?'

'It's only a matter of time for us all,' I reply. 'But Lincoln's Inn remains for the moment in good health, God be praised. If I notice any dead lawyers, I'll ensure you are the first to know about it.'

'Thank you kindly, sir,' she replies.

'May the Lord have mercy upon us, every one,' adds the other devoutly. 'And on our sinful souls.'

'Amen to that,' says the first. Then they both giggle like young girls, and are on their way. The Plague has changed their lives for the better. They will never be this important again, and they know it. The requirement that they live apart from other people when not performing their duties is no hardship to them.

I head along the Strand, towards Post House Yard, where I shall find Sir Samuel Morland. It is with relief that I pass through the great brick arch of Ludgate and into the City. The Plague, as I said to Ruggles, has found its way inside the walls, but it is still relatively rare in these narrow streets for all that. Even here, however, people progress in a strange corkscrew motion along the street—first one side and then the other, to avoid contact with those approaching. Anyone might have the Plague, and most of those who do have it won't know until they collapse onto the cobblestones, clutching their guts in both hands. There are two ways of dying of the Plague—quickly and slowly. I have never stayed to watch anyone die slowly, though you often accidentally hear cries of pain from deep inside the shut-up houses. But I have seen a man die quickly of the Plague: well at dinner time, then, having discovered the scarlet tokens of the disease on his skin during the afternoon, dead by supper time—perhaps of shock as much as anything else. They called it lucky that he suffered so little.

But, today, I need to cross the road only occasionally to avoid another politely cautious citizen. This is a ghost city. The gentry have left and many of the tradesmen have closed up their shops and factories. Blank shutters, barred with iron, guard the windows until their owners return. We who remain go out as little as we can, passing quickly from our home to our place of work or from our place of work to the marketplace. Because, for all our bravado, everyone is afraid all the time. Anyone can give you the Plague at any moment—your wife, your child, your butcher, your baker, your candlestick maker, your landlord, your housemaid, and above all the nurse appointed by the parish to take care of your family.

Many sure cures and preventatives are on sale. I notice from a bill pasted to the wall that John Sly at the sign of the Blazing Star in Aldgate is offering to provide me with an excellent drink of sovereign virtue, used in the time of the last Plague and approved by eminent physicians (strangely, unnamed). Henry Eversden at the Greyhound will sell me Dr Theodore de Medde's famous Antipharmacon for 3*d* or a Universal Elixir at 2/6 per 5-oz. glass. Mr Francis Hall at the Green Dragon in Cheapside has available an excellent electuary at 12*d* an ounce 'by appointment of His Majesty, the College of Physicians of London and by their special care and advice'. Powdered toad is also rumoured to be effective, though opinion is divided over whether it should be eaten or hung round the neck in a muslin bag. Then there are lozenges in many different colours. All apparently completely effective. With so much good physic on offer, it is, on reflection, a wonder that anyone need ever die.

I cross the road to avoid passing too close to a door with a red cross painted on it, only to find myself right by another such door on the opposite side. As I approach it, the door opens suddenly and a young woman in a ragged grey dress appears, carrying a large sack on her shoulders. We both draw back slightly, trying to sum up as quickly as possible the danger that we may each pose to the other. Then she smiles at me.

'Don't be afeared, sir; it's not me that's got the Plague. It's them inside. I'm just the nurse, going about my lawful business.'

It is the word 'lawful' that I find suspicious.

'What's in the sack?' I demand.

'Just old clothes and bedding, sir. I'm taking them to be burned, one of my employers having sadly died of the Plague a moment or two ago.' She wipes away what might well be a tear.

'That's good of you,' I say.

'No, really, sir. That's all that is in there and that's the plain truth. I'm no thief, sir. I'll open the sack for you. You can rummage around in the shit-covered, Plague-infected bedding that somebody's just died in as much as you like, sir.'

She makes no attempt to lower the sack to the ground. She is not expecting me to say that that is what I would like to do.

'Are they all dead, your people?'

'Yes, sir. Whole family. May they rest in peace. God's honest truth, sir. Not a scrap of breath in any one of 'em.' She dares to give me a conspiratorial grin.

'Really?' I say.

'As God is my witness. But why not go inside the house and see for yourself, sir, if you so wish? I'm not going to stop you.'

I shake my head. If she doesn't rob her former employer, somebody else will very shortly. And, if not, the Brokers of the Dead (another profitable new line of business) will seize any goods, nominally on behalf of the parish but on terms that are quite generous to the brokers themselves. She may as well have whatever is in the bundle. If her employers are dead.

'Don't sell any silver too cheaply,' I say to her. 'Get them to weigh it and check the weight yourself. Don't let them put their thumb on the scales. They're all a pack of thieves in Westminster and they'll steal the coat off your back if you let them.'

'You have to make your money as best you can in these times, sir,' she replies. 'The pawnbrokers are crooks, to be sure, but fair play to them all the same. They have to feed their children, like the rest of us.'

As I walk on, I think I hear a groan behind me, from inside the house that has no living people in it. A year ago, hearing that groan, I would have gone in at once to see if I could be of assistance. I would have fetched a doctor.

But it is not a year ago. It is today, and everything has changed. Changed in a way we would never have foreseen. And perhaps, thinking about it, I must have just imagined that groan. I watch the woman make off down the street with her sack. The old bedding makes a merry clinking sound. London will never be the same again. We shall never be the same again.

CHAPTER

4

I am not sure whether Sir Samuel Morland has come up in the world or whether the world has declined around him. He has possession of two rooms at the General Letter Office—the centre of his web of intrigue. But, as Arlington said, his trade is no longer valued as it once was. Few fear Morland. Even fewer respect him. Changing sides has gained him no friends. He is, it is true, now a Knight; but he is not a Knight of the Garter, as he had devoutly wished to be. The blue sash has been denied him. The King had to draw the line somewhere. Still, Morland seems happy in his current job, secretly intercepting, reading and copying other people's letters for his new masters. It is what he enjoys doing.

In many ways, in fact, he is still the same old Morland that I knew six or seven years ago: smooth-skinned, sleek-haired and, like Arlington, pleased enough with the world and more than pleased enough with himself. Nobody knows his trade as well as he does.

'Do you know how Dorislaus used to open letters in the old days?' he asks me, flicking back a lock of blond hair. 'A hot knife under the seal! Can you imagine? Then, when the letter had been read and copied, he'd just put a dab of new molten wax under the old wax and send it on its way, expecting that nobody would notice any difference in colour or texture.'

'So, how do you do it?' I ask.

'I have perfected the Spanish method,' he says. 'You can open a letter and re-seal it with no possibility of discovery. Arlington gave me a sealed letter of his own as a test. I opened it, made three copies, sealed all four and asked him if he could tell me which was the original.'

'And could he?' I ask—though there would be little point in the story if the answer were: 'Yes, unfortunately he did and I looked an idiot.'

'No,' says Morland, smirking at me. 'He could *not*, sir. Arlington stared at one and then the other and then the remaining two. "Sir Samuel," he says to me at length, "it is the third letter." "No," I say. "Then it is most certainly the first," he says. "Wrong again, my Lord," I say. "Then it is the last one," he says. "Not that one either," I replied to him.'

'At that point did he guess it was the second?' I ask.

'I am not implying that Arlington is a fool,' Morland snaps. 'And I would advise you not to mock him either. He pays both of us. Indeed, he has set me up here, with instructions to open and copy whatever I see fit—any letter that I believe may be treasonous.'

'That must be time-consuming,' I say. 'With so many traitors in our midst.'

'Not at all,' smiles Morland. I think he may be about to boast to me again. 'I have also perfected a way of copying letters very quickly. A side of paper takes only a minute for two or three copies.'

'A minute? Why, Sir Samuel, how can that be?' I ask, because that is what I am expected to say, and in the long run it will save time to say it.

'I know and the King knows and my Lord Arlington knows,' says Morland. 'And that is all that ever shall know.'

'I congratulate you, Sir Samuel,' I say.

'A skilful Prince ought to make a watch tower of his General Post Office. That is what I have done for His Majesty. All of the mail passes through here. There are eight clerks of the road who deal with mails on the six great highways to Holyhead, Bristol, Plymouth, Edinburgh, Yarmouth and Dover. Domestic mail leaves on Tuesdays, Thursdays and Saturdays. It arrives on Mondays, Wednesdays and Fridays. Mail for France, Italy and Spain leaves on Mondays and Thursdays. Mail for the Low Countries and Germany on Mondays and Fridays. The timing of return mails from abroad is of course less certain, depending as it does on tides and winds…but perhaps that is not what you have come to discuss?'

'I do of course find your discourse on the postal service of immense interest. I could happily listen to it all day—indeed I already feel I have. But my Lord wishes me to discover the where-abouts of a certain letter that has gone missing. It was carried not by the post but by a certain Mr Fincham. It was coming from the Duke of York and intended for the French Ambassador.'

Morland nods. 'We know Mr Fincham. He visits us from time to time. He is moreover mentioned in other letters that we have intercepted.'

He goes to a drawer and selects a bundle of papers, which he proceeds to riffle through. Eventually he pulls one out with a flourish.

'See, here…' He shows the paper to me. The wording is clear, but the ink quite pale, which may give a clue as to Morland's copying process, which I am determined I shall discover before too long if only to annoy him. 'The French Ambassador writes that he will communicate with the Duke via Monsieur Fincham, in whom he has every confidence. Father Horncastle has offered his assistance but he is not to be trusted. In another letter the authorities in Paris advise the Ambassador to warn the Duke that Father Horncastle is not known to the church in France and also to advise Fincham not to turn his back to him.'

'You mean that Fincham might have been in danger from this Horncastle?'

'Perhaps.'

'So, who is Father Horncastle exactly?'

'He claims to be a priest.'

'Clearly. I had not assumed he was thus named because he is progenitor of a large family. Does he have a first name?'

'It is more than likely. Most people do. But we do not know it. Horncastle is undoubtedly an assumed surname. He may not yet have invented a Christian name to accompany it.'

'And do you know where he is to be found?'

'In the Duke's own household. That is clear from a number of references to him. Hence presumably the need for caution. It is not uncommon for the Duke to take Catholics under his wing. Interestingly, we *think* we may have met Horncastle ourselves. A man visited my Lord Arlington a week ago and offered to sell us certain letters that he hoped to obtain by stealth and deception from the Duke of York, who, he said, had taken him in when destitute and protected him from unspecified enemies.'

'And my Lord refused such a contemptible offer?'

'We said to come back when he actually had the goods.'

'What did he look like?'

'Slightly built, sallow complexion, stooped posture, dark, rather sparse hair, cheaply dressed.'

'So, you think this so-called priest may have killed Fincham to get the letter to sell to you?'

'Or to sell to somebody else. He implied that there were other potential customers if we were ungenerous. But he preferred to sell to us, out of loyalty to His Gracious Majesty King Charles the Second. He was very insistent on that point.'

'His loyalty to the Crown does him credit at least.'

'The words were as ashes in his mouth. He is almost certainly a recalcitrant Republican.'

'A Republican posing as a priest in the Duke's own household? That shows some skill in deception.'

'There are many half-trained and untrained priests plying their trade in the twilight world of English Catholicism. The standard of learning and sanctity expected would not have been high.'

'So, shall I seek him out amongst the Duke's retinue?'

'That would be awkward, if we wish our interest in the matter to remain obscure. Fortunately we also have another address for him—in St Giles.'

'He told you?'

'We had him followed. He will not be expecting you. Not at all.'

Morland writes directions on a sheet of paper and hands it to me. I thank him.

'It is my pleasure to be of service,' he says. 'And then, as I understand it, you will seek out my Lady Pole, who also knew Fincham?'

Arlington has briefed him well—or he has found a way to gain access to Arlington's private papers.

'Yes,' I say.

'A good friend of yours, isn't she?'

'In the past.'

'I thought, when I first knew you, that you and she might marry.'

'She married Lord Pole,' I say.

'So she did. Hence her now bearing the title of a Viscountess. But he died two years ago.' Morland raises an eyebrow.

'I believe that is true,' I say.

'You have not seen her since?'

'No,' I say.

'Or thought to seek her out?'

'No,' I say.

'Or written to her?'

'No,' I say.

'Beautiful, talented and now a widow,' says Morland. He runs a moist tongue over his lips.

'True in all respects,' I say.

'But with no money, of course.'

'I am not looking for an heiress,' I say.

'That is imprudent of you. A bride with no dowry has been the ruin of many a young man.'

'I am not looking for anyone,' I say. 'Rich or poor.'

Morland smiles as if he knows more about me than I do myself. Which he does not. And especially not about this. I realise why, for all his many talents, men consider him a knave and a fool.

Then, just as I am about to leave, I ask him: 'I suppose that Father Horncastle did not introduce himself as such, or you would have been certain that you had met him?'

'No, as you have guessed, he used a false name. Another alias.'

'And what was that?'

'Your name, oddly enough. He said that he was called John Grey. A strange coincidence, no doubt. I'm sure that it has no bearing on Lord Arlington's decision to employ you.'

CHAPTER 5

'There's a gentleman to see you, Mr Grey,' says Will as I enter my chambers.

My eyes stray across the room to a well-dressed man in his early thirties, standing by the window. His hair is glossy and carefully combed. He wears a pale blue silk suit, well cut to disguise a premature portliness. His expression implies I have already kept him waiting too long.

'Let me introduce myself,' he says briskly, as if he has been allocated fewer hours to his day than other people. 'Mister Samuel Pepys. Clerk of the Acts at the Navy Office. I have been sent by my master, His Royal Highness the Duke of York.'

He clearly expects me to be impressed by one or other of these facts, without wasting any more of his valuable time.

'Why don't you take a seat, Mr Pepys?' I say. 'Then I'll see if I can assist you in your business.'

'I'll stand, if you don't mind.'

'I don't charge any more if you sit. But it's your choice.'

Pepys looks me up and down. He is suddenly strangely hesitant. 'It is a delicate matter, Mr Grey,' he begins.

'Most of the problems brought to me are,' I say. 'You may speak freely, sitting or standing.'

'What I have to say may not go beyond these walls. Do I have that assurance?'

'If you come as a client. Confidentiality does not extend to casual gossip.'

'I come on behalf of the Duke.'

'He cannot come in person?'

Pepys's expression tells me that I ought to know that I would have been summoned to attend upon the Duke, not the other way round. I think he would very much like to put me in my lawyerly place. But that will require more time than he has. He takes a deep breath.

'He and the King have left London on account of the current difficulties.'

'They have cut and run, you mean?' I say.

'Surely you would not question the Duke's courage? His conduct at the Battle of Lowestoft was beyond reproach—even when the Earl of Falmouth's brains were blown out scarcely a yard from him, he did not flinch, sir. He stood his ground, noble blood and offal covering a cravat of Brussels lace that cost him five hundred Pounds. *Five hundred Pounds*! He was the hero of the hour, sir.'

'Not everyone who runs is a coward. There is such a thing as expediency.'

'There is such a thing as duty, sir,' Pepys replies sternly. 'The Duke, as heir to the throne, cannot risk his life for no purpose. A glorious death in battle is one thing. To expire squalidly from the Plague is another entirely. It would be irresponsible for a man in his position. His brother the King would not allow it.'

'It is a shame that the King does not extend this prohibition to all his subjects.'

'The Duke is his immediate concern,' says Pepys coldly.

'Until the King has a son,' I say, 'I mean a legitimate son, I can see that the Duke's life is a matter of the greatest moment. Of course the King could legitimise one of his Royal bastards— a son of Lady Castlemaine's, perhaps. But he chooses not to. However, you have not come to consult me about the Royal succession.'

'You have hit the nail on the head, Mr Grey,' says Pepys. 'I have not come to consult you on that.' He looks at me, as if still trying to work out the best way to approach his problem. 'It concerns a letter. A letter written by the Duke.'

'To anyone in particular?'

'To the French Ambassador. As you know well, Mr Grey. I am aware that you have already been asked by Lord Arlington to locate it.'

So, the matter is not as secret as Arlington had hoped.

'The court is always full of rumours,' I say. 'That is how it passes its time. You should know better than to believe them.'

'Is this one not true then?'

'You must ask Lord Arlington.'

This is not a satisfactory answer. Pepys had hoped for better from me. 'But you *have* visited Lord Arlington today?'

'Yes,' I say. Somebody will have seen me there. There is no point in dissembling, even for enjoyment.

Pepys pauses again. He is having to check his displeasure, because he is not sure what I know and he wishes to do so. I too am curious to discover what he knows. So, I also curb my tongue and wait to see what he will say next.

'*As you will have been told by Lord Arlington,*' Pepys says with some emphasis, 'the letter was entrusted to a man named Fincham, who was in the Duke of York's service. He was waylaid and killed close to the residence of the French Ambassador, to whom the letter was nominally addressed.'

'Nominally?'

'The letter is in fact to a lady. A lady with whom the Duke wishes to be better acquainted.'

'A French lady?'

'Well done, Mr Grey. Again, you are right. A French lady. Hence using the French rather than the Spanish or Swedish Ambassador as an intermediary. The Duke has an interest in a maid of honour at the court at Versailles.'

'And he wishes to keep the correspondence from the Duchess, no doubt?'

'The Duchess? What possible concern can it be of hers which mistress her husband takes? No, it is not the Duchess that presents the problem—it is that the King is amorously inclined towards the same lady. He would be wrath indeed, Mr Grey, if it were known that the Duke was paying his own addresses to her. The Duke could expect at the very least his removal from the office of Lord High Admiral. But, more to the point, his disgrace would weaken the position of his father-in-law, Lord Clarendon. Buckingham, Arlington and my Lady Castlemaine are all scheming to have Clarendon removed as Lord Chancellor.'

I know Clarendon. He is almost as round as he is self-important. In the days when he was merely Sir Edward Hyde, he was the King's right hand during his long exile. He returned expecting to be royally rewarded, and so he was. He's the Earl of Clarendon, Lord Chancellor of England. But power is held on a lease only. I suspect Clarendon's lease has only a year or two to run and there is no option for renewal; Buckingham and Arlington are in the market to snap it up.

'So, you mean that it might be in Arlington's interest to regain the letter and use it against the Duke in order to unseat the Lord Chancellor?'

Well, it's not an invitation to dine anyway. I revalue the document from two hundred to four hundred sovereigns.

'You understand the ways of the court very well, Mr Grey,' says Pepys. 'Yet again, I congratulate you. I shall not need to waste time explaining things to you as I might with others. I had been told you were a man of intelligence and discretion. I am delighted to discover that I was not misled.'

'Thank you,' I say. 'You are too kind.'

'My pleasure,' says Pepys.

We smile at each other.

'You know the Duke's household?' I ask.

'As a clerk in the Navy Office, I am the Duke's servant. I cannot be expected, however, to know everyone he employs.'

'Do you know a man named Father Horncastle?' I ask.

'Should I?'

'He is reputedly part of the Duke's household.'

'Mr Grey,' says Pepys, examining his well-manicured nails, 'I think we both have information that would be useful to the other. You have been asked by Henry Bennet, very recently ennobled as Lord Arlington, a man who wears a nose patch and whose days in power are most certainly numbered, to find a certain letter. As you will have gathered, I have been asked to find the same letter by His Royal Highness, James Duke of York, the heir presumptive to the throne and in all likelihood *your next King*—a man of quick temper and unforgiving nature, who never forgets an act against him, however small and however long ago it was committed. I am not asking you to do anything dishonourable. I am merely suggesting that we should work together for the good of the kingdom. And our common good. The Duke will pay well—better than Arlington certainly.'

'How much?' I ask.

Pepys pauses, then says: 'Five hundred guineas. The letter must be returned to the Duke unopened within the next week.'

Well, well. If Pepys, after due consideration, is offering me five hundred as an opening bid, is the letter really worth a thousand? And I have agreed to let Arlington have it for a hundred. Will is going to have to work hard on my expenses for us to break even.

'And you assure me the letter is merely about a lady?' I ask.

'I would not say "merely",' says Pepys. 'Which mistress the King takes is a matter of national importance. The King listens to Lady Castlemaine as he does not to his Privy Council. The Duke was ill-advised to pay his addresses to the same lady as the King, I freely admit that to you. But if we can get the letter back, all will be well. The King may enjoy his lady-in-waiting.

And the Duke will be very grateful. Just tell Arlington you couldn't find it.'

'I would have thought that the King could concede this French lady to the Duke,' I say. 'He already has Mistress Gwynn and Lady Castlemaine, and indeed the Queen. Is that not enough for him?'

'Once the King takes a fancy to a lady, nothing will dissuade him—*cazzo dritto non vuolt consiglio*, as they say in Italy.' Mr Pepys winks at me, one man of the world to another. He seems to be speaking from personal experience. 'I too have a fancy for Mistress Nell Gwynn. And for my Lady Castlemaine. But it is sweet Nelly mainly who glides into my dreams. How about you, Mr Grey, you must have a favourite actress or two?'

'No,' I say. 'I do not.'

'I wish that my Lady Pole would take to the stage rather than merely write plays,' says Pepys. 'There is a beauty, Mr Grey. There I think is a fine leg, if she would but show it. But she says that she would rather play the whore with her pen than her body. A merry wit, sir. Do you know her work, Mr Grey?'

'A little,' I reply. 'Critics say that it is poorly polished—that she does not understand the unities of the drama.'

'What of it? These are plays for our own times, sir, not for the ancient Greeks. She entertains us. That is the thing for the modern audience. For comedy she is better than Wycherley. I have met her, sir. The King himself introduced me to her. "Mr Pepys," he said to me, calling me by my name, "*Mr Pepys*, this lady is the greatest playwright of our age." And I agree. If you yourself had met her—'

'I have,' I say.

'Have you indeed? At the theatre?'

'In Essex. I grew up with her in the same village.'

'And was she such a beauty when she was younger?'

'Possibly. It did not strike me so then,' I say.

'Did it not?' Pepys takes from his pocket a large silver watch, the plumper and more successful cousin of my own, and consults it. 'I have to meet the Duke of Albemarle shortly,' he says. His voice caresses the title—also a new one, but a new Duke is still a Duke. 'The *Duke* awaits me. I need to know, Mr Grey, whether you accept His Highness's commission. Will you recover the letter for us, my dear sir?'

'I am not free to accept the commission,' I say. 'There must be other servants of the Duke who are capable of doing the job.'

Pepys's face shows only contempt. 'There are few in the court or at the Navy Office that I would entrust with the simplest task,' he says. He places a friendly hand on my arm. 'You, on the other hand, Mr Grey, are known for your efficiency and your ingenuity. Perhaps, with the exception of myself, you are the only person I would trust to recover the document with the necessary secrecy and discretion. The Duke needs somebody with the courage to recover it and the honesty to return it, unread. Such men are few, as we both know well.'

I shake my head. Pepys pauses as if considering a new approach.

'I think that you studied at my old college,' says Pepys. 'Magdalene?'

'Precisely. Magdalene. A small college, but all the more reason why its sons should offer one another support, don't you think? If I were to appeal to you as a fellow Magdalene man…'

'It could have no possible bearing on the matters we have discussed,' I say.

'A thousand guineas,' says Pepys. 'That is my final offer to you.'

'Please convey to the Duke my deepest respect for His Royal Highness, but pray inform him that I am not in a position to consider his offer.'

Pepys draws in a deep breath. 'If you ever come to your senses, Mr Grey, you may find me at the Navy Office.'

'I shall ask my clerk to show you out,' I say.

'So, Will,' I say when he returns, 'did you hear all of that?'

'My ear was, as ever, to your door, Mr Grey,' he replies.

'What is your opinion?'

'I am beginning to think a hundred guineas plus expenses is very cheap,' he says. 'That letter, whatever it is, must be worth two thousand guineas at least.'

'That would explain why Fincham died,' I say. 'It's a lot of money to be carrying around with you.'

'And I don't believe his story about the French lady,' says Will. 'Why entrust your *billet doux* to the Ambassador, whose loyalties must be to the French King and who will reveal all to him? Why not just entrust the letter to the post?'

'Unless the lady is very close to the French King. Unless the French King, too, wishes to encourage the liaison with the Duke. In which case, why? The Duke needs no influencing in favour of France or of the Catholic faith.'

'I sense these are dangerous waters, Mr Grey. I should not care to swim in them myself.'

'I think Pepys is right in one respect. Arlington has a use for the letter that he has concealed from me,' I say. 'He and Buckingham and my Lady Castlemaine have formed a party against Lord Clarendon. That is well enough known. Something that disgraced the Duke, whatever that thing is, might indeed bring down his father-in-law and lead to further promotion for Arlington. So, I wonder what is really in the letter?'

'I think we should find it, read it and then sell it to whoever will pay us most,' says Will. 'That's my advice, Mr Grey.'

'No,' I say. 'I have agreed to give it to Arlington for a hundred sovereigns. And if we find it, he'll have it for that. Plus expenses. Somebody has to play the honest man, and I fear, Will, that that needs to be us. Like Lady Pole, I'll keep my virtue relatively intact.'

'I remember Lady Pole,' says Will. 'She came to visit you for a few days when you lodged at Mistress Reynolds's and she stayed for several months.'

'She's an old friend,' I say. 'Old friends can do that.'

'But you haven't seen her since?'

'No. She was married to Roger Pole. Viscount Pole.'

'Not a friend of yours, Lord Pole?'

'No.'

'But you knew her Ladyship when she was a young girl?'

'Yes,' I say.

I think back more than twenty years. I think of her chasing me round the cherry tree in full blossom, her blonde hair streaming in the wind. I think of her making me cakes of mud for my dinner and actually expecting me to eat them. I think of her getting me drunk on her father's best wine.

'And did she, as a three-year-old, show the same coruscating sarcasm and wit as she does now as a playwright?' Will enquires politely.

'Yes, Will,' I say. 'She certainly did.'

CHAPTER 6

Aminta Pole is sitting up on the stage, frowning at a sheet of paper that she holds. The theatre is in gloom except for the candle that burns on the table in front of her. Behind her are some painted arches and gardens, now partially dismantled, and several costumes piled up in an untidy heap on a chest. A lock of hair is hanging down across her face. Her finger touches the lock for a moment, then quickly runs down the document that is causing her so much unease. It must be six—no, almost seven—years since we last met. For a moment I simply stand there, at the entrance to the theatre, looking up at her. She sighs, then turns and finally sees me.

'Why,' she demands, 'have you come here dressed as a Puritan?'

'I haven't,' I say.

'Black woollen coat,' she says, 'black breeches, black stockings, demure white collar and cuffs. If that's not Puritan, I don't know what is. I'm assuming you are wearing them by choice, not as a result of some drunken wager. Or is it that you don't have a mirror in your house?'

'If the light were better,' I say, 'you would see that the coat and breeches were laced with silk.'

'What colour silk?'

'Black.'

'Black. And you think that makes you a Cavalier?'

'I make no claim to being a Cavalier,' I say. 'I had hoped that you would begin by saying how pleased you were to see me.'

'Oh, I am pleased to see you, John,' says Aminta, 'dressed in whatever ridiculous attire you prefer. But as you see the theatre is closed until the Plague quits London and there are many bills to pay that I have no money for until we have customers again. And it is not you but your coat that looks out of place in a theatre—unless you wish to audition for the part of Mr Sourface, the Anabaptist.'

'Is there such a part?'

'There will be. You have just inspired me to write it. Jump up onto the stage, cousin. Though I have no objection to talking down to you, your face is half in shadow and I want to see if you are any less ugly than you were before.'

I advance towards her and jump up onto the stage as requested.

'Quite nimble for a fusty old lawyer,' she says. 'And only slightly uglier than you were.' She takes both of my hands in hers and kisses me lightly on the cheek. I feel the smoothness of her skin and smell an almost forgotten fragrance of lavender and clean linen. 'There,' she adds. 'Now have I proved I am pleased you are here?'

'It's been a long time...' I begin.

'That is scarcely my fault, cousin,' she says. 'You knew well where to find me. The playbills have been posted all over London. For a shilling you could have made my acquaintance most weeks of the year. A bargain in my opinion.'

'I have attended some of your plays,' I say.

'Have you? Really? You've actually seen some? Which ones? What do you think of them? Am I as funny as Wycherley? I am, aren't I?'

'They were very witty,' I say. 'Though the actors spoke the words, I heard your voice.'

'Thank you. But better than Wycherley? People tell me I'm much better and my natural modesty prevents me from disagreeing with them.'

'I haven't been to any of his plays.'

'Of course not,' she says. 'Because you're a Puritan and prefer a bad sermon to a good comedy. He's actually rather clever and unfortunately a lot better than me. As you'd know if you only took a proper interest in these things. I have followed your career anyway. Your fame as a lawyer has spread far and wide. You must be very rich.'

'I can afford to lace my black suit with black silk,' I say.

'You could afford to lace Lincoln's Inn with black silk. You are renowned as a man of law and as the creature of my Lord Arlington, as that man Bennet is now styled.'

'I am not Arlington's creature,' I say. 'I merely work for him sometimes.'

'We are all somebody's creature,' says Aminta. 'This is the Duke of York's company, so I suppose I am the Duke of York's creature—at least for another day or two until the money runs out. Then I shall be my own creature again. I think it is better to be somebody else's creature, as long as they pay well. Does Arlington pay well? Should I become his creature too? I'd like to be a spy. Do you have to lie a lot, or does Arlington exempt you from lying as a Puritan?'

'I'm not employed as a spy,' I say. 'And I am not a Puritan, so I lie as much as I need to. But sometimes my Lord has a problem that he cannot resolve with the resources he has.'

'And you resolve them for him?'

'Sometimes, as I say. I recovered papers, purporting to prove that the King had married a certain lady while he was in exile in the Low Countries.'

'And is he in fact married to the lady concerned?'

'The papers have been destroyed, so no, he isn't.'

'Then you have a talent for that sort of thing?'

'I have had some good fortune,' I say. 'And I know people that Arlington's own agents may not.'

She looks at me, almost with respect, then frowns again. 'Is *that* why you are here?'

'I came of course to see you...'

'No you didn't. I thought just for a moment that you actually wanted to see me. I thought that you had finally overcome your natural diffidence and maladroitness and decided that you would like to visit me for old times' sake. But I was very wrong, wasn't I? You may be able to pull the wool over the eyes of feeble old judges or my Lord Arlington, but you can't lie to me. You never could.'

'Of course, I should have come before—'

'Yes, you should.'

'But various matters intervened in such a way that it proved inopportune...'

'Did they?'

'Perhaps I am explaining myself badly...'

'No, you are doing it very well. You couldn't make yourself clearer.'

'In which case—'

'Just tell me what Arlington wants, John, then leave me to my accounts.'

'It concerns one of your actors,' I say.

'Charles Fincham, I should think?'

'Yes.'

'What has he done now? Has he got himself arrested for drunkenness? Or worse? I have to warn you I don't have the money for my next meal, let alone to bail out an ageing actor of minor comic parts. If he's in prison then he'll need to stay there until the Plague has finished and I can sell a few tickets.'

'I'm sorry to have to tell you that he's got himself stabbed to death.'

'What?'

'He was killed while carrying a letter from the Duke of York to the French Ambassador and his body was thrown into a Plague pit.'

Aminta takes a deep breath. 'Well, John, you have lost none of your ability to break bad news gently.'

'I'm sorry...of course, you knew him well...was he...was he a close friend?'

'Fincham? Certainly not. But I don't like to think of him in a Plague pit, for all that. I wouldn't even like to think of you in a Plague pit.'

'They took him out of the pit.'

'That will be a great relief to him. What was he doing there in the first place?'

'Mistaken identity.'

'So, does Arlington want you to find out who killed Fincham?'

'He wants the letter Fincham was carrying.'

'Good for him. But personally I'd like Fincham's killer caught and hanged, if it's not asking too much. When one of your people dies, it's something you should ensure happens.'

'That could be arranged too. With your assistance.'

Aminta takes a deep breath. 'How can I help you then?'

'Tell me about Fincham. When did he join the company?'

'A year ago. One of the company—Patrick Callingham—said that he had a friend who could do comic parts.'

'And could he?'

'A bit. I mean, I wouldn't give him one of the main roles, but he was fine playing servants or the leading lady's foolish and decrepit father or an old soldier down on his luck. He was really good at being a soldier.'

'He'd actually been one, of course,' I say.

'Yes, with the King's army.'

'And also with Cromwell.'

'Was he? Ah, that explains it. I knew that Callingham had fought with Lord Lambert in the forces of Parliament. It seemed odd that he had known the Royalist Fincham during the late wars. But if Fincham too had been in Lord Lambert's army, before or after becoming a Royalist...'

'And who is Callingham?'

'Who is Callingham? You don't visit theatres a lot, do you? He is our leading man. One of the most distinguished actors of our day. Well, one of the most distinguished actors of the Thirties, anyway—he's getting a bit old now as well. He won't play Hamlet again. But he is still much admired by Lady Castlemaine.'

'The King's mistress?' I say.

'I think there is only one Lady Castlemaine. And you do not need to make interjections as if reminding some dim-witted audience, who would otherwise have forgotten, of the dramatis personae. It is rumoured her admiration extends to taking him to her bed.'

'Does the King know this?'

'He is aware that Lady Castlemaine pays him back occasionally for having to share his own bed with Miss Gwynn. And others.'

'A dangerous game for Callingham.'

'But not an unpleasant one,' says Aminta. 'He was quite fortunate, all things considered. Plenty of younger actors around. Lucky to get the part.'

'So Callingham and Fincham were good friends?' I say.

'Yes, always dining or whoring together. Planning minor frauds on the Duke's company. It was quite sweet to watch them.'

'Could Fincham have told Callingham what was in the letter, or at least that he was carrying something important?'

'That seems very likely indeed, if Fincham had read the letter—or had been warned in advance of its nature. They both spent a lot of their time drunk and Fincham was never discreet.'

I consider all the implications of this.

'There was no falling out between them?'

Aminta considers. 'Now you mention it, there was some minor coldness recently. At least, Callingham seemed a little distant towards Fincham. But nothing compared with some of the feuds that go on within a company of actors.'

'Was there anyone in the company who might have actually wanted Fincham dead?'

'No. Had he regularly taken leading parts, there might have been some jealousy towards him, but he accepted very minor roles that nobody else wanted. He was generous in his praise of other members of the company. He upstaged nobody. He paid for drinks. He was, in summary, well liked.'

'Can I talk to the other actors—and the manager?'

'If you can find them. The manager, Davenant, left as soon as he could. Those who had friends outside London have gone to them. Callingham had not left when I last heard. But everyone who can is leaving London. I had thought to go to Edinburgh—the Plague has not reached Scotland—but I doubt if people will ever travel all that way just to watch a few plays. What was in the letter anyway?'

'Arlington claims not to know,' I say. 'Mr Pepys, of the Navy Office, says that it is from the Duke of York to a lady at the French court, of whom the King and the Duke are equally enamoured. I am inclined to disbelieve both of them.'

'So, you have met Mr Pepys,' says Aminta.

'You know him?'

'He attends *all* of the plays,' says Aminta, 'primarily to lust after the leading ladies. When you next see him, please ask him to keep his nose out of my actresses' smocks.'

'If I see him,' I say. 'Do you know of a Father Horncastle?'

'No, not at all. Is he somebody else who knew Fincham?'

'Yes. Apparently. Did you know that Fincham occasionally did work for Lord Arlington?'

'I suspected he was working for somebody. He always had more money than you might have expected an actor to possess. And his acting talents, such as they were, might have assisted him as a spy. So is Horncastle also a spy? What did he look like?'

'Slight build, sallow complexion, dark, rather sparse hair. He might have called himself John Grey.'

'Really?'

'It's a common enough name.'

'Very common indeed. I think, however, you mean Lancelot Jones. He visited Fincham once or twice.'

'I don't know Jones.'

'When I saw him, I thought I had previously made his acquaintance—you know how it is—somebody you might have met years ago? He had an irritating way of sniffing that I was sure I'd encountered before. And a strange whining tone that was not unfamiliar. But if I have met him it was under some other name entirely.'

'Fincham had been warned to beware of Horncastle.'

'Good advice, no doubt, but I don't think he took it,' says Aminta. 'He had at least two long conversations with him. So, if that is the way you are thinking, there is indeed every chance that Horncastle too knew that Fincham was carrying letters for the Duke of York. He may have even known, if Fincham's tongue was loose enough, that Fincham was one of Arlington's informers and playing some sort of double game.'

'I need to find Callingham and Horncastle,' I say. 'Let me try Callingham first. He seems to have known Fincham as well as anyone. You say that you have his address?'

'Yes,' says Aminta.

'And you will give it to me?'

'No,' says Aminta.

'But...'

'However, I shall take you there.'

'Thank you, but...'

Aminta holds up a single slender finger. 'As I said, I have a strange longing to be the creature of my Lord Arlington. You make it sound very attractive. Lying. Gratuitous deceit. Plague pits. Money. But especially the last of these. There is frankly nothing for me to do here, other than look at a list of bills I have no way of paying. I need either money or to be somewhere else. Or both. So, I shall assist you as much as I can.'

'That will not be possible,' I say. 'It is no role for a woman.'

'Then good luck with finding Mr Callingham,' says Aminta, picking up her papers again. 'How long do you have to recover this letter by the way? A day? Two days? A week?'

'Very well,' I say. 'What I meant was: thank you for your offer to accompany me to his house. I accept.'

'I think you may need me to gain access to Father Horncastle too. Though I do not know which is his real name, I would certainly recognise him again. He has an unusual face. Not the sort of face you see everywhere, or that you would want for yourself. But you could still waste a lot of time looking for it. Yes, I can be of value to you there too.'

'I am not sure that it is worth your risking dying of the Plague in order to become Lord Arlington's creature but, so be it, if that is what you wish.'

'I do wish. Let us turn to practical matters then, cousin John. How much will you pay me?'

'Pay you?'

'I believe you are not working free of charge. Nor is your clerk. And I have, as I said, no other source of funds. I think you might let me have a fair share of what Lord Arlington pays you.'

'A shilling in the Pound,' I say. 'That's what I pay Will.'

'Plus expenses,' says Aminta.

She holds out her hand and we shake.

'I do think you should have placed a limit on my expenses,' says Aminta. 'But the deal is done.'

'We should go,' I say. 'Or everyone in London may be dead of the Plague before we get to them.'

The Plague Road

From My Lady Pole's Esteemed Poem,

The Puritaniad

When Plague descended on the Town
And gentry fled and trade fell down
Theatres closed and what was worse
There was no need of tales or verse
Then actors too did quit the city
At least if any had the wit, he
Followed doctors, lawyers, courtiers
With their wives and sons and daughters
Crammed in coaches. And on waggons
Men heaped chests and sacks and flagons,
Then flew with contents of the pantry
Ever out towards the country.

Yet one lawyer who will feature
In my tale, A-------n's creature
(A rather pious dull young man
In short, a very Puritan)
Stayed right there to make some money
Though of clients he had none, he
Thought to put a little by, in
Other ways, I mean by spying.

CHAPTER 7

I am walking arm in arm with Aminta through the City. We are approaching the great Gothic cathedral of St Paul's, with its fantastic stone buttresses and gargoyles and its massive spire-less tower. The more heavily infected western end of the town and its suburbs lie behind us. For a moment we quit the bright sunshine and enter the vast shadow that this cathedral casts. Here, for now at least, we may breathe more easily, though there is no way of knowing if passers-by have come from Plague-free Woolwich or from infected St Giles, bringing disease on their very breath.

'Do you take any precautions against the pestilence, cousin?' asks Aminta.

I shake my head. 'Nothing—other than keeping myself to myself and not entering other people's houses more than I have to.'

'No purple lozenges or powders or trinkets? No paper with ABRACADABRA written on it, stuffed into your pocket?'

'None.'

'Perhaps you think that Puritans are exempt from contagion, if this is a punishment on the wicked City?'

'The King noted recently that Quakers were dying as much as other men. He was relieved that piety was not in any way a preventative. Some say that you cannot catch the Plague if you have venereal disease. If so, that would explain why the court is so far untouched.'

'My Lord Rochester could walk through a dozen pest houses unscathed.'

'Do you know Rochester?' I ask.

'He attends theatres and he has attended mine. But he had no interest in meeting me. I should have been interested to meet him, because I have never met anyone as wicked as he is rumoured to be. I should have liked to enquire about fighting and wenching and drinking. I try to make my characters as real as I can, and rakehells are popular with our audiences. But alas, I must make do with lesser models of vice. Still, your concern for my own virtue—if that's what it was—is touching.'

Her grip on my arm tightens for a moment. Then she says: 'And here we are.'

'Callingham lives here?' I ask, looking at the inn in front of us. 'I scarcely needed your help to find this.'

'Of course not. But you haven't found Callingham yet, have you?' she says. 'Let's go inside and see if we can locate him.'

I cover my nose and mouth with a cloth as we enter the inn, descending a couple of worn stone steps to an earthen floor, which is covered in dirty rushes, once gold, now grey and crushed underfoot and mixed with discarded bones and ash from men's pipes. The ceiling is low and the cracked plaster is smoke-blackened. The whitewash on the wall has yellowed and is flaking. Only a little light penetrates the thick green glass of the windows. Two customers seated at a table look at us suspiciously.

'Where are you from?' asks one.

'I live at Lincoln's Inn,' I say. 'There is no Plague there.'

'And the woman you've brought with you?'

'Essex,' replies Aminta with easy assurance. 'The woman he's brought is from Essex. Thank you for enquiring.'

The two men return to their drinks, reassured by this last lie. The landlord enters from some back room that I had not previously noticed. He is clutching a wet rag in his hand, as if about to undertake some cleaning.

'Good day, Lady Pole,' he says to Aminta. 'And good day to you, sir,' he adds, noticing me.

'Is Callingham here?' asks Aminta. 'Is he moreover sober and not currently fornicating? Can we go up to him without fear of embarrassing anyone?'

He shakes his head. 'Callingham? Gone, like everyone else. He said there's no work for him here and no point in dying of the pestilence while he waited for some.'

'When did he leave?' I ask.

'This morning.'

'Did he say where he was going?'

'He *said* he was going to Guildford—that he had friends there. He *said* if anyone asked to say that's where he was to be found. But...' He looks at Aminta and then at me.

'Yes, he can be trusted,' says Aminta. 'Where is Callingham really?'

'I'd say Stepney,' says the innkeeper. 'If I were talking to a good friend of his, as Lady Pole is, I'd say look for him in Stepney. There's a widow there he was fond of. Name of Sparrow. Of course, I've told other people Guildford, since that was what Mr Callingham wanted and I don't doubt he had good reason.'

'What other people?' asks Aminta.

'Well, there's the one calling himself John Grey for a start—runty, ferrety little man. He's been back.'

'Back?' I say. 'So, he's been here more than once, this Grey person...'

'The first time might have been three or four weeks ago? When the Plague was hardly started here, anyway. I noticed him outside, skulking, watching—looked like a nasty piece of work. Then one evening he collared Mr Callingham as he was returning. They went up to his chamber here. After Grey left, Mr Callingham came down and called for brandy. He was shaken, right enough. His face was whiter than my sheets. "If that man comes again, I'm not at home," he says.'

'Callingham was scared?'

'Yes. Or maybe angry. Difficult to tell. Can't always read what an actor's feeling. It's part of their trade, I suppose.'

'You didn't hear what they said?'

'No. I've got good doors here. Too good. Old oak, near four inches thick. Can't hear a blasted thing through 'em. Gets in the way of proper innkeeping. Need to do something about it really.'

'If Mr Callingham returns,' says Aminta, 'could you very kindly tell him I was looking for him?'

'If I were in Stepney, I'd stay there,' says the landlord. 'The further east you go, the less Plague there is. It's all of the boatyards and the ships docked out that way—the smell of tar prevents the Plague settling there. That's what they say. If I could move this inn to Stepney, I'd be a happy man.'

This last seems unlikely. He scowls at us and then, suddenly noticing the wet rag he has been holding, starts mopping his counter furiously.

'So,' says Aminta, 'you can already see how valuable I am to you. The innkeeper would most certainly not have told you where Callingham had gone, especially if you had announced yourself as John Grey—common and unassuming though the name is.'

'So Horncastle…alias Grey alias Lancelot Jones…has frightened Callingham off…'

'Not necessarily,' says Aminta. 'Callingham seemed angry, according to his landlord. But I think Horncastle was fishing for information about Fincham. At least, I can't see what other business he would have had with Callingham.'

'Everything points to Horncastle having killed Fincham and to Horncastle now having the letter Arlington wants.'

'We might assume so,' says Aminta.

'Then it is Horncastle I shall seek out next,' I say. 'But first, I shall return to Lincoln's Inn for some dinner.'

'You do not need me further?'

'I think not. I am grateful for your help, Aminta, but if Horncastle has killed to obtain the letter, he may be willing to kill again to retain it. I would not put you in such danger.'

'But you would not expect me to return to Westminster alone? The streets of London are unsafe at the best of times. But now, in this time of Plague, with madmen running round the streets, naked or nearly so...'

'Of course not,' I say. 'Perhaps you would like to join me for dinner, then Will can see you home...or I could escort you back to Westminster now if you prefer...'

'I'd be delighted to join you,' says Aminta. 'I too am hungry after our morning's work. Then we shall both go and hunt for Father Horncastle.'

'But I've said—it will be dangerous...for a woman. And I know where to go.'

'Yes, but you don't know what Horncastle looks like, and I do. You have to take me.'

I sigh. 'You will need to do exactly as I tell you, without questioning my word. Do you think you can do that?'

'But of course, cousin,' she says. 'When have I ever done otherwise?'

'Will,' I say, on my return to Lincoln's Inn. 'I'm afraid I must ask you to go out for some more food...'

'I have already obtained it, Mr Grey. Knowing that you were visiting Lady Pole, I assumed that she might return with you. There is ham and pike and a salad.'

'Thank you,' I say to Will. This is prescient, even by his standards. But pike as well as ham was unnecessary. And expensive. I shall explain this to him later. 'I am afraid, however, Aminta, that I have no wine to offer you...'

'I took the precaution, Mr Grey, of buying two bottles of canary. Not cheap in these times of Plague, but the grocer assured me it was excellent. And perfect for serving to a lady guest. One bottle is already open. Would you both care to sit at the table, where it will be my pleasure to serve you?'

From My Lady Pole's Esteemed Poem,

The Puritaniad

And so our hero, baptised John,
Was sent by the Lord A-------n
To find a letter that he needed
Since John perhaps knew more than he did
Who and what and where—and why
'Twas stolen from a murdered spy.
Though John at first was quite resistant
He soon obtained a fair assistant
With sparkling eyes and golden tresses,
But better still who knew addresses
That John was likely to require
That girl, I think, was worth her hire.

CHAPTER

8

The house to which we have been directed by Morland is in a narrow, sunless alleyway to the west of the City, in the parish of St Giles-in-the-Fields. It is the most feared corner of London—the one in which the Plague was first reported and where it still burns with its brightest flame.

A Plague doctor is quitting the road as we enter it. He wears a sort of cassock that covers his entire body, large leather gauntlets and, most distinctive of all, a head covering that fits snugly over his skull and that supports a massive beak-like structure in front. This beak contains herbs, which filter the air the physician breathes. He turns to look at us briefly through the bright glass eyehole in his head covering. It must be stifling inside the costume, but it must so far have preserved him from the disease. We do not stop and enquire about the health of his patient. Nor does this strange bird pause in his flight. Nobody wants to stay long in the parish of St Giles-in-the-Fields.

'Horncastle is a brave man if he resides here by choice,' I say. 'With a poor sense of smell,' adds Aminta.

The street in front of us is more rubbish tip than road, and large black rats scurry freely in the rotting household waste. I sometimes wonder if the rats are aware how much they owe to their human neighbours and whether they would show any gratitude if they were. I think they take us for granted. One looks at me and holds my gaze with its shiny black eyes for several seconds before scuttling off. The houses themselves are ancient, London-soot-caked, half-timbered, their upper storeys stretching out precariously over the roadway and their narrow gables arching up to the sky. There is a strange chill in the air, even on a day like this, as if the sun never reaches this spot.

Two houses here have red crosses and the dread words on their doors: *'Lord Have Mercy'*. A watchman stands in front of one of them, a buff jerkin encasing his ample body, a pikestaff in his hands and a flagon of ale on the ground beside him.

'We are looking for a man called Horncastle,' I say to him, 'though he may be calling himself John Grey or Lancelot Jones.'

'You've come to the right place, sir,' he says, tipping up the broad brim of his hat to reveal an honest, freckled face and a fringe of ginger hair. 'Right for Horncastle at least. But you're too late if you want to speak with him; he's gone.'

'Gone where?' I ask.

The watchman looks significantly at his flagon then back at me. I stretch out my hand to him, getting no closer than I have to, and pass him a shilling.

'To the pest house,' he says, quickly pocketing the coin. 'He's dying of the Plague, may God have mercy upon him. His landlord was caught sneaking out of the building with a pack, as if hoping to travel somewhere. Two of the Searchers of the Dead happened to be passing, early though the hour was, and, thinking there might be business for them, asked him where he was going. They didn't like his story and called me over and we detained him. Sure enough, when they looked inside the house they found Horncastle, lying on the floor with the tokens of the sickness on his chest and a great sweat all over him. We told the landlord that we were shutting the house up with both of them in it, but the snivelling little man said he had no money for a nurse and that we'd have to call for a cart to take Horncastle to the pest house to be looked after. So we did, and that's where he is now, if he isn't already dead and buried. As for the sneaking, penny-pinching landlord, he's shut up inside his own house for forty days. Quarantine. And if he wants to eat and drink decent while he's there, he'll need to find a civil tongue. Cursing and blaspheming he was. It would have shocked a bishop.'

'Which of the houses is his?' I ask.

With a twitch of his pikestaff, he motions towards the house opposite, bearing a very newly painted cross, the dull red pigment still gleaming damply. 'I'm guarding both houses until they can find another man to do that one; I ought to be paid double by rights—until the new man comes. Two houses, two fees. Not that I shall be—mean bastards that the City aldermen are.'

I readily acknowledge that lounging in front of two houses is harder work than lounging in front of one. 'When did all this happen?' I add.

'This morning. Just after I came on duty. Seven of the clock, as near as a man without a pocket watch might tell.'

'What's the landlord's name?' I ask.

'Saunders,' says the watchman. He spits and then wipes his mouth.

'Can I speak with him?'

'I wouldn't if I were you, sir. It's all right for me. Tough as an ox. Not a day's illness in my life—not even when I was a little 'un. The Plague can't touch the likes of me. But you, sir, or your lady... That's another kettle of fish, as we say in Islington. Delicate constitutions you gentry have. That's why you never see a gentleman doing a decent day's work. It's mainly gentry dying of the Plague, so I hear, and quite right too.'

'He's a lawyer,' says Aminta. 'He's not gentry of any sort.'

The watchman nods. 'He'll have a strong stomach then, like me. But you can only go in if you don't mind staying there forty days. Once you're in, I can't let you out again. Not for any money. You could offer me thirty shillings and I probably couldn't do it for you. That's the law of the land, that is.'

'Thank you for explaining the legal niceties, but he may have a letter that I need,' I say.

'What, *that* again?'

'Again?' I ask.

'When they were taking Horncastle away, just as they were leaving, his landlord, Saunders, tucks a letter into Horncastle's doublet. There, Father Horncastle, he says, you'd better take this with you if it was so important.'

'Even though Horncastle was dying, Saunders thought he should have the letter?'

'That's right, sir. It was obviously of great consequence to Horncastle. For some reason. But people get strange ideas. Take my wife's mother for example...'

Eager though I am to hear what his mother-in-law thinks on all things, I am obliged to cut him short.

'And what did Horncastle say when he received it?' I ask.

'Nothing much. He scarcely knew where he was. He said that it wasn't really his, but he didn't seem to know what he was saying, poor man—it's always a shock to them when they learn they've got the Plague and maybe only hours to live with nothing but an excruciating death to look forward to. And everlasting bliss with the Lord above, of course. But you've got to get through the excruciating death first. I've seen it before—a sort of distraction overwhelms them. They can't think straight. But Saunders insisted and eventually Horncastle allowed the paper to remain where it was and settled back into the litter. Mr Saunders was a kind man to think of that, as well as being a mean bastard in other ways, but his kindness will be to no avail if Horncastle dies in the pest house, as I fear he must, for few return thence.'

'Horncastle said the letter wasn't really his? What did he mean by that?'

'How should I know that, sir? If I knew that, I'd have the power to read men's thoughts, and not even I have that, whatever you offered me by way of inducement. The man was raving and in a fever, sir. He might have meant anything or he might have meant nothing at all. What I *do* know was that there was a big fuss over the letter then, and now you seem to be about to make a fuss all over again. What's in the letter anyway?'

'I have no idea. Like you, I lack the power to read men's thoughts, even for ready money. But, if it's what I think it is, a man has already been killed for it.'

'Valuable then?'

'Apparently. Saunders would have been better off being less honest and keeping the letter for himself. I'd have paid him well. But it is at the pest house with Horncastle?'

'Or in the pit,' says the watchman. 'If Horncastle has passed away, I doubt they'll search his clothing or want his letter if they do search. Folk who get a letter these days won't open it until it's been dunked in vinegar or hung out on a pole for days on end to get the Plague off it. Who'd take a letter off a fresh corpse if they didn't have to? I think it's probably under several feet of soil by now. The landlord may have read it first, of course.' He motions again to the padlocked house.

'Mr Saunders!' I yell up at the first-floor window, thinking I see a shadow move. But there is no reply.

'I've heard nothing for a couple of hours,' says the watchman. 'Before, it was get this and get that for him—food, ale. Oaths and curses if I was too slow and no more than sixpence for my trouble. But the present silence, though a blessing in some ways, does not bode well in other ways. I do not doubt that Saunders is now sick too—maybe already dead with great black buboes under his armpits and in his groin. But I won't be going in to check free of charge—I'm only being paid for this house here. Just the one. My colleague who watches at night can do that if he likes. He'll be relieving me in a few hours' time. Whether he's sick or whether he's dead, Saunders isn't going anywhere in the meantime.'

'I'll need to go in and speak to him,' I say.

'Your choice, sir. Like I say, you can go in whenever you wish but, if you do, you can't come out until next month.'

I look up at the window. This time, I'm almost certain I see a figure behind the grimy glass.

'Mr Saunders!' I call again. 'Can I speak with you, sir?'

There is no reply. The window remains firmly closed.

'Wasting your breath,' says the watchman.

I consider my options. It would seem that it is at least two hours since Horncastle was taken away. Probably more. He may live a day or two or may be dead already. Time is not on my side. They could be shovelling dry earth onto the letter even as we speak. Saunders, conversely, should be available for the next forty days.

'Which pest house was Horncastle removed to?' I ask.

'Westminster,' he says. 'Tothill Fields, close to the new pit.'

'If Saunders appears, don't let him leave,' I say. 'I'll be back.'

'Let him leave? I know my duty better than that,' he says indignantly.

'Good. Whatever bribe he offers you to let him go, I'll double it if you keep him there.'

'Thank you, sir,' he says. 'It's always a pleasure to deal with a real gentleman.'

'And don't leave your post.'

'I'll be here when you come back, sir. You may depend on that. I'm your man, sir.'

'I'll take you back to your lodgings first,' I say to Aminta. 'A pest house is no place for a lady.'

'There's no time to stand here arguing,' says Aminta. 'And there's no time to escort me home. We'll go to the pest house together and we'll go now. Don't forget, you need me to identify Horncastle, dead or alive.'

Though I have been to a pit, I have never been inside a pest house. But I am about to. The house at Tothill Fields is a long, ramshackle building, two storeys high. It must be doing good business, because it is being extended as I watch. Next to one of the orange brick walls, a low wooden shack is being constructed by some of the bravest carpenters in London, who are hammering hard and trying to ignore the screams and groans from the patients. They are working as fast as they can because, though work is hard to find these days, they do not wish the job to last longer than it has to. Other than these men, the citizens of the parish have elected to avoid the lonely building in the middle of the grassy field. Travellers passing this way give it a wide berth and only Aminta and I tread the dusty dirt path towards its wide-open door.

'Horncastle?' asks the Master of the pest house once he has been summoned from within.

'He may be calling himself Father Horncastle,' I say.

The Master removes his hat and runs his fingers through short, grey hair. 'Yes, we had a man of that name admitted this morning. I was surprised, in view of the authorities' disapproval of his religion, that he confessed to being a Roman priest. But that was how the men who carried him here said he called himself. *Father* Horncastle. Perhaps seeing death approaching he saw no cause to dissemble about his faith.'

'May we speak with him?' I ask.

The Master raises an eyebrow. This is not a common request. 'I have said—he saw death approaching, and he was not wrong to do so. He died an hour ago. Quick deaths are not uncommon, mercifully.'

'Did you call for a priest to give him the last rites according to his beliefs?'

'The chaplain we had here sufficed. Horncastle was in no state to notice. And, as a Papist, he would have gone to Hell as fast one way as the other.'

I look at Aminta. If Horncastle killed Fincham, then he has met his just deserts, but we are not here to bring him to justice.

'Did he bear a letter?' I ask. 'Perhaps concealed in his clothing? He has not been buried yet?'

'He will be buried tonight,' says the Master. 'As is seemly. I do not know what was in his clothing. If you wish to enter, then you may look for yourself. The lady may prefer to remain outside.'

But Aminta shakes her head. She has not come all this way to be turned back now.

This is worse than anything I could have imagined. The low beds are packed so closely together that we have to squeeze between them, trying to avoid the buckets of shit and vomit that block the way. The muffled cries that we could hear from the outside have become deafening. One man, his filthy, ragged nightshirt soaked in sweat, is being held down as a gleaming steel knife is applied to his swellings by a surgeon. An assistant holds out a bowl to catch whatever will be released. I do not stay to see whether the operation is a success. But, however great this man's pain, he does at least have a bed to himself. Three wretches are crammed into the one next to him. One is well dressed and raving. The second is almost naked and groans softly as he stares up at the ceiling. The third has a quiet smile on his face and has probably been dead for some time.

The high windows are open and unshuttered, casting a clean, cruel light on the scene below, but doing little to reduce the stench of sweat and urine and rotting flesh. Aminta is holding a small lace kerchief to her nose, but I doubt that it is doing any good. A blanket held to the nose would not be enough.

'It is the circulation of the air that drives away the miasma,' says the Master, waving his arm at the room in general. He is proud of what he has to show us. 'Thus, it does not have a chance to settle on healthy individuals. Men of science have noted that places that are close, confined and dark, such as houses in valleys or prisons, are much more liable to contagion than situations upon eminences, where the air is much agitated. The malignant effluvia cannot so well fix in an air so tumultuously hurried about. So, I have ordered that the windows should be always open. You have no doubt already felt for yourselves the beneficial effects.'

I nod. The air is still and very hot. Perhaps there will be a breeze later.

'Is there anything you can do for the sick, other than lancing their buboes?' I ask.

'We feed them good, wholesome food,' says the Master. 'Eggs. Broth. Cordials. Most are incapable of doing that for themselves and could die of hunger and thirst without our aid. We provide blankets, though they often throw them off in their delirium. We tie them down with strong ropes, if needed, so that they do not harm themselves or us. We leech them as a matter of course. There is little else to be done.'

'Do many survive?' asks Aminta.

'We have some success, my Lady. Those whose swellings are successfully lanced and who do not die of gangrene may recover. But your friend, Father Horncastle, did not. When he was carried to us he already had many small spots about his face and body. Such tokens, in my view, always predict a swift death, and so it was for him. Lord have mercy on his misguided Pope-worshipping soul.'

There is a loud scream behind us and a muffled curse. I think the surgeon has quickly wiped his scalpel on the dirty rag tucked in his belt and moved on to another patient, who does not sound grateful for his attention. I do not look back and the Master does not even seem to notice it.

'Father Horncastle is at the rear of the building,' he says, 'where we keep the newly dead in decent and respectful conditions for the short time before their burial. It is fortunate you are here so soon after your friend died. He will probably be stacked quite close to the top of the pile. Please follow me. You'll find it's faster to walk across the beds than to try to go round them. Just be careful of the patients. If one grabs your legs in their delirium, you could have a nasty fall.'

In fact there are only three bodies at the back, lying in an orderly fashion next to each other. A young woman, her hands crossed before her as if in contemplation of salvation, is stretched out next to a child wrapped neatly in a shroud. The child's face is pale grey but otherwise beautiful—an angel sketched in charcoal. Slightly further off is a tall, gaunt man, with a dark black beard, wearing a patched suit of brownish wool and new cream-coloured stockings. I am surprised that nobody has decided to risk the Plague and claim the stockings for their own.

I frown. 'Where is Father Horncastle?' I ask, surveying these three. None match the description we have been given of a ferrety little man. Perhaps we are indeed too late. 'Has he already been buried?'

'I told you: the burials here are at night. None of today's departed have departed, as it were. Your friend is still right there in front of you, though perhaps sadly changed by his disease.'

'That's definitely not Horncastle,' says Aminta, at my shoulder. 'Not unless the Plague causes you to grow six inches. The man I saw was shorter by half a foot and had no beard.'

'Well, the men who brought him said that was his name,' says the Master testily. 'Father Horncastle of the Society of Jesus. I made a note of it myself. And though he never confirmed it, he certainly never denied it.'

'He's not even dressed as a priest,' says Aminta. 'Look at him.'

'Of course,' says the Master. 'I too thought it odd that a priest should not wear black, but most Papists, and even more so their priests, are obliged to conceal their allegiance. In any case, it matters little to us what our patients choose to call themselves. If a man wishes to go to his God under an alias, then that is between him and St Peter.'

I drop to my knees and feel inside his doublet, because one button is undone and a small corner of paper peeps out. I withdraw it carefully—one sheet, folded. It has a blob of very dark red wax still sticking to it, but no longer sealing it closed.

'I can soak that in a bucket of vinegar,' offers the Master. 'Or I can scorch it in front of the fire. Both will remove the taint of the Plague.'

I shake my head and unfold the letter. But, other than the wax, the paper is completely white on both sides. Totally unblemished. Unsullied by any pen. Not a word is written there. I hold it out for Aminta to see.

'Duped,' I say. 'This is not Horncastle, and this is not the letter. Very clever of somebody, or at least cleverer than I have been.'

'The watchman said that Horncastle's landlord pressed it on him,' says Aminta, 'even though, in his frenzy, all Horncastle could do was to protest it was nothing to do with him.'

'Of course. He'd never seen it before. It was pressed on him at his door, in such a way that the watchman would be bound to remember and tell us if we asked about a missing document. A sheet of plain paper, with a blob of wax added too quickly for it to stay sealed even for an hour or two. Done so that we would go chasing after it. If we were stupid enough. A trap of the utmost simplicity, which a baby should not have been deceived by.'

'We never saw his landlord, imprisoned in the house,' says Aminta. 'He kept well out of sight...'

'So, my guess is that this gentleman in a brown suit in front of us is the landlord,' I say. 'As for the real Father Horncastle, hopefully he is the gentleman of mean appearance and little gratitude, who is still under lock and key inside the house, with our trusty and largely incorruptible watchman outside. If the guard is as honest as he claims, then Horncastle will not have been able to profit by his trick. But if conversely the watchman is complicit in all this, as he may well be... I am a fool, Aminta. We must return at once to St Giles. If Horncastle is still there, we shall have our man. Otherwise I need at least to question our worthy watchman a little more closely.'

But when we reach Horncastle's lodgings, the watchman is no longer standing guard outside. I curse myself for not having bribed him properly before we left. The door is slightly ajar and the padlock is hanging loose on its bracket. I give the door a gentle push and it creaks open. Though the light is poor, I cannot fail to notice the figure sprawled on the rush-covered floor, face down. He wears a buff-coloured jerkin. A pikestaff lies beside him. A broad-brimmed hat is not far off. For the second time in an hour I kneel beside a body. This one has not died of the Plague.

'A case of rope fever,' says Aminta. 'I wonder who he caught it from?'

The thick cord has been wound twice round his neck and pulled tight. It has bitten into his flesh, which is red and raw under the ligature. I roll him over. His eyes are bulging and wide open and his thick, purple tongue is hanging out.

'Horncastle!' I yell at the top of my voice. But there is no answer from within the house. It does not take long to search and confirm that there is nobody here except a dead watchman. An open window at the back of the house, and some discarded boards that might have been blocking it up, suggest a possible escape route. I try all of the likely hiding places for a letter—the real letter. There is nothing, though in an upstairs room I find fresh new paper and bright red sealing wax.

'I think our bird has flown,' says Aminta. 'Though not before killing the man who sought to cage him. I wonder why he left via the rear rather than the front door, if it was available to him? But he has gone, whichever route he took. What now, Cousin Grey?'

'We must find Callingham,' I say. 'Apart from Arlington he's the one person who has definitely met Horncastle—and spoken to him at length. But, now that Horncastle is free, Callingham may well be in danger himself. First we will need passes, certifying our good health, if we are to travel to Stepney. We will not be allowed out of London without them. So, that unfortunately means returning to Arlington to get them.'

And I have a feeling that Arlington will not be happy with my progress.

My Lord Arlington is elsewhere. But Joseph Williamson is here. Or hereabouts. He has kept me waiting for half an hour while he deals with some other task, but I have profited from it by giving his clerks some instructions. There are things I shall need.

Williamson is to Arlington what Morland once was to Thurloe. He is his right hand. But Williamson is not treacherous. I've had to trust Williamson before. He has not betrayed my trust. Not yet anyway.

Williamson's office is spacious and panelled in honey-coloured wood. I'd tell you what sort of wood it was if I knew. Not cheap but not showy. That's Williamson's taste.

The room is ornamented with the marble busts of Roman emperors, which sit on top of his cabinets, staring blindly into the distance. They serve an unexpected but wholly practical purpose—a paper might be listed as being filed under Claudius or Nero or Augustus. His clerks are expected to know which emperor is which. He does not tolerate mistakes in filing. He does not tolerate mistakes in anything. He is a tall, good-looking man and, like Pepys, he believes that everyone in London except himself is a fool. Arlington tried to dismiss Williamson once but had to recall him after a couple of days. Williamson works hard and a tithe of his work every day is devoted to making himself a little more indispensable. Only Williamson really understands how this office works. Only Williamson will ever be allowed to know how this office works. Only Williamson knows the code names of all of the agents. Only Williamson knows where they all live. Some information is too important to file, even under Augustus.

'So, Horncastle outsmarted you?' he asks me. 'For the price of a sheet of paper and a blob of red wax, he managed to send you to Westminster while he made his escape? Do you not think it would have been better to search the house first?'

'Yes,' I say.

'Was the watchman in league with him? He effectively prevented such a search.'

'If so, Horncastle showed little gratitude. I think that Horncastle has been cunning and that the watchman has paid the penalty for his officiousness.'

'So, Horncastle killed the watchman, doubtless having lured him into the house on some pretext, then chose to leave by a rear window rather than the front door. I suppose he would have known all of the obscure lanes and alleyways and the best route to them. Where is he now, I wonder?'

'Still in London,' I say. 'At least until he can obtain the paperwork necessary to leave. The magistrates must be issued with his description at once and told not to issue him with a pass.'

'That was done yesterday,' says Williamson. He retains a trace of a northern accent. He comes, I think, from Cumberland and, like Thurloe, is the son of a clergyman. He taught at Oxford and has a reputation as a scholar. 'It seemed a wise precaution, however your own investigations were proceeding. He will not be given a letter certifying him as being in good health, even if he is. And without such a document, the guards must not sanction egress.'

'Then we may still find him before he can flee the city,' I say.

'Of course, passes can be forged,' he says, 'and, though I scarcely believe it, I am told that gatekeepers can be bribed. There are many ways to get out of here if you are clever enough. But I do not think that Horncastle is a man to waste money on bribes, which may be his downfall. Unbribed officials can prove surprisingly honest. And yet our man is cunning. He will be sniffing round the gates of London, as a rat in a courtyard scurries from corner to corner, waiting for us to let our guard drop for a moment. What we don't know is where he will choose to hide in the meantime. He has to sleep, after all.'

'You know him better than I thought.'

'We've met him only once. It's more that I know the type. I've encountered plenty like him. The Low Countries were full of them in Cromwell's time, buying and selling each other for a few crowns or a pint of gin.'

'Others are looking for him,' I say. 'Mr Pepys of the Navy Office visited me and suggested that I might like to work for the Duke of York.'

'And would you?'

'I have a contract with Lord Arlington.'

'So you have. And, if you want to be paid, you'd better find Horncastle before Pepys does.'

'Callingham may be able to help us locate him,' I say. 'If we can find Callingham. We can go to Stepney today.'

'Passes are already being prepared for you and for Lady Pole, as you have requested,' he says. 'But do you think it wise to take her with you?'

'She knows Callingham,' I say.

'True. Are you sure she can be trusted in other ways?'

'Of course. Her family has always been loyal to the Stuarts.'

'To the Stuarts... You see, even now, you think of His Majesty merely as one of the Stuarts. A man with an illustrious name, but still a man like others. You do not instinctively use his Royal title. You may even harbour lingering doubts that he has been personally appointed by God to rule over us.'

'I must protest, Mr Williamson. You mistake me entirely. I am absolutely loyal to his Majesty the King...'

'Of course you are. Now. But when Cromwell was running things, when he was a puffed-up little Highness, you were loyal to him, were you not?'

'Yes, naturally.'

'Precisely. That is why I trust you, Mr Grey. There are three types of people. First there are those who support the established government, whatever it is—you, for example—and as a servant of the established government I approve of such people unreservedly. Then there are those who look entirely to their own advantage—take Pepys for example. I have no fear of him, because I understand him perfectly. Finally there are those whose principles oblige them to support one side or another, come what may, even to their utter ruin—like Lady Pole's father, Sir Felix. I mistrust men of principle, whichever side they may be on. And women of principle.'

'Then you misunderstand her. Having watched her father bankrupt himself giving loans to the Stuarts...I mean to his late Majesty...she knows how foolish it is to espouse a lost cause. She is not stupid. In any case, as you say, she has never wavered in her support for the King. You have nothing to fear from her.'

Williamson raises an eyebrow.

'I have known Aminta since I was about five years old,' I say. 'I have no cause to distrust her.'

'None at all?'

I think back many years. I am sitting on the floor with an empty wine bottle in front of me. The contents, which are the legal property of Sir Felix, Aminta's father, are in my stomach. The room is spinning round. I hear Sir Felix's footsteps approaching. Aminta, who until a moment ago had been hospitably pouring the wine, is nowhere to be seen.

'Hardly any,' I say.

'She is the servant of the Duke of York, whose letter you seek—a letter that may not be to his credit. You doubtless know from Pepys that the Duke wants the letter back very badly indeed.'

'Lady Pole has merely written a play or two for his company of actors,' I say. 'She is his servant only in the most nominal sense.'

Williamson's eyebrow arches again.

'Truly,' I say. 'Her loyalty is to her Profession and her Art, not to her patron.'

'Then why does she wish to help you?'

'She is an old friend. And I think she hopes to commend herself to my Lord Arlington. She seeks a new patron.'

'Does she? Even so, it seems to me to be an unnecessary risk. You do not need to take her with you, John. I am sure that you could find Callingham merely by asking after him. It would be easy to leave her behind. You could make it appear an accident. Or you could tell her, if you wished, that I would not issue a pass for her.'

'Thank you for that advice,' I say.

'Which you will not take. Just don't blame me if I prove to be right. I would also give you one other piece of advice, John— never try to be clever with Arlington.'

'I don't understand you, Mr Williamson.'

'Yes, you do. If he thinks he's outsmarted you—on your fee, for example—just let him think that. If you are having an argument, let him win it. How old are you, John? Twenty-five, twenty-six?'

'That's close enough.'

'One day you may have Arlington's job or mine for the asking, but not yet. I have no plans for retirement to my country estates, even if I had some. Arlington's power will last a little longer—there's a lot more to him than people think. So remember who pays you. Curb your tongue. I tell you that as a friend.'

I bow to him. 'I am honoured that you should regard me as such, and accept your advice with gratitude,' I say.

Williamson frowns at me for a moment, strangely unsure of my sincerity, then laughs. 'Find that letter, John, and you can tell Arlington that he looks a bloody fool in that nose patch, and he'll still have to grit his teeth and employ you.'

'Can you not shout at the guard that you are on an important secret mission for Lord Arlington?' says Aminta.

'The point of an important secret mission is that nobody knows about it.'

'So, we have to shuffle forward in this queue?'

'Precisely,' I say. 'Just be patient. Much espionage work consists of doing very little while you wait for others to do what you want them to do. In this particular case we are waiting for the guard to check the passes of two travellers fleeing the Plague. A little irritation on our part is normal. Please feel free to express it. But too much haste would invite suspicion.'

I have collected a pass from one of Williamson's clerks. It claims that Mr and Mrs Grey, travelling together, are in good health and free of the Plague or any other infectious disease. Now 'Mrs Grey' and I are attempting to leave via the Barbican gate, but so are many others. The man ahead of me is arguing with the guard and looks likely to be arguing for some time. The guard is expressing doubts that the pass the man holds is actually his. Passes are now a tradable commodity and may change hands several times before they reach the final owner. The man is insistent that the person described in the document is himself, but he is unwilling to bribe the guard. His reluctance suggests that the pass may indeed be valid, but the guard nevertheless hopes that money will be forthcoming because it often is. And while this deadlock persists, we and others must wait.

'Why do I have to be Mrs Grey?' asks Aminta.

'Williamson's clerk thought that it would be more convincing if you were my wife rather than some female unrelated to me in any way whom I had decided to take out of the City for immoral purposes. Even these days, some people disapprove of that sort of thing.'

'And the gatekeeper would be suspicious of a Puritan doing that anyway?'

'If you object to being thought a Puritan's wife, then you may return to your lodgings and I can proceed alone.'

'Do I look like a Puritan's wife?'

'You look charming as always,' I say.

But Aminta decides not to accept this olive branch.

'The pass might at least describe me as Lady Aminta Grey, thus ensuring that the guards understood the extent to which I have married beneath me.'

'Would it help if I addressed you as Your Ladyship?'

'Yes, I should like that very much.'

'Sadly it would make the guard ahead of us even more suspicious and grasping than he is now. If we are to get beyond the city walls then I shall require you to be a modest and obedient Puritan woman, albeit a well-dressed one, who obeys her husband's every command.'

Aminta sighs and we shuffle forward another couple of steps. The man ahead of us has proved, one way or another, that he is who he claimed to be—or has at last resorted to his purse. There is just a heavily laden pedlar and a sailor ahead of us, and then Mr Grey and his obedient Puritan wife may show their fraudulent papers and be on their way.

CHAPTER 10

We reach Stepney in the last of the evening sunshine. Here at least everything still seems as it was. Golden light reflects off newly cleaned windowpanes. Honeysuckle clings tightly to the walls though its scent floats freely. No door yet bears a red cross on it. No Searchers of the Dead strut the broad streets. Children play together in the dusty road, one family mixed with another. A dog stretches himself out by a wall, happily ignorant of what is happening to his cousins in the City. Stallholders are clearing their goods away in a leisurely manner after the weekly market. Men sit outside the tavern with pint pots in their hands and talk without enquiring first where the others have come from. Only our own arrival causes a slight stir. One of the men points in our direction, and the dog almost opens one eye but then thinks better of it.

'We have passes of good health,' I say, approaching the tavern. 'There is no need to fear us.'

'But you're from London?' asks one of the men.

'Of course they are,' says another. 'Why else would they need passes?'

The others nod. Our possession of a pass is good, but our not being there at all would be even better. This isn't the first time there's been Plague in England. Everyone knows that it is spread by travellers. We're travellers.

'We are searching for Patrick Callingham,' says Aminta. 'He may be staying with a widow named Sparrow.'

The men nod. They know Widow Sparrow. They are not surprised she has another man.

'Is it right you can't get the Plague if you've had the French pox?' asks one of them.

'So it is said,' I concede.

'Widow'll be safe enough then, even if your passes are forged, as most seem to be. Keep going through the village, then turn left by the church. Hers is the big house with bay windows and a green door. And then you can take yourselves and your bloody London Plague somewhere else.'

'The pestilence will be here soon enough,' says Aminta, as we walk away from the tavern. 'Then it will be others saying to them, "Don't come here with your bloody Stepney Plague".'

'Man is like a wolf to man,' I say.

'Who says?'

'Your late husband,' I say. 'He said it to me more than once. But he used to say it in Latin. He was a clever man.'

'That's right. After all, he married me,' says Aminta. 'Which you never did.'

'Here's the church,' I say. 'The house we want must be just down there.'

The Widow Sparrow is not what I expected. She is a small, neat woman, who has at some time in the distant past upset her neighbours, rather than the brazen harlot that I had been promised.

Her residence is a clapboard cottage with two small projecting bays, a newly thatched roof, an apple orchard and lavender edging the well-swept path to her door. If order and cleanliness could protect a man from the Plague, this is where he would live. She quickly sizes us up before confirming that Mr Callingham is indeed staying with her, until the Plague has abated in London, and leads us upstairs to his chamber.

Callingham conversely looks every bit the actor down on his luck. His green velvet suit is dishevelled, his hair uncombed and his doublet and shirt gape open to reveal the grey down on his chest. His brow is creased, his jawline is slack, his nose redder than most. It is not immediately apparent why Lady Castlemaine might have been attracted to him, though I must concede there is a sort of decayed nobility in his face and a glint of mischief in his expression. One small detail that Aminta omitted in her description of him is that he has only one eye. A black patch denotes the loss of his left one at some time in the past.

'My Lady Pole!' he enunciates, with great clarity, so that those at the back of the stalls will hear him. 'Have you too fled the City? Bringing with you this...this...'

I am not sure how he plans to describe me towards the conclusion of this sentence, but a look from me stops him in his tracks.

'I am here on behalf of Lord Arlington,' I say. 'I have some questions for you.'

Callingham shows no concern at this. 'You are very welcome, sir,' he says, 'to my humble dwelling, here in the depths of the country. I regret that in my current reduced condition I cannot offer you wine, though perhaps Mistress Sparrow has some strong ale that I may obtain on credit.'

I call for wine—Arlington shall pay for it—and allow Callingham to settle happily in his chair.

'So how can I help Lord Arlington?' asks Callingham.

'Fincham's dead,' says Aminta bluntly, proving that her gibe about my breaking bad news was uncalled-for. 'Stabbed in the back while carrying a letter from the Duke of York to the French Ambassador. Then thrown into a Plague pit.'

Callingham is unfazed that he will need to go whoring with somebody else in future. I recall Aminta's information that there might have been a recent coolness between them. 'Poor man,' he says. 'The only surprise is that he survived so long.'

'You expected somebody to kill him?' I ask.

'He was playing a dangerous game.'

I say nothing and wait for him to continue. It is usually the best way.

'Fincham and I served in the same regiment,' Callingham says, stretching out his legs, as if in preparation for a long tale. 'It's not very fashionable now to have fought for Parliament. The Duke of Albemarle did and it's done him no harm. But old soldiers like me and Fincham have to earn our money as we can. I'd done a bit of acting before the war—I was quite well known then, if I do say so myself—so when the Republic fell and the theatres opened again I thought, well, why not return to the sock and buskin? And I didn't do that badly for a man with one eye— it's surprising how few parts really require two. I have played a one-eyed Iago, Macbeth and Theseus with equal success... Then I ran into Fincham. Now there was an unfortunate man—no money, and everyone chasing him for unpaid debts. So, I said to him, why not take up my line of business? It pays well enough when there *is* work and there are lots of pretty girls on and off the stage, if you know what I mean. With some greasepaint on he didn't look bad at all and he could say the words nice and clear— what more do you want from an actor? He was happy.

'But we cannot live for ever in a prelapsarian state of innocence. A very pretty young actress joined us—Kitty Hammond—and for a while Fincham was happier than ever. But young actresses attract attention like wasps round a jam pot. A nobleman spotted her on stage and offered her more than Fincham could ever have afforded. Fincham did his best, buying her ribbons and laces and the other fripperies that young women can be bought with—present company excepted, Lady Pole. The nobleman soon lost interest but then there was that clerk from the Navy Office—Mr Pepys. And he had money to spare as well.

'In short, Fincham realised he needed more than the theatre would pay him if he was to keep Kitty's rather fickle affections. He was always on the lookout for any chance to supplement his income. First he found ways of being helpful to the Duke of York—it's his company of actors and the Duke needed people to run errands of one sort or another. I don't *know* why he chose Fincham out of all the rest of us, but I can make a good guess. Fincham changed sides in 1660 in more than one way—found a new religion, and I don't mean yours, Mr Grey. The Duke continues to observe the rituals of the Church of England, but many of his closest servants are Catholics, and it is said that it is only a matter of time before the Duke becomes a Catholic too. Anyway, one day Fincham says to me: "You know, the Duke's not paying me nearly well enough for some of the things I'm doing." "No?" I say. "No," he says. "What sort of things?" I ask. "Can't tell you," he says, "but there's plenty who'd give good money to know. If you had a secret—a big one, a valuable one—who would you go to with it?" "What do you mean?" I say. "I mean treason," he says. "High treason." "Well," I say, "my Lord Arlington's your man for treason…"'

Callingham pauses and looks at me at this point, but I still say nothing. 'Anyway,' Callingham continues, unabashed, 'I told Fincham that he'd need to be careful, if he was about to sell some of the Duke's secrets. Oh, I will be, he says. And I'll tell you something else, he says. A friend of ours has shown up in the Duke's household. Who? I say. We knew him at Colchester, he says. He's calling himself Father Horncastle now—Jesuit priest, if you don't mind. Wants to renew the acquaintance. I've kept out of his way so far, and I'm not planning to talk to him unless I have to.'

Again, Callingham pauses to gauge my reaction.

'What do you mean, "knew him at Colchester"?' asks Aminta, who has been silent for a while, perhaps smarting under the lace and ribbons slur upon the integrity of her sex.

'I mean the siege of Colchester,' says Callingham. In describing his conversation with Fincham he'd become somehow smaller, almost furtive, but suddenly he was the actor again, his face lit up by the footlights. 'The great siege of Colchester, when the man of blood, Charles Stuart, took up arms against his people again but fell like Icarus—or was it Daedelus?—when the hot sun of the Republic melted the wax of tyranny.'

'You mean, when His Majesty the King attempted to regain his rightful throne,' says Aminta.

'I use the language of the time, my Lady. I say only what everyone said then. I am a loyal subject of His Majesty. But I do not suffer from the forgetfulness that so many people have now and imagine that I was always a Royalist. But to return to the subject of my story... I wish you to see the scene unfold before you, exactly as things were in the Year of Our Lord one thousand six hundred and forty-eight—the famous town of Colchester behind its thick, ancient walls, built by the Romans and now topped by the brass cannons of the evil tyrant...or rightful, God-anointed King, entirely as you prefer. Surrounding it were the forces of Parliament, with our own massive earthworks protecting our positions. Parliament's gunners pounding the walls day after day. Hundreds of stout pikemen and musketeers, waiting for the order to storm the city once the walls were breached. Brave troopers on horseback ready to follow them into the town or to chase the Royalist curs if they fled. From the battlements of the castle you might have seen a thousand pikes glinting in the sun, you might have heard the neighing of a thousand horses, eager for battle. Then the brassy crack of our cannons and the splintering of stone as the great balls crashed into the city.'

'Haven't you taken some of that from my play *The Siege of Famagusta?*' asks Aminta. 'It's very good, anyway.'

'Possibly a little,' says Callingham. 'One siege is much like another. We never did break through the walls, of course. Fairfax wasn't one to waste men unnecessarily and a frontal assault is always costly. We waited and eventually we starved them into surrender. But there was some action for all that, clearing Royalist fortifications outside the city walls. And when that order came, all of our men were overjoyed to see a bit of action—or almost all. Fincham and I caught one skulking coward trying to sneak away from the battlefield. We had him hauled up before Fairfax, but the villain gave him some story about misunderstanding his orders and mistaking east and west. Fairfax didn't hesitate to execute the Royalist commanders after Colchester fell—Lisle and Lucas both died by the castle wall—but he didn't want to shoot any of his own men if he didn't need to. So our deserter was simply dismissed and allowed to go on his way. But he swore vengeance on both of us...'

'And you say that was Horncastle?'

'That was Horncastle. And he never forgot his injury. In fact he came to visit me at my lodgings earlier this year to repeat his threats. I sent him away with a curse. Horncastle is a coward and wouldn't try anything on me. But to stab Fincham in the back in revenge for our handing him over to Fairfax— yes, he would do that. Kitty will be broken-hearted. I could weep.'

Callingham looks for a moment as if he will indeed weep, then, remembering that he was once a soldier, he pulls himself together and wipes a tear from the corner of his eye.

'So, did Horncastle threaten Fincham as well?' I ask.

'He must have done. "I'll get my revenge on both of you," he said to me, pulling a terrible face and shaking his fist. Yes, he was quite clear about that.'

'Inadvisable if he was really planning to kill Fincham,' I say. 'Better to say nothing than to threaten all and sundry in a way that will be remembered after the body is discovered.'

'Horncastle has a certain cunning—enough to prop a body against a wall and leave him for the dead cart to collect. But he is not a clever man. He would not have forgone the pleasure of threatening us merely to avoid detection. He wanted us to know he was getting his revenge.'

'So what is Horncastle's real name?'

'You mean, what was he calling himself at Colchester?'

'Yes.'

Callingham frowns and shakes his head. 'It was a long time ago... Jenkins? Jennings? Johnson?'

'But Fincham at least knew his real name?'

'If that *was* his real name then. Charles Fincham had known him longer, I think—perhaps even before Colchester. Yes, he would certainly have known it. But Fincham did not remind me. He merely said that the man was calling himself Horncastle now.'

'So, Horncastle joins the Duke's household, posing as a Jesuit priest, but Fincham, who is also working for the Duke, recognises him. In short, Fincham was in a position to expose him as a coward and a fraud?'

'I hadn't thought of that, but it is true. He could have done.'

'Then Horncastle visits Fincham to threaten him?'

'Indeed! So he does! I think you need look no further for his killer.'

'Do you have any idea where he might be found now he has fled his lodgings?'

'None at all. But do *you* know where he might have gone, Mr Grey? It is a matter of some importance to me. I had assumed his threats were empty, but if Horncastle has killed Charles Fincham, then I must fear for my own life too.'

'I think he is still in London, but not at his old lodgings, which were to be sealed up once it was known his landlord had the Plague. He escaped from them, killing his guard.'

'The guard too? If you hear any more, Mr Grey, I should be grateful if you would let me know. I do not doubt that in a fair fight I could defeat Horncastle. An actor must be proficient in swordplay after all. But if he attempts to ambush me as he did Fincham and this other poor man...'

'I shall,' I say. 'The moment I have news, I shall send a message. Horncastle has killed twice but we shall ensure that he does not kill again.'

Callingham picks up his glass and drains it. Then he places the empty vessel back on the table in front of him. 'Fincham was a brave man. He didn't deserve to die like that, even if he was an idiot to get involved in things he did not understand.'

I spend more of Arlington's money on two beds at Widow Sparrow's for the night. Then in the morning I hire a coach to take Aminta and me onwards to Braintree, where Aminta says Kitty is to be found in these times of pestilence.

'That is something else that you could not have done without me, cousin John,' she says, as we rumble along the parched roads under yet another clear blue sky. 'I'm sure Callingham did not know whither Kitty had fled. But I do.'

'Callingham seems to admire Kitty.'

'Kitty was widely admired. And she was flattered by the attention she received. But she liked Fincham best. He was a decent man. He was kind and he was loyal to her, unlike the other men she had known.'

'I thought you said that Fincham and Callingham whored together? Kitty can't have exactly approved of that.'

'Oh, that was before Kitty joined the company. Anyway, that is what you men do, isn't it? Marriage does not seem to have blunted Mr Pepys's appetite. You must have enjoyed one or two of the ladies of the town, cousin John?'

'Certainly not,' I say.

'I'm sure my father did. I am sure he would still, were it not for the expense and the distance to London.'

Both Aminta and I are aware that her father did not need to travel to London for entertainment. My mother's house was much closer and my father was away a great deal. I look at Aminta and wonder, as I have whenever I have thought of her over the past seven years, whether I am more closely related to her than might be convenient. More closely related than I am comfortable with.

I succeed in producing a carefree smile. 'I do not doubt it for a moment,' I say.

11

Kitty has been crying on Aminta's shoulder for five minutes. Aminta glances across at me, and she is right to glance in that way. Once again she is doing something that I could not have done.

It is at times like this, giving comfort to somebody who has just learned that the man they might have married is dead, that I see Aminta as she might have been. She is, after all, the daughter of the lord of the manor. Had she not chosen very badly whom she married (a man who, even if he had lived, was a poltroon), had her father not ruined himself, had she not had to face an impoverished exile as a supporter of the Stuarts, then this would have been her role in life—visiting the sick and the bereaved, bringing kind words and soup to her admiring and devoted tenants. She may now be an impoverished writer, but it is clear to everyone she meets that she is a member of the gentry. I, conversely, as she has so often reminded me in the past, am merely a lawyer, albeit one with moderately illustrious ancestors on my mother's side of the family. Better by far that she breaks the news to Kitty. It's not a job for a lawyer.

I take a turn round the garden of the inn that Kitty's father runs. Here in Braintree, too, the Plague seems very far away. The sun continues to shine and the birds sing in the trees. The shade dapples the grass. There is a scent of hay and roses. It is like every summer I can remember. Only a small group of armed men checking passes, just before we entered the town, reminded us that fear of infection is spreading outwards like a dark mist, to envelop the countryside around London. The Constable challenged us in a most threatening way, but a combination of our coach and our certificate of health persuaded him to let us through. Had we arrived on foot, I think we would have been turned back as vagrants. Even then we were warned that to attempt to travel further would be pointless—the whole of Essex is starting to erect barricades to prevent travellers spreading the disease. One city is rumoured to be hanging anyone arriving from London as a matter of course, though nobody could say which city it was.

When I return, Aminta is sitting talking to Kitty, who has a glass of brandy beside her. She is a sweet little thing—small and dark with large brown eyes. I can see that she might have appealed to Pepys and to the unnamed nobleman as well as to Fincham. I am introduced and I add a few poor words of condolence of my own.

'It is my fault,' she says. 'I have led a wicked life and God is punishing me for it. I should not have become an actress. I'm sorry, my Lady, but it is true. I have allowed myself to be led astray. If I had remained here, Charles would not have died.'

Of course she may be correct in this last statement. If Callingham is right, Charles Fincham became entangled in espionage only to earn money to buy her ribbons. On the other hand it is unlikely that God has time to punish individuals for minor infractions when (if certain preachers are to be believed) He has set His heart on punishing the wicked more generally by smiting us with pestilence. Fincham seems to have died because, like so many agents, he was incautious when changing sides, and he had forgotten an old quarrel.

'Did you ever meet this man Horncastle?' I ask.

She shakes her head. 'Charles told me of him,' she says. 'He came to visit him.'

'Did he mention his real name?'

'I didn't know he had another name. Charles seemed to treat him with contempt.'

'He wasn't worried by him, then?'

'Worried? Yes, I think so—but not afraid, if that's what you mean. He was very thoughtful after Horncastle's visit. When I asked him what the matter was, he said that there was something he had to do, and that there was some risk, but after that everything would be all right.'

'You mean that he would have the money he needed?' I ask.

'Was Horncastle offering him money, then?' says Kitty.

'I'm not sure,' I reply. 'Perhaps he did and Charles turned him down. He clearly did not fear Horncastle, who seems a contemptible creature. But he was, in that respect, unwise.'

'Please catch him for me, Mr Grey,' says Kitty. 'To see him hanged is the one thing that I will live for.'

If Horncastle has killed only one of the two men we think he has killed, then he most certainly deserves to hang. In these days of the Plague, lives are cheap, but still not that cheap.

The journey to London is easier. Nobody is concerned about our bringing disease back into the city. It's already there. A little bit more won't hurt. We pass groups of men on the road, armed with muskets and pikes and pitchforks, but they simply watch us with mild curiosity as we pass by, stupidly quitting the safety of the countryside for what seems to be certain death in London.

'I'm sorry that Kitty thinks God has punished her for being an actress,' says Aminta. 'As a profession it doesn't pay nearly well enough for that. She had a great deal of talent and was very popular with the male members of the audience.'

'I'm sure she was,' I say. 'Who was her noble admirer, by the way?'

'The Earl of Rochester,' says Aminta. 'Kitty was wise enough to see that that would lead nowhere good. She was dazzled at first by his title, but was always aware of his reputation. She learned quickly to fend him off.'

'Would Rochester have seen Fincham as a rival?'

'I doubt that he would have noticed Fincham. Rochester would run somebody through with his rapier at the merest hint of an insult—or more likely would pay somebody else to do it. But I don't think he was even aware of Fincham as an actor or as a possible rival. I don't think he played any part in Fincham's death, if that is what you mean.'

'And Pepys?'

'Pepys lacks Rochester's aristocratic arrogance. But he is naturally cautious. If he entertains one of my actresses, he takes two coaches home, switching coachmen at a convenient point. That way nobody knows both where he started and ended his journey, and nobody can tell his wife. I don't think he would risk killing somebody for love. Mr Pepys regards half the women of London as his rightful property. If thwarted in one direction he can always find solace elsewhere—the wives of navy contractors, for example, who are often compliant on their husbands' behalves. He is enthusiastic, but easily put off by the slightest hint of danger.'

'You're right,' I say. 'We need not look further than Horncastle. He had a triple motive—Fincham was in a position to expose him and cause him to lose a comfortable place. He wanted revenge for Colchester. And he wanted to get his hands on the letter and to sell it. Perhaps he first offered Fincham money for the letter, then killed him when he would not take it.'

'What I don't understand,' says Aminta, 'is why Horncastle would give them such a clear warning of his intention? Grimacing and shaking his fist seems to be over-egging the pudding.'

'Have you seen no revenge tragedy in your theatrical career? That is what revengers do. There's no point in revenge if the victim has no idea why they are to die.'

'I have always enjoyed a good revenge tragedy. Comedy pleases the crowds, but you need tragedy if you want to offer them the rape, murder, mutilation and incest that they so enjoy. Very well then, we are in a revenge tragedy and, if we are to observe its rules strictly, it is now for us to avenge Fincham's murder. And then of course die horribly ourselves, because that is one of the other conventions.'

'It is fortunate we are not in a work of fiction and so may avoid that fate. Hanging Horncastle would be good; but it is merely a bonus, for all that I would like to help Kitty. Our main task is to find Horncastle, recover the letter and collect our reward for returning it to Arlington. Let's not forget that.'

It is late afternoon by the time we return to Lincoln's Inn. Will is waiting for us.

'Bad news, I fear, Mr Grey,' he says. 'My Lord Arlington requests your presence. He has found both Horncastle and the letter himself. You have had a wasted journey and we have lost our fee.'

CHAPTER

12

I read the letter again.

> The Duke of York presents his compliments to His
> Excellency the Ambassador of France and hopes that
> this will be to his satisfaction. The Duke awaits a
> response as before.

'And that is the letter?' I ask. 'That is what Fincham died
for? That is what Pepys's master, who knew the contents, was
prepared to offer me so much money to recover?'

'It would seem so,' says Arlington. 'The original was in
code: a simple substitution code, which Horncastle was, however,
unable to decipher. He has been carrying this around for the past
two days in the belief that it was of great value. When he brought
it to me, and we had it made into plain English, I had, sadly, to
tell him that it was worth nothing.'

Williamson, standing at Arlington's side, nods. 'It is, to say the least, enigmatic in its brevity.'

'You've checked for invisible ink between the lines?' I ask.

'Of course,' says Williamson. 'That was our first thought when we read this. We immediately applied a candle to the original paper. What you see is all there is.'

I look at the coded version of the letter, the thing that Horncastle delivered. Three rows of letters, in groups of four, on one side of the paper. Nothing at all—not a single mark—on the other. I pass it back to Williamson.

'And he came to you?' I ask. 'You did not need to seek him out?'

Arlington smiles. 'It was always a possibility. Either you would find him, at some cost to His Majesty, or he would come here free of charge. It was only prudent to allow for both outcomes. Happily, as you see, I am not put to the expense of paying you. I should have been annoyed to discover that I had had to lay out good money for this trifle. I hope, however, that you have not spent much in your investigations. The payment of your expenses was of course also as much contingent upon your success in retrieving the letter as was the payment of a fee. I would have liked to have given you your expenses at least—particularly because, as you pointed out, they were unlimited—but, as you also said, we must keep to the terms of the contract. Since you are a lawyer, I am sure you would not wish it otherwise.'

'Thank you. I was aware of the terms. And you have charged Horncastle with Fincham's murder?'

'Not yet,' says Williamson. 'Strangely, he denies it.'

'And the murder of the guard?'

Williamson shrugs. 'The same. He says that the guard was alive and well at the front of the house, when he left via the back. Through his earlier demands, Horncastle had made the guard grateful for a little peace and perhaps slightly too incautious. Thus he could, at his leisure, remove the boards that had been used to seal up the rear window. He had no need, he said, to inconvenience the guard in any way.'

'Well, somebody killed the poor man,' I say.

'So they did,' says Arlington. 'We are about to talk to Father Horncastle again. I thought you might care to accompany us. I am sure that you must now know a little about the case after your holiday in Essex. You may have some valuable insights to offer.'

'Having declined to pay me for my investigations, you would now like me to undertake further work for nothing?'

'Yes please, if you would be so kind, Mr Grey. I have a feeling that it would be most helpful, and also perhaps instructive for you. Father Horncastle is being held at the Tower. There are other places in which we could have imprisoned him equally safely, but I do find that the Tower focuses men's minds in a way that other prisons do not. All that stone…it weighs upon a prisoner. I have a carriage waiting. We can be there in fifteen minutes.'

I have been led along an underground passage smelling of piss and river water. The flagstones are green with one or the other. The Thames is, I think, close by and disconcertingly above us; only wet stone holds it back. This is not where you send somebody whom you wish to make comfortable. There is no sunlight down here, even at this time of day at the height of summer—not in this low, subterranean thoroughfare. A man with a flaming torch precedes us. The walls flicker black and red, as they say Hell does, but Hell is reputedly not this cold or damp. Arlington follows the torchbearer, a kerchief held to his nose. A clerk with a large ledger and a quill pen is at his elbow, anxious that the light does not outpace him. Then comes Williamson, with long purposeful strides. I bring up the rear. We proceed briskly but with care—the floor is slippery and nobody would wish to fall on the slime that covers it.

It is Arlington himself who produces a key and unlocks the door to the cell. He has not needed to ask the torchbearer which way we were going. He knows where this stinking hole is. He has visited before.

Horncastle is squatting in a corner. He has no stool to sit on, nor straw to lie on, nor jug to drink from nor pot to piss in. He has already been there some hours at least. He knows Arlington can keep him there for ever if he wishes, until he is skin and bone and sores, and until he forgets what daylight is. He looks up, his rat-like eyes gleaming between strands of lank, black hair. He glances uncertainly at the leather-jacketed brute holding the torch, then he sees me and grins.

'Good to meet you again, Mr Grey,' he says. 'Always a pleasure doing business with a gentleman like you.'

'Ah, so you already know each other, Grey?' says Arlington. 'Excellent. Then perhaps you can introduce us.'

'His name is Esmond Underhill,' I say. 'We met some years ago when I was working for John Thurloe and Samuel Morland. He is an extreme Republican and a double agent of the very lowest kind. He is most certainly not a priest. He lacks principles of any sort. Anything he has told you so far will be a lie.'

'And I'm so pleased to meet *you* again, Mr Grey,' Underhill says. 'Didn't I always say we were destined to be friends? We have a great deal in common. Delighted that you have found the time to visit me, though I can offer you no refreshment on this occasion.'

'Thank you, Mr Grey,' says Arlington, ignoring Underhill. 'Mr Morland thought that you might know the man. The fact that he had called himself "John Grey" suggested you had met before and that he had cause to dislike you. We were fairly certain that Horncastle was an assumed name, and the gentleman here was understandably reluctant to reveal his true one. You have saved us a great deal of work in identifying him. Of course, we do have other ways of persuading men to tell us the truth, which we may still decide to use if we have to.'

Williamson and I exchange glances. I'm not sure he approves of what Arlington is hinting at any more than I do.

'You can't torture me,' says Underhill, puffing his chest out. 'I know my rights. You can torture prisoners in Scotland but not here in England. It's against the law. Ask Grey.'

'I can do as I wish here in the Tower,' says Arlington. 'I can certainly leave you to rot. Nobody knows you're here. Nobody would care very much if I chose to have you racked, or at least nobody who counts for anything. Everyone has rights, but you'll find you need money or friends to exercise them to their full extent. As things stand, I can make you scream as much as I choose.'

Most men would accept the truth of that, but not Underhill, for some reason.

'You wouldn't dare,' he says, squaring up to the Secretary of State for the Southern Department. 'I have a value to you and you know it. Lay a finger on me and I'll tell you nothing. Anyway, if you were going to kill me, you'd have already done it—and if you wanted to try torture, you shouldn't have brought Grey. He's no friend of mine but he's straight enough. If I'm found dead here, he'll testify against you. He won't be bribed neither. You know that too.'

Arlington looks at me. It is just possible that he has miscalculated. He wouldn't have had Underhill tortured because he too values precedent and the law. And Williamson wouldn't let him. But he would have wanted to keep Underhill in doubt of that fact. My presence here has helped in one way but impeded him in another. Underhill may be a puffed-up sparrow dictating terms to a hawk, but this hawk needs to be cautious for some reason.

'Do you really think Lord Arlington is going to make any pacts with a double murderer?' I say. 'You can hang only once but, in the meantime, I'd be quite happy to see your arms pulled out of their sockets.'

Underhill grins again, quite an achievement for a man in his position.

'Except you wouldn't allow them to do it, and you know it,' he says. 'And, anyway, I didn't kill either of them. I've already told them the guard was alive when I left. All I needed to do was remove a few poorly nailed boards and squeeze out of the back window. Easy as anything.'

'You had the letter Fincham was carrying,' I say. 'You can hardly say you had nothing to do with his death.'

'Arlington's got the letter now. Does that mean he killed Fincham?'

'This is getting you nowhere,' Williamson says. 'Just keep to the facts, Mr Underhill.'

'If I'm being threatened with torture, I'm not telling you anything at all.'

Arlington clearly wishes he could torture Underhill and get the whole thing over with, but we all know he can't. Not here. Not now. 'All right,' he says. 'You'll come to no harm if you've broken no laws.'

'That's correct,' says Williamson. 'We can promise you that at least.' Though he plays a subordinate part in today's discussions, there is a reassuring solidity in everything he says. Underhill already trusts him in a way he doesn't trust Arlington.

'I was following Fincham,' Underhill begins. 'I can't exactly deny I was doing that. So was your man, my Lord—don't think I didn't see him. Fincham has a very loose tongue. By the time he set out to deliver the letter, half London was probably on his tail. He didn't have a natural talent for the work. Not like me or like Grey over there. Fincham headed first for Mr Morland's office. I thought he was going to hand the thing over to you. But just before he got there he started to act nervous, as if he was aware he wasn't alone. He clearly didn't want to be seen informing on his master, whatever Morland would pay him for the goods. He hesitated, then he changed direction suddenly. One moment he was there and the next he had gone. In short, Fincham gave us both the slip—me and your man—which was a big mistake because neither of us wanted him dead and somebody else out there did.

'Well, I guessed where he was bound for, so I headed towards Westminster, using all the shortcuts I knew. When I finally caught sight of him again, he was walking quickly down the street, maybe a hundred yards ahead of me. The light was already fading, but I could tell who it was. I called out to him and he turned, but at that very moment it was as if he jumped sideways into an alleyway. I cursed and ran to him, but when I found him he was already on the ground. He was half against the wall, slumped forwards. Then I saw the knife. Somebody had clearly grabbed him as he went past, dragged him in and stabbed him in the back, exactly when I called out—but, seeing me, they'd run off. The question was whether they'd got to the letter first. I lifted Fincham a bit and I heard a sort of rustling noise from his doublet, so I think to myself—well, that's where it is, then—you're in luck, Esmond Underhill. Fincham may be dead but whoever killed him didn't get the letter. So, I undid the top buttons on his doublet, and what do you know? There was a letter, looking very much like what I was after and without even a spot of blood on it. I eased it out very gently and slipped it into my pocket. Then Fincham gave a groan, which was a bit of a shock, as you will imagine, because I thought he'd snuffed it.

'He tried to speak to me, but he couldn't get the words out, bless him. So, I put my head close to his and said, who did this to you, my old friend? However things turned out, I thought it might be useful to know… Anyway, he looked at me, smiled and then said, "Underhill, my old comrade". But those were the only words he said to me and they were the very last words he ever spoke. His eyes just glazed over, though I thought I still saw his chest moving. Well, like I say, it was getting dark so it was only then that I noticed another body right by—and you could see it was somebody who'd died of the Plague. So I decided not to hang around to see if Fincham was going to tell me any more. Since the knife was in his back, the chances were that he didn't know who'd stabbed him anyway, and I was starting to get nervous in case his killer *hadn't* run off. I patted him on the shoulder one last time, in a very friendly way, and legged it. Fincham was still alive, more or less, when I left him.

'When I got home I carefully eased the seal away and opened the letter up. I couldn't read it because it was in code and there wasn't much of it anyway, but if somebody had killed Fincham for it, it had to be more than it seemed. I knew my duty and brought it to His Lordship's office. And now, contrary to all principles of justice, I've been thrown into this cell. There's gratitude, Mr Grey.'

'Your indignation is uncalled for,' I say. 'You knew the risk you were taking showing your face here. It's not just that you were in possession of the letter. We know that you'd already threatened to kill Charles Fincham. He would hardly have wasted his dying breath calling you his friend.'

'I called him a friend. He called me a comrade. I take that as the higher compliment. Anyway, why would I threaten to kill him?'

'Because he accused you of cowardice at the siege of Colchester,' I say.

'Fincham accused me of cowardice? Whoever told you that?'

'Patrick Callingham,' I say.

Underhill laughs. 'Callingham certainly accused me of cowardice, but my Lord Fairfax saw through his design.'

'Callingham says you ran away.'

'Let me tell you what happened,' says Underhill. 'Callingham had just arrived at the siege from God knows where, claiming the rank of corporal. Fincham and I were both serving in Lord Fairfax's army. When we were ordered to clear some outlying Royalist positions, Callingham was put in charge of our section. Now, we were dragoons, but that day Fairfax needed us to fight on foot because that was the job that needed to be done. Callingham may have known cavalry drill, but he had no idea how infantry should be commanded. Well, he led our section forwards but then...have you ever been in a battle, Mr Grey?'

'No,' I say.

'Lord Arlington has, though. So he'll know what I say next is the truth. By the time we'd fired a volley and the Royalists had fired a volley, and we'd fired another, you could hardly see ten yards ahead of you for the smoke. Another couple of discharges and you could scarce see the man next to you. Callingham calls us on, but he's used to being on a horse above it all and he's lost on foot—taking us God knows where, sideways to the correct line of our advance. So I try to lead the men back towards the Royalist positions. Callingham realises I'm right but knows he'll look a fool so he accuses me of going the wrong way and trying to duck out of the fight.'

'So what then?'

'A musket ball comes flying out of the smoke from the direction I'd been trying to lead us and takes Callingham's eye out. That made me laugh, I can tell you—still brings a smile to my face now. So, I help him back to the dressing station and he tells the surgeon I'd been trying to run for it and should be arrested.'

'And were you arrested?'

'Callingham was a corporal. I was a trooper. What do you think?'

'And then?'

'As I say, Fairfax saw it was nonsense and dismissed the charges.'

'Why?'

'Because plenty of others witnessed the event. Fincham came forward and gave evidence for me—so there's another reason why I wouldn't have killed him. He was a good man. Not long after, I was made corporal myself. Does that sound as if they thought I was a coward?'

'But you never forgave Callingham or Fincham?'

'I never forgave Callingham. I told you, Fincham had nothing to do with it. He'd advanced with the others and taken the Royalist positions, just as I'd tried to do. He was a brave man. His dying words were to call me comrade, and comrades we were.'

'He knew who you were. He could have exposed you to the Duke as an imposter,' I say.

'Why would he do that? We were friends. I was safe enough.'

'Paris had already warned the Duke that you were no priest and that you should not be trusted.'

'Had they? Well, that explains a lot, but I won't be going back there again. Look, once I worked out what he was up to, I went to visit Fincham at his lodgings. I tried to persuade him to come in with me. He'd pass me whatever he was carrying and I'd sell it and we'd split the proceeds. When he wouldn't, and when I knew he'd finally been given something really important to carry, I followed him, thinking I might pick his pocket, or something... But I didn't kill him. I had no reason to kill him at all.'

'Why did you think *this* letter was particularly valuable?' asks Williamson.

Underhill hesitates, considering his options, one of which may be to tell the truth.

'I've told you before that the Duke was always sending messages to the French Ambassador. Usually in code. There were rumours in the Duke's household that this one was special. And I'd overheard one or two things... So I thought I'd get proof of what I'd already told you. Even though you hadn't believed me.'

'That was very public-spirited of you,' says Williamson.

'Thank you.'

'And who else have you tried to sell it to?' asks Arlington.

Underhill looks for a moment as if he might tell him, but thinks better of it.

'Nobody. I'd have come sooner but...I was delayed.'

Arlington shrugs. He has the letter now, even if he doesn't understand it. He is also willing to give Underhill considerable benefit of the doubt over the deaths of Fincham and the guard. Arlington needs the information Underhill has more than he needs a hanging. There are plenty of other men to hang if necessary.

'So, let's go back a step,' says Williamson. 'Why did you join His Highness's household in the first place and why did you choose the name Father Horncastle? Was this also out of a desire to be of assistance to us?'

'I'm glad you asked me that, Mr Williamson,' says Underhill. 'After Oliver died and Charles Stuart came in, I thought to seek my fortune abroad. I travelled in many strange and wonderful places, but mainly Holland, now I come to think about it. Unfortunately I made enemies along the way—dangerous Republicans, for sadly such people still exist—and was obliged to return and go into hiding in my own country. I needed to change my name and find somewhere that my enemies would not find me. So, I took on the guise of Father Horncastle and arrived at the residence of the Duke, claiming to be an English Catholic priest hunted by the authorities. The Duke, who is the best-known secret Catholic in the land, took me in and gave me work and protection.'

'You expected to get away with that?' I say. 'That the Duke would not see through you?'

Underhill grins. 'I once had to hide out at the English College at Douai for a bit—long story. I can pass as a lot of things, including a priest. The point is that *I* saw through the *Duke's* plans and came at once to you, as an honest man should.'

'That was a lucky chance,' I say.

'Precisely,' he says.

'Let me put another possibility to you,' I say. 'While you were in Holland, our enemies, the Dutch, recruited you to infiltrate the household of the Duke of York, High Admiral of England, and send back whatever information you could. That was your only reason for returning to England. The Dutch gave you a new name and forged papers to assist you. As a hardened Republican, you were more than content to betray your own country, but you decided you could make more money by selling whatever you had discovered to us.'

Underhill smiles. I am not so far from the mark.

'Good,' says Arlington. 'I'm sure that is true. So, do you have further information for us about the Duke's household?'

'I might have,' says Underhill. 'And it would give me great pleasure to tell you. But first I want to be moved out of this stinking hole.'

'I shall consider your request,' says Arlington.

'So, I am to be released?'

'Sadly not,' says Arlington.

'Then I'm telling you nothing more.'

Arlington nods to the clerk and turns to go. The interview is over.

'You have no right to hold me here,' says Underhill.

'I probably don't,' says Arlington. 'And much good may that do you. Come, Mr Grey. Come, Mr Williamson. I think our work here is finished for the moment.'

As we proceed back down the slimy passageway, Arlington says: 'Some of what he told us may be the truth. We shall discover in due course which parts those were. I think you are right, Mr Grey, that somebody supplied him with papers and a name—the Dutch, probably. I've asked our agents in Amsterdam and The Hague if they know anything about him. When it became clear to Underhill that the Duke didn't trust him, I think he approached Fincham to see if a deal could be done—and then Callingham, as somebody who might know what Fincham was up to, when Fincham wouldn't help. Only when all else failed did he actually try to follow Fincham and steal the letter.'

'Was one of your agents also following Fincham?'

'Yes, of course, but he had nothing to do with Fincham's death, if that's what you mean. If he had, I'd have had the letter all along. And I'd probably have had enough time to work out what on earth it meant.'

'What do you propose to do with Mr Underhill now?'

'Nothing,' says Arlington. 'Nothing at all.'

A door slams shut behind us and the noise echoes down the long, dark passageway.

I arrive back at Lincoln's Inn, tired and hoping that Will has no further news for me of any sort. I should like a bottle of canary and a peaceful evening. Perhaps Will has anticipated my wish and has already laid out everything on the table.

I open the door to my chamber. Will is not there, but Aminta is. That, however, is not the main thing that strikes me about my room. I blink twice but my eyes are not mistaken. Accompanying Aminta is a child of about six or seven, wrapped only in a large shawl.

'Will has gone out to find a dress for her,' says Aminta.

'Why?' I ask.

'Because she doesn't have one,' says Aminta.

'I mean why is she here?' I ask.

'I honestly had no choice,' says Aminta.

'Perhaps you'd better explain,' I say.

'Of course,' says Aminta, 'but, before I begin, let me reassure you that it is quite possible that she does *not* have the Plague. Whatever she may tell you.'

CHAPTER

13

'After you left us,' says Aminta, '…can I pour you some more wine, by the way?…no?…it's quite good…well, after you'd gone, I decided to return to my lodgings. I set out for Westminster but, having travelled a short way, I found the street blocked. An altercation was taking place between a magistrate and the inhabitants of a house that the authorities were trying to shut up. The owner of the house was leaning out of a first-floor window and remonstrating with the magistrate. There had, he said, been sickness in the house but it was not Plague; or, if it was the Plague, then nobody else in the house yet showed any signs of sickening. Even if the Plague was amongst them, however—and he wasn't saying that it was—were the healthy members of the family to be condemned to remain and die with the sick? The man said he had a sister in Salisbury who would take them all in, if they could be permitted to leave the house and travel there. Once in Salisbury they would undergo any quarantine that the law demanded.

'The magistrate, who had clearly been called out to adjudicate on a dispute between the householder and the Searchers of the Dead, was insistent. Everyone in the house must remain there. That was the law. That was what happened elsewhere. He could make no exceptions.'

'So the girl is from the house?' I say. 'You've brought me a child from a house shut up because of the Plague?'

'Don't jump ahead in the story,' says Aminta. 'It may have a completely different ending. Where was I? Oh, yes, the officious magistrate. Well, the man's neighbours for the most part supported him against the City authorities, albeit that his imprisonment was nominally for their protection. They had succeeded in wrenching off the padlock that the guard had attached to the door and were now preventing him from fastening a new one. But the guard was still standing in front of the entrance with his halberd. It was, you might say, a stand-off. The magistrate had the law on his side but he was heavily outnumbered and aware that feelings were running high. He could not be certain that, if things turned nasty, even the guard would necessarily choose to protect him against this angry mob—not if other, safer alternatives presented themselves. The guard, too, was looking anxious, because if things turned nasty the magistrate might be able to run faster than he could with his pike, which would mean that he was caught first. Had I been the magistrate, I would have threatened and blustered a bit, and then left while I was still in one piece, taking the guard and his weapon with me. But, fair play to him, he bravely stood his ground.'

'So, at what point do you abduct the child?' I ask.

'Am I telling this story or are you?'

'You are,' I say.

'Precisely,' says Aminta. 'I am telling the story. Fortunately the householder was not yet inciting the crowd to violence, as I have heard some have in the past. He continued to lean on his windowsill, smoking his pipe, and to argue calmly and reasonably against the policy of shutting up houses, with great patience and at surprising length.

'The crowd was enjoying it, but I felt that the householder's speech was rather too long and lacked the variations of light and shade that I would have given it. After a while I decided that I was not going to get through the throng anyway, and so I retraced my steps and tried to work my way round the back streets. A narrow alleyway offered the best chance and I took it. As I was hurrying along, however, a small gate opened and a woman appeared with a child wrapped in a shawl.'

'In other words, this child,' I say. 'The one you have there in a shawl.'

'The shawl certainly suggests a coincidence,' says Aminta. 'But you'll never know if you keep interrupting. Where was I?'

'Child wrapped in a shawl, a bit like the one you have.'

'Thank you. I realised, at the same moment, that I must be at the back of the house that was being shut up. "Take her, please!" exclaimed the lady. "We cannot all get away, for they know that my husband and I and our maid and children are in the house. If we tried to make a general escape by the back gate, then they would discover quickly that we had gone and would search for us. In any case, one of the other children is already ill, with some disease that is in no way the Plague, and cannot travel. But little Sophia is well. I have wrapped her in a new shawl that can have no taint of the Plague on it. If you take her now, nobody will suspect and she at least may live. My husband's sister dwells in Salisbury, hard by the cathedral. Martha Thatcher, she's called. If we do not survive and you cannot return her to us, take her there. Take this ring too—my sister-in-law will recognise it as coming from me and she may then sell it or do as she wishes with it to pay for the child's lodgings. My husband will keep the magistrate talking for at least another quarter of an hour—he has scarcely covered half of the legal precedents yet. You will have all the time you need to get away, even if they do eventually suspect it is a trick and that one of us has gone. You have a kind face, my Lady. Please do this for us and may God bless you and *everyone who helps you save our little Sophia*—and may you *and they* never find yourselves in our terrible position."'

'She said all that?' I ask. 'Those precise words? With that emphasis?'

'I may have improved on it slightly, just here and there. Can I pour you some more wine?...no?... Anyway, the point is that, before I could say anything in reply, the girl was thrust into my arms, the ring into my hands and the gate slammed shut.'

'You banged on the gate of course and attempted to return the child.'

'Possibly.'

'But you doubtless received no response.'

'None at all,' says Aminta.

'You then attempted to take the child back to the guard at the front of the house?'

'I wasn't sure of the way to the street in question—there was a left and a right, or maybe a right and a left. It was complicated.'

'I see. And then?' I ask.

'I told the nice lady to run,' says the girl.

'And did she?'

'No, she walked quickly to this big house. A man let her in and said he would find me a dress.'

'Did he say whether I would mind your being here?'

'He said you wouldn't mind,' said the girl.

'Which was very generous of you,' says Aminta. 'We are both most grateful. And you are, as I hope I made clear, in receipt of a mother's blessing of remarkable clarity. I suppose I couldn't pour you some wine?'

'So, where will she stay?' I ask.

'With me until we can take her to Salisbury.'

'We?'

'The pass you have says Mr and Mrs Grey. It would look odd if I were travelling alone.'

'But not their daughter, whatever she's called...'

'Sophia,' says the girl. 'The lady told you. My name's Sophia. I have the Plague.'

'No you don't,' says Aminta. 'Look, John, we could just add her name to the pass. Nobody in her family has actually died. Not yet. Who would know anyway?'

'Excellent,' I say. 'We are to carry a child with the Plague, abducted from under the nose of the magistrate, to Salisbury, misusing a pass that I have been supplied with for official purposes. Would you like me to break the law in any other way?'

'If you are too scared to act as any decent person would, then we can hide her in the carriage as we pass through the gate,' says Aminta dismissively.

'You have money for a carriage?' I ask.

'No, but you do. Anyway, we could probably sell the ring, if you are also too mean to pay yourself.'

'I am not going to Salisbury,' I say. 'You have taken it upon yourself to flout the law. You must accept the consequences, Aminta. The girl is yours to look after until you can return her and the ring to her parents. There is every chance one or other will survive the forty days quarantine and come looking for her.'

'You *promised…*' says Sophia.

At this point Will returns to find the three of us glaring at each other.

'Good afternoon, Mr Grey,' he says brightly. 'The dress has seen better days, but it was the best I could find at short notice. I took the liberty of paying for it out of the cash box. Three shillings. I think it will serve little Sophia well enough until you all get to Salisbury, where doubtless these things can be obtained.'

'We're not going to Salisbury,' I say.

'Aren't you, sir? Lady Pole said you were.'

'No, Will, we are not. Lady Pole and this child are just leaving.'

'They won't stay for supper then? I have ordered food and the grocer's boy will be delivering it shortly.'

'Yes,' says Sophia. 'We shall stay for supper. And then, if we can't go to Salisbury, I shall have the Plague here.'

It is early morning. The sun is shining through my window. It is another cloudless summer's day. I have been awoken by a banging at my outer door, but it stops and I turn over and fall into blissful slumber again. Then, as if from very far away, I hear a hand knocking politely on my bedroom door. I open my eyes again. Aminta and Sophia left after supper, without any offer from me to assist in their travel plans, so only Will and I are here.

'What is it, Will?' I call.

'It's Lord Arlington, sir. He presents his compliments and says he wants you to go to Salisbury straight away. May I show him in?'

CHAPTER

14

I am sitting in front of an open window in my dressing gown, as yet unshaven. Arlington sits opposite, a cup of chocolate, which Will has just made for us, in his hand. I think he has not slept last night. His jowls, too, are dark with stubble and there is grey beneath his eyes. But the nose patch is fresh and glossy.

'We heard yesterday evening from The Hague,' he says. 'Our agent reports that a man very much like Underhill was there, calling himself Grey. He did not in fact consort with any of the known English extremists—quite the reverse. Our man says he steered clear of any of his fellow countrymen—though it is not impossible that they steered clear of him. He did, however, have contact with the secret service of the Dutch—that is to say, the people with whom we are now at war. He vanished suddenly from The Hague a couple of months ago, leaving a number of unpaid bills, as spies often do.'

'Interesting news, if a little old,' I say. 'But your agent has responded very quickly. I cannot see how you can have asked the question and he responded so quickly.'

'We asked for a report some time ago,' says Arlington, 'when we were first approached—and not just at The Hague but in other places where Underhill might have been. The information reached us as slowly as these things usually do. Having received it last night, I thought that I would return and question our prisoner further in the light of this new intelligence.'

'Very wise,' I say. 'And what information did you get from him?'

'Nothing,' says Arlington. 'He still refused to say who had sent him to England. He disregarded my threats that he would not be released unless he talked. He is one of the few men that we have housed in that fetid pit who genuinely seemed at home there.'

'Presumably if you leave him where he is, he will eventually change his mind. Not even Underhill can prefer to live in such a place.'

Arlington nods. 'His cockiness will diminish if he really thinks he will end his days in the Tower. What he now insists he wants, however, is to tell the King in person. What he has to say is so important that only His Majesty's ears may hear it.'

'And the King is now where...?'

'The court is in Salisbury, we think. His Majesty recently left Hampton Court to travel there with the Queen. Whether they stay long depends on whether the Plague has reached Salisbury yet. If it has, then they will go to Oxford next.'

'Send our man under armed guard to Salisbury then.'

'He won't go under armed guard. He says that I'll have him killed on the road. He will only go with you. He trusts you for some reason, while at the same time using your name as an alias whenever he is doing something particularly vile.'

'So I am to accompany Underhill and his guards?'

'No guards. Just you. Those are his terms.'

'Underhill is dictating terms? You scarcely have to accept them, my Lord. He willingly admits to betraying his current master, the Duke. He is almost certainly a Dutch agent and a murderer. His position is not the strongest. Just leave him to rot for another month. He'll change his mind.'

'How can we be sure we have another month? What if he knows of some immediate danger? If there is a plot against the state—by the Dutch or by the Duke—I cannot delay taking action.'

'You really think he will tell the King what he won't tell us?' I ask.

'I have no idea. But if he does not reveal all, then it will be the King's failure, not mine. If what he reveals is trivial, then the King can dismiss it as such, not me. And if Underhill accuses the Duke of treason, then it will be on his head alone. I shall have done all I can, however things turn out.'

'I see the advantages,' I say. 'Is that Mr Williamson's advice too—to send him to Salisbury?'

'I have not had time to consult him. Get Underhill safely to the King and our original agreement stands. One hundred guineas. Plus reasonable expenses.'

'That's a lot of money for a couple of days' work.'

'Don't underestimate the work,' says Arlington. 'He may try to escape.'

'And if he does?'

'Do whatever you have to,' says Arlington. 'I shall not blame you if you have to shoot him.'

'It could be inconvenient if I arrived at the court without him. And you will have lost the information he has.'

'Better dead than at large and selling whatever information he has to the Dutch or Spanish or Lord Clarendon. And the King is not expecting him. If he does not arrive, he will be none the wiser.'

'There is unfortunately the small question of legality,' I say. 'I mean, if I have to shoot him and a local magistrate wonders why I have done it.'

'If you have to prevent his escape, then I promise you that you will suffer no penalty. You have my word.'

'Thank you,' I say. 'Could I, however, please have that in writing?'

'Do you doubt my word as a peer of the realm?'

'I do not doubt your good intentions, my Lord. In the event of my having to prevent his escape, I would just prefer to have something that I can show the authorities there and then before they hang me.'

Arlington looks around him, testily. 'I shall send you something as soon as I have paper and pen.'

'I am a lawyer,' I say. 'I am never without both.'

I, too, look around the room. Will has tidied up and taken the spare paper to his own office below. I feel in the pockets of my dressing gown and bring out a blank folded sheet, with just the smallest trace of very dark red wax still adhering to it where a seal once was. I blink at it, not realising at first what it is. Then I see that it is Underhill's counterfeit letter—the same that I chased after yesterday, yet now lacking all but a purplish fragment of the hastily applied sealant. Very well then, let Arlington write upon this. How fitting that the false paper that Underhill used to dupe me may prove to be his death warrant.

I carefully smooth the sheet out on the table, rubbing out the creases as best I can. You'd scarcely know that it had spent a couple of hours in the pest house. I decide not to tell Arlington, who might fret unduly, and go to fetch pen and ink from my desk.

He looks at it, then, seizing on the least impediment, pushes it back across the table. 'If this is the best you have, I shall write it on fresh paper once I have returned to my office.'

But I have no plans to let him escape his promise so easily. 'This is adequate for the task, my Lord,' I say. 'And it would be a great comfort to me to have it.'

Arlington is not well pleased but takes the pen and writes. I examine the results.

'This merely says that, in the event of my prisoner attempting to escape, I may take any action I consider prudent,' I point out. 'It does not authorise me to kill him.'

'I would have thought that my words allowed for that,' says Arlington. 'It is perfectly clear to me and, I would hazard, to any magistrate. They would scarcely arrest anyone bearing a document signed by the Secretary of State. And, if you are troubled in any way, I shall double your fee.'

'One hundred for Underhill alive and two hundred for him dead?'

'Plus reasonable expenses.'

'Underhill is a double agent and Fincham's murderer. This way he gets safely out of London and is rewarded by the King. Why should I want to do that?'

'For the money. Anyway, he's not Fincham's murderer. So don't try to push the price up by pretending that he is. We need to get him to the King to tell him whatever it is he needs to tell him. It would be a pleasure in some ways to hang Underhill, but my duty is to get him to Salisbury and the King.'

'Fincham was by all accounts a good man,' I say.

'Very well. One hundred and fifty guineas.'

'Two hundred,' I say.

'Two hundred guineas for the prisoner delivered to the court in Salisbury or Oxford, dead or alive.' Arlington pauses. 'But if you and he are captured by some third party...you should not feel under any obligation to risk your own life to rescue him.'

'Thank you. I doubt that I would have done. But surely Underhill will then disclose to his captors whatever he knows?'

'Those are my instructions to you, Mr Grey. You are to prevent his escape *at all costs, short of endangering your own life*. Payment will be made on your return to London. You will need new papers to travel to Salisbury. The roads are becoming difficult. Old passes are not being accepted.'

'I reached Braintree without too much trouble.'

'I receive reports almost hourly. Even in the last two or three days things have got worse. Villages are arming themselves. Constables are puffing themselves up with their own importance. Barriers are being erected across the main roads. Bridges are blocked. And it will have been easier for you travelling with Lady Pole as a family than travelling alone as you will be now.'

'In what way easier? Two carriers of the Plague are surely no more welcome than one?'

'I mean less conspicuous. Less likely to attract attention. Would Lady Pole perhaps accompany you to Salisbury? Her theatre is closed. You should speak to her.'

'Her home is still London, but I shall do everything in my power to persuade her to allow me to take her to Salisbury. But I thought you did not trust her?'

'If anyone is on the lookout for Underhill, they will be watching for two men, not a family. Underhill could be listed on the pass as your servant.'

'Not as himself?'

Arlington pauses. 'It may be better if people on the road do not know who he is.'

'Why? Is he in some way in danger?'

'Not under your watchful eye, Mr Grey. Let Morland know what the passes should say. He's expecting you. He'll also give you a warrant to collect Underhill from the Tower. Then you should set out for Salisbury without delay. If this is done quickly, and due caution is observed, there should be little risk.'

'I thought that there was no danger?'

Arlington touches the plaster on his nose. 'Indeed. What possible danger could there be to a family and their servant fleeing the Plague, as so many are?'

I fold the letter permitting me to kill Underhill and place it carefully in my pocket. All I need to do now is to tell Aminta that I am not merely willing but contractually obliged to escort her and Sophia. For those who enjoy irony, this will be an interesting journey in many ways.

'Thank you for that reassurance, my Lord,' I say. 'I'm most grateful.'

CHAPTER

15

'Salisbury?' says Aminta. 'Arlington will pay you to take us to Salisbury?'

'Correct,' I say. 'But in exchange we have to escort and protect Charles Fincham's murderer.'

'Though he denies it…'

'I cannot think of a single past occasion when Esmond Underhill has told the plain unvarnished truth. You are, however, correct. He claims to have been Fincham's friend. He claims Callingham is a coward. But I don't believe him.'

'If we don't take Underhill, what happens then?'

'Somebody else takes him, I imagine. Underhill would not be able to resist a troop of dragoons, for all that he may prefer to travel with me.'

'Then he may as well come with us. We are delivering him to justice, as Kitty would wish us to do. I am sure that the King will not release him if Underhill's guilt is apparent.'

'Unless of course he amuses the King and receives a Royal pardon,' I say.

'You are too cynical,' says Aminta.

'To be fair, Underhill is not the sort of merry rogue who could persuade the King he deserved another chance. For once I think we may rely on His Majesty's impartiality.'

'Then it is decided.'

'Not quite. There is another consideration, Aminta. Arlington knows of some danger that he was not prepared to share with me. He seems to think that somebody will try to take our prisoner away from us. And, though he says he wants me to get Underhill to Salisbury, he is surprisingly willing to overlook the matter if I fail. I am in fact permitted both to kill Underhill if he tries to escape, and to give him up if we are outnumbered. This is a strange business. Finally, Arlington has clearly talked to the crafty Morland about his plans but not the honest Williamson. I would rather it had been the other way round. I would advise against your coming, Aminta. Will can accompany me, in case I need a second pair of eyes and ears on the road.'

'I have to come,' says Aminta. 'Even if Underhill is guilty or Arlington is lying.'

'Why?' I ask.

'Do you believe in signs?' Aminta clasps her hands in front of her. Her knuckles are white.

'Signs? Of what sort?' I ask.

'From God.'

'I doubt that God would be incautious enough to act through Arlington,' I point out.

'But think—only yesterday I was handed a child and asked to take her to Salisbury. Now we are sent by Arlington to precisely that town. What can that be but a sign of God's will?'

'You were always free to travel to Salisbury, if that is what God intended. It is just that Sir Samuel Morland will now supply us with forged passes. I see nothing miraculous in that.'

Aminta shakes her head. 'When I was handed Sophia yesterday it was as if God was asking me to do one good and charitable thing. It was as if He was offering me a deal. If I saved Sophia, then He would look after me and those I love during this Plague time. For a moment I didn't know whether to accept, then I found myself walking away from Sophia's house as fast as I could, clutching her hand firmly in mine.'

'If God and Arlington are in league, then I would check the terms of the contract very carefully.'

'Don't mock me, John,' she says. 'Not here. Not now.'

Outside the sun is shining on Lincoln's Inn Fields. If it weren't for the silence, for the lack of people going about their business, you wouldn't know anything was wrong.

'We all know that we could be dead of the Plague tomorrow,' I say. 'It makes some prayerful. It makes others drunk. It makes some charitable. It makes some crueller than we could have imagined. None of us are what we were before the pestilence struck. I am not mocking you, Aminta. I am mocking myself. Perhaps getting Sophia to Salisbury is your test. Perhaps getting Underhill safely to the King, when I would prefer otherwise, is mine. I shall obtain passes for the four of us from Morland and I shall hire a coach to go to Salisbury and back. You and Sophia must be here by eleven o'clock. Bring no more than you need to stay one night in Salisbury, and one or two at an inn on the road. It is best that we travel light and are prepared to change our plans and our route if we have to. God willing, we shall both have accomplished our respective labours before the sun sets tomorrow and whatever evil Arlington has foreseen will not happen.'

'God willing,' says Aminta.

And she finally unclenches her hands.

Aminta has scarcely left the building when Will announces that there is a lady to see me. For a moment I think that she must have forgotten something, but there is a troubled look on Will's face.

'I am about to leave for Salisbury,' I say.

'This one won't be kept waiting,' he says, looking over his shoulder. 'Especially not for Lord Arlington.'

I check my watch. 'I have five minutes,' I say. 'Tell her not a moment more.'

But, before Will can say anything to anyone, my visitor sweeps into the room, in an almost deafening rustle of silk stockings on silk petticoats on silk skirts. She pauses, head on one side, to take me in and she seems not entirely displeased. For a moment I stare back, barely remembering to keep my mouth closed. It is as if some mythical beast, of which I had read a great deal but never quite believed in, had just landed in the room and carefully folded its bejewelled wings over its golden scales. But it really is her. In the flesh. Black curls frame the smooth skin and even features of her face. The second largest pearls I have ever seen are strung three rows deep round her slender throat. But only the second largest, because the largest I have ever seen are suspended from her ears. Any discomfort they cause must be compensated for by their ability to strike her rivals dumb with envy. Her dress is cut fashionably low at the bust, with white lace peeping out from the pale grey silk. The same grey silk clings tightly to the trim bodice before flowing in cascades from her waist to the floor. A rich perfume of Hungary water wafts around her. In her hands she carries an ivory fan, with a long trailing ribbon. So this is Callingham's famous admirer.

'I think, Mr Grey, that we have not met before,' she says. 'But I've heard a great deal about you. The cleverest of Lord Arlington's young men. And this is where you live?'

'Good morning, Lady Castlemaine,' I say. She waits for me to say what an honour it is to make her acquaintance. She waits for me to compliment her on her jewels.

'Would you like to take a seat?' I ask. 'How can I help you?'

She inspects the two chairs that I possess and shakes her head sadly. 'Let me come straight to the point, Mr Grey,' she says. 'You have been recommended to me as one of the most astute young men in London. Nobody had told me that you were also one of the best looking. But it is your intelligence that I require this morning, not your body.'

She taps me on the chest with her fan, which involves standing very close to me.

'Then perhaps I should inform you of my hourly rate…'

'I never pay bills,' she says. 'There is always something more interesting to do with money, don't you think?'

'I don't work free of charge, my Lady,' I say.

'Nor do I, as you can see,' she says, fingering her necklace. 'But the work I am offering pays in a different way.'

'Why don't you take a seat and explain?' I say.

She looks again at my chairs and sits down with a sigh on the newer of the two.

'You don't approve of me, do you, Mr Grey?'

'I neither approve nor disapprove of clients. I resolve their problems in exchange for cash. So far you have revealed neither a problem nor an intention of paying. But I am happy to listen a little longer in case you do.'

'Thank you. But you think that my being the King's mistress is not to my credit?'

'You said that you were coming straight to the point, Lady Castlemaine. Perhaps I have prevented you from doing so. If you just want to talk, I am happy to oblige, but my clerk will bill you for it.'

'At the usual rate, no doubt.'

'No, I have a special rate for people who waste my time,' I say.

She laughs. 'You must be even better than they say if your other clients put up with this rudeness,' she says. 'Lord Arlington, for example. Are you this rude to him?'

'I don't discuss clients,' I say.

'Does he pay well?'

'That is entirely between me and him.'

'How much is he paying you to escort Mr Underhill to Salisbury?'

'Sadly I can answer no part of that question.'

She laughs again. It is not an unattractive laugh. Neither high nor low. Neither masculine nor feminine. It invites friendship and confidentiality. And possibly rather more. It is the laugh that the sirens would have laughed. She shifts in my chair and there is another rustle of silk on smooth bare skin. 'Do you think that I have plucked from the air the first name I could think of and the first city? I know exactly what you have been asked to do.'

'Then you'll also know exactly how much he's paying me,' I say.

'What we are offering is far more valuable,' she says. 'If you help us.'

'Who is "we"?' I ask.

'The Duke of Buckingham,' she says. 'And one or two others.'

'Lord Clifford?'

'Well, John…I may call you "John", I hope…if you were of our party, then I could of course tell you. And do much else for you besides.' Lady Castlemaine reaches across and places a hand on my knee. I feel its warmth through my breeches. Their Puritan blackness is no protection. 'I could do a great deal for you, if you would let me. It would give me enormous pleasure to be of assistance to you.'

'Really?' I say.

'You are still too young to realise how ambitious you might be,' she says. 'You know you are clever, because all clever men do. But talent alone will get you nowhere. The world is full of poor clever men. They sit alone in dusty chambers and drink small beer and wonder where they went wrong. I was poor once, but now I'm rich. And let me tell you, it's so much nicer being rich. Of course, I'm not rich and *clever* myself, because I am only a woman. Being somebody's wife or mistress is as high as we can aim. There it is. That is how God made us, apparently—you can't condemn me for being what I am. But you, John—there's nothing you couldn't achieve, if you have friends. Powerful friends, who will see that well-paid places slip into your hand. Friends who will dress you in silk. And introduce you to some pretty actresses, or whatever meets your fancy. Even though I am merely a woman and somebody's mistress, I could make that happen. In return for a little help now and again.'

'So you want me to betray Arlington for a silk suit and a pretty actress?'

'And my undying gratitude. Face the facts, John. You'll have to betray him sooner or later. He's an upstart. He won't last. The dukes of Buckingham have been a power in the land since King James's time. You need a patron who is worthy of you. Not a ridiculous clown with a nose patch. Ask Lady Pole. She's a Clifford too, in case you'd forgotten—a distant cousin of Lord Clifford, but a Clifford for all that. As for your family—your mother's family, I mean—they've been lords of the manor since the Conquest. Your loyalties should be with us, John. With the people who matter.'

'You seem to know a lot about me,' I say.

'Take it as a sincere compliment that I do. Would it surprise you if I said that I know your mother?'

'No,' I say. 'I see a great deal of my dear mother in her. It was my mother's misfortune to be a contemporary of Charles I rather than Charles II, a time when Royal mistresses were less in demand. My mother would have enjoyed being a Royal mistress. She probably wouldn't say 'no' even now.

'I'm already as rich as I need to be,' I say.

'Nobody is ever that rich, John.'

'You want me to hand Underhill over to you, I suppose? You want me to ignore my existing agreements and go against my word. You want to use whatever information Underhill has, in the most underhand manner, against your enemy, Clarendon?'

'Thank you, John. That would do nicely. Shall I ask your clerk to invoice me?'

'I'm sorry, my Lady,' I say. 'I am, as you say, pre-contracted in the matter.'

Lady Castlemaine stands and places a hand on my shoulder. I look up into her blue eyes.

'Who would you rather be in bed with?' she asks. 'Me or Arlington?'

It's probably a genuine offer. She took Callingham and I have half his years and twice as many eyes.

'I never get into bed with my clients,' I say. 'I am not ungrateful for your offer, Lady Castlemaine, but I have work to do. Will can show you out.'

Morland puts his head on one side and smiles at me. Arlington has certainly taken him into his confidence. I wonder what he knows that I don't?

'One pass for Mr and Mrs Grey, their daughter Sophia and their manservant, Ezekiel Lowerdale. All certified as having been examined by a doctor appointed by the College of Physicians of London and found free of the Plague. And another similar certificate for Mr William Atkins, your clerk.'

'Thank you,' I say.

'Does my Lord Arlington know of the existence of little Sophia?' he asks.

'You tell me,' I say. 'I imagine you know the answer.'

Morland smiles again. 'Your own child? Some bastard, perhaps?'

'A distant cousin. She is travelling to Salisbury.'

'To stay with even more distant cousins, no doubt?'

'Precisely, Mr Morland.'

'I thought your family was from Essex?'

'That does not prevent me having distant cousins.'

Morland fingers a golden lock of hair for a moment. 'It is of course no business of mine. But it is as well to know so that I do not betray any confidences inadvertently.'

I nod. Morland still reserves the right to betray me intentionally. That is understood by us both.

'My Lord Arlington implied that there might be some risk. Do you know what he might have meant by that?' I ask.

'I am sure that he has told you all he can.'

'So am I. The question is what it is that he can't tell me but that it would be useful for me to be aware of anyway. I don't think he's told Williamson either, but I think you may know.'

Morland makes a poor pretence of considering this. 'I am a mere postman,' he says. 'A cipher clerk. A copier of other people's letters. There is no reason why he should tell me anything.'

'I didn't say he had; you may have told him. As you say, you have your sources of information.'

The cipher clerk says nothing but is flattered to be reminded.

'If the Duke of Buckingham was interested in our plans, should I be concerned?' I add.

Morland considers this. 'I think not. The Duke is of the same party as Lord Arlington. His interests are the same as ours.'

'Entirely the same?'

'There are no two courtiers whose interests are identical in all respects. But Buckingham and my Lord are equally opposed to Lord Clarendon.'

'Good,' I say. 'Then hopefully that alliance will remain intact for another day or two, until I reach Salisbury. I'm just warning you that Buckingham is apparently not well inclined towards Underhill.'

'According to whom?'

'Lady Castlemaine. I also get the impression that it might suit Arlington if Underhill doesn't reach the King.'

Morland looks sideways at me, a manner he has when he is about to impart something of importance.

'Why?' he asks.

'I am authorised to kill him if he tries to escape. I am enjoined to surrender him to a third party if I have to. What am I to make of that?'

'I doubt that my Lord wishes you to make anything of it,' says Morland. 'But, if you will accept my advice, don't expect gratitude from Arlington for keeping Underhill alive.'

'I'll fulfil my contract,' I say. 'And I don't expect gratitude for anything from anybody.'

Morland, once one of the most important men in the country and deputy to the Secretary of State, looks around him, at the piles of paper, at the bottles of ink, in short, at his small empire of postage.

'I think you are very wise, Mr Grey,' he says.

'Just sign here, Mr Grey,' says the gaoler.

I write my name on a slip of paper, acknowledging receipt of one Esmond Underhill, prisoner of His Majesty, in good working order with all limbs intact and unbroken, as required by the laws of England (though not Scotland).

'Is this necessary?' I ask.

'We just need a record that Mr Underhill was delivered into your custody, alive and well. If he doesn't reach Salisbury safely, then it's not our fault.'

So, Arlington is covering his back then, as well as part of his nose. If Underhill goes missing it will be none of his doing.

'I offer no guarantee that I can deliver him to Salisbury in the same condition,' I say.

'You are not being required to,' says the gaoler. 'I simply need a record of his departure, just as I have one of his admittance. And having got to know the prisoner personally, as you might say, I wish you well of him. He is in the next room, washed, shaved and with new linen upon him. And he is all yours.'

Underhill is less grateful than I had expected. He sits, in donated clothes that are slightly too large for him, on a wooden stool in an otherwise bare room. The doublet and breeches are of rough blue serge, which probably scratches where it touches the skin. The shirt is nearer to grey than it is to white. The stockings are perhaps intended as a pair, but are ill-matched. He holds a broad-brimmed leather hat in his hands.

'You're late,' he says to me.

'I had to procure a carriage to take us to Lincoln's Inn and thence onwards to Salisbury. There are few available with so many people wishing to leave the capital. They are not cheap. Fortunately Mr Morland was able to direct me to a driver who was free to take us at a reasonable price.'

This well-considered answer does not please him as I had hoped.

'Of course they're not cheap,' he says. 'And good luck to the coachmen, I say. Let the lords and ladies pay a decent wage for once. I'm sure Arlington's already given you the money to pay the going rate.'

'I also had to get health certificates.'

'You've checked the driver's own health certificate, I hope?' says Underhill.

'If coaches were plentiful, we could afford to be fussy. We'd be lucky just to get a seat in a coach, let alone a whole one to ourselves, as we have. He looked well enough.'

'You can sit closest to the driver then. It's a while since I had information this good to sell. I'd like to live long enough to collect the cash. I don't want to die of the Plague or a knife through my back. Who already knows I'm leaving with you?'

'Arlington,' I say. 'Morland, of course. The gaoler. The Duke of Buckingham, apparently. Lady Castlemaine. And the people we shall be travelling with.'

'People? What people?'

'Lady Pole and...her cousin, Sophia. You will travel as our manservant, under an assumed name. If anyone is looking for you, they will not be watching out for a family travelling together.'

'So, I am to be a *servant*?' Underhill looks at me incredulously.

'I think you will have no difficulty in playing the part—and you are dressed for it. It is, after all, just for a day or two while we travel. Then you may resume whatever you regard as your proper station in life.'

'If Cromwell had lived—or if one of the generals had replaced him as the people wished—there would have been no ladies and gentlemen with their lackeys. There would have been no noblemen strutting about with gold-headed canes. There would have been no rich men in their carriages and poor men driving them. We would all have been equal.'

'We have a long journey ahead of us, Mr Underhill,' I say. 'Perhaps you can save your political lecture until then?'

Underhill shakes his head. 'I had thought better of you, Grey. You were one of us once—a good Republican of sound principles. But I see you have taken Arlington's gold.'

'True,' I say. 'I have taken Arlington's gold, as you would if he'd been willing to hand it to you. On this occasion, he has given it to me to protect you. So, just remember that I'm all that stands between you and a musket ball through the head on the Salisbury road. Arlington may not have been able to have you tortured, but as your master I can have you flogged whenever I choose.'

'Except,' he says, 'legally, you're no master of mine. So you can keep your whip for your wife and your dog.'

Aminta has brought a box, contrary to all my instructions, and Underhill is, in his capacity as our devoted servant, now loading it onto the roof of the coach, watched by the coachman. The coachman is not party to any of our secrets and we shall need to play our respective parts when he is present. Underhill gives one final heave and looks resentfully up in my direction. When the revolution comes, I shall be made to load boxes without end for the common people.

Aminta and I observe all of this from my window.

'Perhaps,' I say, 'I should have made myself more agreeable to Lady Castlemaine.'

'No, you were right not to bend to her will as others do. She is scheming and avaricious. I think that the King is growing tired of her demands. But I thought Arlington and Buckingham were united in their desire to see the downfall of Clarendon.'

'Not at the moment,' I say. 'Something seems to have caused a rift in that Cabal. My Lady seemed ready to seduce me there and then to get her hands on Underhill.'

'What a shame that Pepys does not have Underhill in his pocket,' she says. 'He would give a year's salary to be seduced by Lady Castlemaine—not that she would have to try very hard. I wonder who informed Buckingham that something was afoot?'

'Who can say? The gaoler? The torchbearer? Arlington's clerk? Morland? The court does not keep secrets well.'

'Then we should assume a lot of people know we are going to Salisbury.'

'Except Williamson,' I say. 'He is to remain ignorant, it would seem. The sooner we are all in the coach and on our way the better.'

I wait until Aminta too has descended, with Sophia in tow, before giving Will some final instructions. 'Take this pass and go to Stepney. Seek out a one-eyed man named Patrick Callingham at the Widow Sparrow's. Don't get your hopes up: she is nothing like what they say. Tell him that we have Underhill with us for the moment but that I have no idea what will happen to him after we reach Salisbury. If he has anything to fear from Underhill, then he may like to move his lodgings again. I can't promise that Underhill won't come looking for him. Then, Will, take five guineas from the strong box and, as I asked you before, *go into the country*. The Plague is getting worse daily and you may be able to save yourself.'

'Thank you, Mr Grey; but, as *I* said before, I'll stay as long as you do. You may need me here when you get back, which should be no more than three or four days' time, if all goes well. How did you manage to get a coach? They're as rare as hen's teeth these days.'

'Morland found it. The driver's called Luke. That's all I know about it.'

'It looks well built anyway, and new enough. It should get you there and back.'

'And a driver named after an Evangelist inspires confidence, I'm sure.'

'So it does. I look forward to seeing you and Mrs Grey back here soon.'

I think again of my mother counting on her fingers and concluding that Aminta could not possibly be my half-sister. Perhaps she was genuinely convinced because, when Roger Pole died, my mother encouraged me to seek Aminta out. She pointed out that it was high time I was married. She said that I should at least write to the newly widowed Lady Pole. But I didn't.

'She's not really Mrs Grey,' I say to Will. 'It's only what it says on the pass.'

'More's the pity,' says Will. 'You'd be lucky to get yourself a wife like that. Still, you have the journey to Salisbury to convince her that it is worth marrying a mere lawyer. Edinburgh would have given you a better chance, but at least the King isn't still at Hampton Court.'

From My Lady Pole's Esteemed Poem,

The Puritaniad

So, we set off, a merry band
A lying paper in our hand
That swore as God above was witness
We'd none of us got Plague or sickness
Not wife nor husband nor their daughter
(No reference there to how we'd caught 'er
Thrown from a house locked up for Plague.
Official passes can be vague).
Our servant too was free from fever
(Small mention here that he had ever
'Scaped a place from where they'd carted
One who'd recently departed.)
With such a pass who could refute
Our right to journey on this route?

CHAPTER 16

Arlington is right. Things are getting worse very quickly out here in the country. We pass through Westminster without trouble but, as we bowl along, we overtake lines of men and women trudging along the road, fleeing the City in a desperate migration westwards. They carry bundles with them—clothes, cooking equipment, bedding, tents. Some of the children clutch dolls or trail hobbyhorses behind them—playthings that have become burdens. Here and there we see small dusty piles by the roadside—possessions that have proved too heavy to carry beyond this point. There are cooking pots and blankets and a child's hoop. All abandoned as unnecessary lumber. Sophia points to the hoop, but I promise her one when we get to Salisbury. The people who left these things may already be dead of the Plague. Indeed, a mile later there is a body stretched out by the grass verge. Face down, head resting on his arms, the man could have just collapsed there from heat and exhaustion, but there is already a stiffness to him that confirms he will not rise again. Nobody has dared to approach the body or remove it for burial. Soon the crows will come for his eyes.

We stop shortly after to give the horses a brief rest and water. I hail one group of migrants as it reaches us. A man detaches himself from his friends and approaches us cautiously, a kerchief soaked in vinegar held to his nose to protect him against such infections as we may have.

'Where are you heading for?' I ask.

'Southampton,' says the man. 'If we can get there. I've had word it is free from Plague—or was a week ago. But the inns refuse to serve us in case we have the sickness, and the farmers will not let us approach because they fear we shall steal from them. We left London yesterday afternoon. We slept in some woods last night. I do not know where we will sleep tonight. We hope that the people of Hampshire will prove friendlier than those of Middlesex, may the Devil shit on their grandmothers' graves.'

'Then God speed you to Hampshire,' I say. They trudge on but we quickly overtake them again once we have restarted, a long, thin line that grows longer and thinner as the stragglers tire and those in front lose their patience with those behind. But the speed of even the fastest is painfully slow. We wave and again wish them a good journey, but when we reach the pleasant town of Staines it is clear that this will not be easy for any of us. There is a barrier across the road; several large logs have been rolled into place and a number of men sit on them, armed with whatever weapons they could find. A fat baker, still in his dusty apron but now also wearing a bright red sash around his waist, waves a rusty sword at us and demands to see passes. I duly descend and produce ours for inspection.

'Who are you?' I ask, handing him the paper. 'By what right do you stop us?'

'I'm Captain Smith,' he says. 'Formerly lieutenant in Lord Newcastle's regiment of foot. Now commander of the Staines Militia, newly raised for the prevention of disorder in these troubled and dangerous times. Nobody passes this barrier without my authority. So, which of you is John Grey?'

'Me,' I say.

He peers over my shoulder.

'And that is your wife and daughter in the carriage?'

'Yes.'

'And that odd-looking fellow in blue sitting opposite them is your manservant?'

'Yes. Ezekiel Lowerdale.'

I hope I have remembered the name correctly. Captain Smith has my pass, which he is holding at arm's length to avoid contagion. He does not contradict me.

'All free of the Plague?'

'As you can see.'

'If you could see the Plague clearly on a man then we would not need this caution. Which part of London do you live in? St Giles?'

'Lincoln's Inn. It's still free of disease.'

'So you say. It's full of lawyers though, isn't it?'

'Yes,' I agree.

He nods and spits on the ground. I suspect he's been on the wrong end of some litigation in the past. 'Where are you going, Mr Lawyer Grey?'

'Salisbury.'

I want to conclude this conversation and move on, but the Captain is enjoying his moment of power.

'Planning on staying here?' he asks.

'Yes. We're stopping for food and drink at your inn.'

'No you're not. Not you or your family or your sour-looking serving man. Strangers aren't welcome at the inn. Or anywhere else here. Maybe you'll have better luck at the next town. They may want the Plague there. We don't.'

'The next town's at least an hour away. My daughter is hungry.'

'You should have brought food from London then. There's nothing for you Plague-people here.'

One of his companions raises an ancient musket, which I doubt he knows how to use, even if he knows how to load it. He squints at me along the barrel and grins, revealing some crooked teeth. The weapon may not be capable of firing at all or it may go off by accident and kill me. I think he would regard either as an amusing joke. He may not have considered the possibility that it may blow his own head off.

'Tell your driver to go straight through the town,' says Captain Smith. 'Keep moving. Don't speak to anyone. Don't give anyone anything. And don't waste your time stopping at the well for water—we've had a new lid put on it and that's padlocked. I wish you Godspeed, Mr Grey, and a pleasant journey.'

He returns the pass to me, then wipes his fingers carefully on his floury apron, removing any Plague that the letter may have contained. He supervises the rolling back of one of the logs while I return to the coach.

'Drive on,' I say, looking up at our coachman. 'We are apparently not stopping here after all.'

The coachman makes no reply, but I think he inclines his head just a little. Well, he's not paid to converse with us. I climb back in. The whip cracks and we are on our way. As we pass through the town, I notice a few people peering from their windows at us. Nobody risks coming out of their houses until we have gone by.

'Not the friendliest of towns,' says Aminta as we gain the open countryside again.

But, as it proves, she is wrong. Staines is the friendliest community we come to all day.

It is just outside Bagshot that our problems really begin. We meet a line of people walking dejectedly in the opposite direction from the one in which we are travelling. There are about a dozen men and women, all with the dust of the road about their stockings and the hems of their skirts, and with three or four children clinging to their mothers' aprons. The men carry bundles of varying sizes and shapes. Most of the children are crying, the tears washing thin clean lines in the dirt covering their faces. All look exhausted.

'Are you heading for London?' I ask in surprise.

'Winchester, sir,' says the man at the head of the line, dropping his bundle to the ground with a sigh.

'You're going the wrong way.'

He laughs bitterly. 'Do you think we don't know that? We left London three days ago and have met with nothing but checks. The way is closed just after the bridge, about a mile yonder. Nobody may pass, whether they have a permit or not. There are armed men and a waggon blocking the road. They threaten to hang anyone who tries to gain access. We are retracing our steps to a lane that will take us round the town at a safe distance from it—if that is not closed off too.'

'Will they let a coach pass, do you think? At Staines they let us drive through so long as we didn't stop.'

'Are you all from London?'

'Yes.'

'They're turning everyone back if they say they're from London. Even gentry like yourselves. You may as well come with us. We can show you where the lane begins. That is our route today.'

'Then what?' I ask.

'One of our company who knows this country says we may strike towards Chobham and thence to Guildford and Winchester. We have two soldiers' tents with us, which the women and children can sleep in. The rest of us will sleep under the trees if there are any to hand. Thank God it's dry at the moment. We have food for another three days, if we are careful. After that, if nobody will sell to us, we'll see what we can borrow from the fields. We're honest men, or we were when we set out, but if they won't let us buy it, then there's food enough in the ground and they can't watch everywhere at once.'

'We'll take our chance down the road,' I say. 'They may prove charitable. But good luck to you on your own journey.'

The man nods and shoulders his burden again, which I now see is canvas and tent poles. It must be quite a weight. The group sets off in silence. They are too tired to talk.

'Drive on!' I call to the coachman. Again there is no reply but just a crack of the whip. He is not as content as he was. I had thought he was naturally taciturn, but he is beginning to realise he has been duped. Of course he has the advantage that he's paid by the day, but that's small comfort to him if we can find neither food nor beds nor stabling. At least, sitting on the box, he has the benefit of a breeze. Here inside the coach it is becoming rather warm. Underhill has removed his jacket, and is busy scratching himself. Sophia, who has been alternately excited and fretful, is now asleep because there has long since been nothing to interest her. Aminta is frowning, though strangely all the more beautiful for doing so, though I shall not tell her that. We lurch forward again towards another unfriendly welcome.

This time, as we approach the barrier, a shot rings out. The Bagshot men at least know how to load their guns. The driver stops and I open the carriage door and step onto the hard, cracked earth.

A hundred yards or so ahead, an old ox cart has been placed athwart the road. There is a small space to pass by on foot on either side, but no room for a carriage. Beyond, I can see the first houses that make up the town—solid half-timbered buildings with red-tiled roofs—and the broad, dusty street passing between them. An inn sign swings lazily and invitingly in the breeze. This is where, in normal times, travellers breathe a sigh of relief and look forward to sitting under the trees in a pleasant garden in summer, or by the fire in the parlour when it is cold. But not in these Plague times.

I approach the barricade at an even pace, aware that several muskets are aimed in my direction. At this range, and with so many guns, these bumpkins may even be able to hit me. About twenty yards from it I am ordered to stop.

'Where are you from?' somebody calls out.

'Essex,' I call back. I am surprised how easy it is to lie.

'Which town?'

'Clavershall West,' I say.

'Is that a town?'

'It's a village. Near Saffron Walden.'

'Never heard of it. Do you have a pass?'

'Essex is free of the Plague. They're not issuing passes there,' I say.

'They say there is Plague in Chelmsford.'

'Not as far as I know,' I say. 'Anyway, why should we care about that in Saffron Walden? Chelmsford's miles away from us.'

We are close enough to see the expression on each other's faces. His is unsympathetic. Mine is doubtless untrustworthy. We both know that the country is full of rumours and that only a few of them are true. But you need only one Plague victim to get into your town for everyone to die. A rumour of Plague is as good as a bill of mortality.

'Looks like a London coach, that does,' he says, indicating our transport.

'I can't say where it was made. But Essex is where we've come from.'

'Anyone could say that. You're all liars in London. You may have money in your purse and silk on your arse, but you've got the Plague on your breath. Stay where you are, or we'll fire.'

'We need food,' I say. I take a step towards him.

'You heard what I said. Stay there and I'll talk to the others. You're a dead man if you move another inch.'

The men on the barrier go into a huddle, then the first man calls out: 'You can't come through the town, because you're London scum, but we'll sell you food and drink if you wish. Best Plague prices. Take it or leave it.'

I negotiate the price of three loaves of bread and some ham and some beer. Plague prices are high, it would seem, but they will not sell me more. They do not want us to remain long within breathing distance. After a while a man comes cautiously round the barrier with a large basket and a leather pail and places both on the ground. 'You can come and take the food,' he calls. 'Leave your money in the bucket of vinegar. Hold the coins up before you drop them in so that we can see you have paid us properly and not cheated us with your London tricks. Take the basket with you. We don't want it back after you've touched it.'

I do as I am bid. I can feel ten pairs of eyes watching me, but nobody threatens to shoot me. I turn and carry the basket back. The bread smells fresh. The ham looks almost good enough to eat.

For a while we sit on the steps of the coach, within sight of the barricade, and consume the bounty that Bagshot has seen fit to bestow upon us. The sun shines from a deep blue, cloudless sky. I, too, am now in my shirtsleeves, my coat hanging from the door handle. The coachman has stretched himself out under the shade of a nearby oak and lit his pipe. Thin wisps of pale grey smoke rise, untroubled by any breeze. He has still said almost nothing to us. Most coachmen are talkative enough. All we know of this one is his name. Sophia plays some game of her own devising in the warm dirt. Aminta kneels down with her, and starts tracing letters in the dust. Sophia looks on admiringly. 'That's an S!' I hear her exclaim. Only Underhill is ill at ease, pacing up and down, but the sun shines on him too.

Indeed, the fine weather that has marked the Plague time looks set to hold, which may be as well if we can neither reach Salisbury nor find an inn that will take us. I think of the group we met earlier. They at least had tents and a supply of food. We could perhaps sleep on the coach, some of us, but not in any great comfort.

'Is this Salisbury?' asks Sophia as I lift her back into the carriage.

'No,' I say.

'How far is it?'

'Not far,' I say.

'Is it because I have the Plague?' asks Sophia. 'Is that why we couldn't go into the town?'

'Sophia,' I say, 'if you want to reach Salisbury, please remember one thing. Never, ever, say to anyone that you might have the Plague. Will you remember that?'

'I'll try,' says Sophia, frowning. 'But what if I do get the Plague? What happens then?'

She has watched at least one member of her family fall sick. She knows it is something that can happen. She has seen the worry on her mother's face.

'You won't get it,' I say. 'None of us is going to get the Plague. I promise. Cross my heart and hope to die.'

Two hours have passed and we have retraced our steps several times. The lane to which we had been directed proved too narrow for our coach and, at our driver's insistence, we have driven some miles back the way we came, revisiting long stretches of road that we passed earlier, going east when we should be going west towards the sinking sun. Eventually our man finds one to his liking, a rough but relatively broad road running more south than southwest. The hamlets that we pass through, if not friendly, at least do not try to detain us or shoot at us. That is some small comfort. Away from the Salisbury road people have seen fewer migrants and are a little more trusting. Plague prices are not yet standard. We are directed to a farmhouse where, we are told, we might obtain supplies cheaply. We follow a track until a new red-brick building appears suddenly before us, hidden behind some trees. There we receive apricots and bread and cheese and cherries and small beer in a wooden flagon. The old couple who run the farm are friendly but cautious. Following their instructions, we drop some coins into a jug of vinegar, where they will stay for some hours or days or weeks until (unlike us) they are considered Plague free.

The coachman is now checking the harness while the horses rest. Aminta and Sophia have been given permission to walk in the farm's orchard, as long as they do not approach the house.

Underhill and I are left, peering through green branches towards the road. Then we hear the rattle of another coach travelling fast and, shortly after, a galloping horse. We see little, however, from this secluded spot. Just a flash of yellow as the coach passes and a shadow across the foliage as the rider spurs his horse on. A small cloud of dust rises slowly above the trees and then hangs in the air, as if it had nowhere else to go.

'We're not the only ones to have been sent this way,' I say.

'Are they following us?' demands Underhill, immediately alert to possible danger.

'We've no reason to think they are,' I say. 'Any more than we are following whoever went this way ahead of us. The people in the yellow carriage are doubtless fleeing London, just as we are. But if you are worried about pursuit, then at least they will not have seen us here. Did Arlington say to you that we might be followed?'

'Why do you ask?'

'Because Arlington is in the habit of keeping some information to himself. It would be helpful if you told me what you knew.'

'Arlington came to see me again yesterday evening,' says Underhill. 'He had more questions.'

'About Fincham's murder?' I say.

Underhill sneers. 'You don't think Arlington's worried about that, do you? He wants the key to understanding the message. He thought I must be holding something back. I told him that was all I had—I thought it would mean something to Arlington even if it meant nothing to me. So he asked me what else I knew about the Duke. But I didn't like the way he asked. I said I'd tell the King. So, Arlington thought for a bit and then said he'll send me to Salisbury with a troop of horse. I said, only if the lawyer comes with us. I'm not having my throat cut the first time I stop to piss. No thank you. So, he's given me you—but no soldiers, unfortunately. If I'd known the roads would be like this, I'd have insisted on a couple of dragoons to force the barricades.'

'You didn't refuse the escort then?'

'Why should I do that?'

Underhill's version of events is not quite the same as Arlington's. One or other of them is lying about the reason for our lack of an armed guard.

'And you think it would be worth somebody killing you for what you know?' I ask.

Underhill smiles. 'Of course. Fincham's dead, isn't he?'

'Why not just tell Arlington? Other than you don't like the way he asks.'

'I'd be giving up the one advantage I have over him: I've got information he doesn't have. That's what's keeping me alive. Once he knows, he's better off having me put out of the way. But I told him: I've been in the Duke's household for three months. I've listened at doors. The King will believe me. He knows his brother.'

'So it is the Duke of York's men whom you fear?'

'Yes, of course. Who else? The Dutch don't have agents out here.'

But he looks over his shoulder all the same.

'It would be helpful to know what the secret was, Mr Underhill, if I am to protect you against those who wish to steal it.'

'Except, I'm not telling you for the same reason I'm not telling Arlington. I'm not stupid, Mr Grey.'

'Very well. It is my job to ensure that you get to Salisbury alive, but if you try to escape, then you should know I am authorised to kill you.'

Underhill smiles. 'But I'm not going to escape. Why should I want to do that? You are going to take me to the King and he is going to pay me well for what I have to tell him. Then I'll be free to go where I wish.'

The long summer day is drawing to its close and we are not at Salisbury. The sun has already set and we travel on in a precarious twilight. If somebody wished to ambush us, now would be the moment.

Three times now the driver has admitted that he has lost his way in these back roads. Three times we have had to find a place to turn because the fork we had taken had narrowed to a dusty path between two hedges—not an easy thing to do with a coach and four. Our driver may not say much, but I admire his skill with the reins. Sophia has long since ceased to ask whether we are there yet and is sleeping against Aminta's arm, a thumb in her mouth. I am beginning to think that we may have to spend the night in the woods after all, when we see the lights of an inn ahead—a soft glow of candles through the trees. It is a solid stone building of some age, its walls golden in the last of the sun. The Royal shield bravely displayed on a post in front of it proclaims that it is the King's Arms. The building to one side of it confirms that it possesses stables. A yellow coach near the stables, its shaft resting on the ground, indicates that the rapidly travelling carriage we saw earlier has got here well ahead of us.

'It's as good as anywhere,' I say to my companions. 'You all wait here and I'll go and see if they will accept us.'

'What about that coach?' asks Underhill. 'Who does that belong to?'

'I don't know,' I say. 'I'll ask.'

The inn has three empty chambers and we can take our pick of them. It is willing to accept our pass without undue questioning. The landlord is pleased rather than otherwise to hear that the men of Bagshot are blocking the road and sending carriages in his direction.

'Trade is bad,' he says with a shake of his head. 'Only those fleeing London are on the road, and they are travelling as fast as they may. Nobody wishes to stop if they don't have to. We have one other gentleman staying here.' He nods in the direction of the dining table where a plump person in pale blue silk suit is eating his supper. Hearing himself referred to, he turns and smiles.

'Good evening, Mr Grey. I am pleased to see you.'

'Good evening, Mr Pepys,' I say. 'What a coincidence that we are both travelling on this road.'

CHAPTER

17

Pepys wipes his lips with a clean white napkin and places it on the table.

'No coincidence, I think, Mr Grey. I am travelling to Salisbury on navy business, since I must from time to time have dealings with the court, wherever it chooses to be. I am assuming your master, Arlington, has dispatched you for much the same reason. We will have both found the usual route blocked and have been obliged to take another road, on which there are few enough inns willing to entertain travellers. Hence I have the agreeable prospect of your company for the evening.'

'The yellow coach is yours?'

'You have been admiring it? No, it is not mine, sadly, but I hope to have one like it one day. Are you travelling alone, Mr Grey?'

'My companions are still outside in the carriage. Lady Pole and a young cousin of hers.'

'Lady Pole? But of course—you said you knew her. I look forward to meeting her again.'

I consider whether Aminta will appreciate fighting off Pepys's amorous advances all evening and conclude that perhaps she may not.

'She is very tired, as is her young cousin, who is travelling with us. Tomorrow perhaps.'

'So, you are not journeying on Arlington's account then?'

'If you will excuse me, Mr Pepys, my friends are waiting for me to tell them whether there are beds here for them. I must go to them.'

'They have room for us,' I say, 'but Mr Pepys has got here before us. The yellow coach is hired by him. I am concerned. He may be travelling on navy business, as he says, or he may be searching for Underhill on behalf of the Duke.'

'Pepys?' says Aminta. 'I am surprised that the Duke does not have a few ruffians in his pay who could strike a little more terror in our hearts. I should fear for my actresses, if any were here, but I think we can deal with any threat he poses to us.'

'He is not necessarily alone,' I say. 'The Duke's ruffians, and I am sure he has some, may not be far away. There was a horseman who passed by shortly after the yellow carriage. I have my pistol with me and some powder and shot, but I could not fight off a gang of them.'

'Is there any sign of this horseman?'

'No,' I say.

'Then for the moment we merely have one plump and lecherous navy clerk to deal with. Pepys is no soldier. Nor is he noted for his bravery. He may not be seeking Underhill—it is quite natural that he would be travelling to Salisbury to consult the Duke. We are not in any great danger, I think. We'll stay here.'

'Excuse me,' says Underhill, 'but may *I* give an opinion? Wouldn't you like to hear what *I* have to say? I am apparently only your serving man, but if there's any danger to anyone then it's to me, I think. Pepys is no threat here tonight but, if he sees me and gets to Salisbury ahead of us, he could arrange for us to be ambushed long before we can get to the King. I say we go on—gain a few miles on him. The sun is down, but there will be a moon shortly.'

'Poor little Sophia is exhausted,' says Aminta, 'and, more to the point, so are the horses. If we carry on, we've no idea how far we'll get with the roads as they are. Mr Underhill can find a bed with our driver above the stables, well away from Pepys. Pepys can't possibly know that Underhill is with us.'

'Again, if I am permitted to express a view on the subject of my own murder,' says Underhill, 'thank you all so much, but I'd rather take my chances on the highway. So, I still say, let's go on, even if it's only to the next inn. Pepys isn't stupid. He's seen you right enough. He knows who you work for. He'll ask around or bribe the landlord to tell him how many meals we've ordered.'

'Stay here in the coach, all of you,' I say. 'Just in case anyone is watching from the parlour window. I'll ask the driver how well he knows the road ahead.'

But a brief conversation with the driver, who is already starting to unhitch the horses, is conclusive. There are few good inns between here and Basingstoke, he says, and the horses cannot go much further anyway. They are living beasts, he says, not automata. We may be cruel enough to force them on, but he isn't. If we go tonight, then we must go on foot. It is the longest speech he has made since we started our journey. Though he does not complain on his own behalf, he too looks tired. I do not press him, but watch him unfastening the straps for a moment, then turn back to the coach.

I plan to report all this back to the others, but it is clear they have overheard most of it. Underhill is not pleased, but Aminta breathes a sigh of relief.

'Aminta, Sophia and I will take a room in the inn,' I say. 'You, Mr Underhill, will remain in your seat until we have engaged Pepys in conversation—give us five minutes, then make a run for the stables over there. We'll arrange for food to be sent to you. Either you must starve or we'll have to trust the landlord that far at least.'

'Let me have the pistol then,' says Underhill. 'You're in no danger. I may need it.'

'I doubt that Arlington would think that was a good idea,' I say. 'Giving you a gun formed no part of his plan, whatever that is. You'll be safe if you stay where you are until morning. If you try to leave, I can promise nothing.'

Though I had hoped to get Aminta to our room quickly, we find Pepys lying in wait. We stop and exchange pleasantries. It will at least give Underhill time to get to the stables.

Pepys, as I expected, lavishes compliments on Aminta's writing. I am not sure that I like the way he looks at her, but that is of course none of my business. She is not my wife, nor can she ever be.

'I think that *The Way of the World* is your finest piece,' he says, 'though I also admire *The Gay Rake*. And of course *The Moroccan Prince*—the harem scene gave your actresses a chance to show themselves to advantage.'

'You are too kind, Mr Pepys,' says Aminta. 'I am sorry that we shall have nothing new to show you until this Plague is over.'

'Conversation these days always returns sooner or later to the Plague,' says Pepys with a shudder. 'We are free of it here at least. But I think that it will not be long before it follows us. My father often speaks of the Great Plague—I mean the one of 1625, the year that the late King was crowned. Forty thousand died in London that year, but I fear that we may surpass even that total before long. And we have no better knowledge now of its cause or its cure than we did then. We are helpless. London will soon be a city of the dead. Everyone will be in their grave or shut up in their houses.'

'They *wanted* to shut me up,' says Sophia.

Aminta hushes her and then looks angrily at Pepys.

'You will frighten the child with this talk,' says Aminta. 'She imagines things. A…friend of hers was shut up with her family. I shall take her up to our chamber to rest.'

Sophia, almost asleep, allows herself to be led away.

Pepys frowns. 'A precocious child,' he observes. 'Imaginative too.'

'Indeed,' I say.

'I wonder what she meant about people trying to shut her up?'

'I have no idea,' I say.

Then he digs me in the ribs. 'And you are a sly one,' he adds. 'Mr *and Mrs* Grey, eh? Don't think I didn't hear you asking for a chamber. Well, I won't give the game away, but I wish I'd asked her first! You must have great powers of persuasion, sir!'

'It is not my intention to take advantage of her,' I say. 'I have offered her my protection for the journey. It seemed…simpler… to pose as husband and wife.'

Pepys grins. 'You have no need to be so coy with me, Mr Grey. I envy you—nothing more. Will you kindly assist me in drinking this bottle of wine?'

I allow him to pour me a glass. He holds his up towards the window to examine the colour. It is pale straw and perfectly clear.

'So,' he adds carelessly. 'You are travelling without any servant?'

'The journey to Salisbury is a short one.'

'But your coach would accommodate an extra person?'

'We prefer not to have the expense,' I say. 'A servant is of little value on the road, when there are waiting men and women at every inn.'

'How wise you are. And, of course, Lady Pole might prefer the…arrangements…to remain between you and her. No servants' tittle-tattle when you get back to London. Well, your good health, Mr Grey.' Pepys, having decided the wine is the correct colour, raises his glass to me and I raise mine to him.

For a while we drink in silence and then Pepys says: 'So, *did* Arlington find what he was looking for?'

'I could not say,' I reply.

'Would it help if I said that I now know the man calling himself Horncastle tried to sell him the purported letter? Which Arlington discovered was less than he hoped?'

'You seem very well informed,' I say. 'But there is nothing I can tell you.'

'Except, that isn't true, is it, Mr Grey?'

I shake my head.

'You seem reluctant to follow your best interests, which I think are not so far from mine. There could be money in this for both of us, if we do but play our cards aright. Could Horncastle have concealed the thing you are now looking for…the remainder of the message…on his person?'

Since Underhill is now wearing a borrowed suit of clothes, I know that he cannot have done so—indeed, I now understand why Arlington so generously replaced Underhill's old suit, which was taken away, in all likelihood to be dismembered and searched, stitch by stitch. I note also that Pepys is very insistent that there *is* a second part to the letter, which as the Duke's servant he would presumably know. But equally I know Underhill cannot have it with him. Nor do I think that Underhill has any knowledge of it. He is as puzzled as we are. So, could Fincham's killer have removed it before Underhill came on the scene? If so, where is it now?

'Horncastle, if that is his true name, seems to have told Arlington that he had more information,' Pepys continues. 'But he will only tell it to the King.'

'If you say so.'

'It would be better if he spoke to me.'

'You should tell him so.'

'I shall, if I can find him. But here's a thing. Horncastle wishes to speak to the King and the King is in Salisbury. Arlington has Horncastle in his hands and you are Arlington's servant. This is the road to Salisbury and you are on it in a capacious coach. Did you by any chance study logic at our old college, Mr Grey? If so, what would you conclude from these various premises?'

I drain my glass and replace it on the table. 'Thank you for the wine,' I say. 'I must order food for my driver. He is sleeping tonight above the stables.'

'So is my driver,' says Pepys. 'They will be able to watch over each other and keep each other company.'

The ceilings are low, here above the stables. Underhill could stand upright if he wished, but I have to stoop a little as I enter. The wooden floors are clean, but the smell of hay and horse from below is all-pervasive. There is a small window overlooking the courtyard.

Underhill is sitting on his bed. The untalkative coachman is already asleep in his.

'Said he didn't want no supper,' says Underhill.

'I've already ordered food for both of you,' I say. 'Perhaps he will feel hungrier in the morning. Have you seen Pepys's driver?'

'There's another chamber opposite. I heard somebody coming and going from that.'

'Then just keep clear of him and be as quiet as you can. He'll be reporting back to Pepys on anything he hears or sees.'

'I am sure he will. It's just as I said, in fact. I might as well have had a chamber in the inn in that case, like you. At least I would have had a good night's sleep before I get shot.'

'On the contrary. Pepys suspects you might be with us but he isn't certain, because he hasn't seen you. He also suspects you've held something back from Arlington. He made it clear there *was* a second part to the letter. Do you have it hidden somewhere?'

Underhill seems genuinely nonplussed. 'I gave Arlington all I had. Why would I hold back anything I could sell?'

'If what you say about Fincham's death is true, could the killer have taken whatever Pepys is talking about? Is that why this other man ran off? Not because he was afraid of being caught with Fincham's body, but because he already had what he wanted?'

Underhill is pensive. 'He wouldn't have had the time,' he says eventually. 'And it didn't look as if somebody had already searched him. Unless Fincham simply gave it to him and was then stabbed anyway. Maybe he didn't give it to Morland because he already had another buyer. I hadn't thought of that.'

Underhill stops suddenly and glances across at the heap of blankets that conceals our own driver. But our man is fast asleep and has not overheard anything. Not that it would matter much if he had.

'Whatever this is about, it's already cost two lives. You'd better make sure you don't fall into the Duke's hands,' I say. 'Stay out of sight.'

Underhill nods. We both know that the snoring driver won't be much help if Underhill is attacked, but I still reckon he's safer here than in the inn.

The driver mutters something and turns away from us. I exchange glances with Underhill, but the snoring quickly resumes. I am happy, on all counts, to be sleeping at the inn. I bid them both a soft goodnight and return to my own room.

Aminta and Sophia have already eaten and are fast asleep in the larger of the two beds. I tiptoe out and return to the parlour and order cold beef and bread for myself. I eat it slowly. We hope to be in Salisbury tomorrow night, but much depends on what sort of welcome we receive at other towns along the road. The landlord brings me a fresh candle and more ale.

'Your driver was slumbering when I took his food up,' he says.

'He's driven all day.'

'But he has taken to his bed early...he does not have any sickness?'

'No,' I say. 'He has good reason to be tired.'

The landlord nods. 'I don't want the Plague at my inn,' he says. 'I can't afford to have the establishment closed down. If your man's got the Plague, I don't want him dying here. He can stay out in the stables. Horses don't get the Plague.'

Little does he know that the person in our group who claims to have the Plague is sleeping soundly above his head, her thumb in her mouth.

'Don't worry. We'll be gone at first light,' I say.

In my chamber I undress quickly and take the small truckle bed that the landlord undoubtedly intended for Sophia. I wonder about our driver, who has said so little and retired so early. Is he deliberately avoiding any conversation with us? Could he have been listening? I shall try to find out more about him tomorrow.

I look over at Aminta and the child together. I pray that Sophia does not in fact have the Plague. I pray that, in the days to come, Aminta's good deed will serve to protect all of us. But it seems a very small deed in a very large world.

The Plague Road

From My Lady Pole's Esteemed Poem,

The Puritaniad

Thus in our coach and four we ride
Through all the friendly countryside.
The towns and villages are one
In their desire to see us gone.
With jeers and oaths men drive us hence
Lest we should gift them Pestilence
They have, they say, no use for passes
Unless it were to wipe their a---s
Dear Lord, please grant that on each rear
A token of the Plague appear
To fright these leering, grinning elves
Who, when they see it, sh-t themselves.

CHAPTER 18

I am dreaming of a horseman, riding through the chamber, his steed's hooves thudding against the bare wooden floor. I awake to find that the sounds I have heard must have been outside in the yard. Then there is a metallic rasp as bolts are drawn on a door somewhere below and there is a hurried conversation. Two voices, but I cannot tell what they are saying.

The moon is shining in through the open window and there is a cool breeze after the heat of the day. In the pale light I can see every detail of the room clearly—the beds, the black-beamed walls, the small table and the two spindly chairs, my gun, loaded and primed on the table—but all strangely drained of their natural colour and turned into a ghostly silver.

I rise cautiously and go to the window. The sharp night air bathes my face and I hear a hunting owl hoot somewhere out there in the black, ferny woods. The silence that follows is broken by the steady tread of a horse's iron-shod hooves on the cobbles. A man and horse come into view, flat shadows against a phantom landscape. The shadow man leads his shadow horse by its reins towards the blank entrance to the stables. They both enter and merge softly into the darkness. There is a flash of light as a lamp is lit inside, but I can see nothing except the glow of the candle on the stone floor. I remain at my post for some time, but the man does not reappear. He will be unsaddling the horse and rubbing it down before watering and feeding it. That may take some time. A lone traveller at this hour may be inconvenient for the landlord but there is nothing to suggest that he poses a risk to anyone else.

I rub my eyes and return to my cramped bed. I cannot say for how many minutes or hours I am allowed to sleep, but I am suddenly awake again and listening to urgent footsteps outside. Has the traveller finished looking after his horse and is he now returning to the inn? But why is he running? Then a shot rings out and there is a cry and somebody or something falls to the ground.

I am on my feet in an instant, quickly pulling on my breeches and stuffing my bare feet into my shoes. I seize the pistol from the table. As I run down the stairs it occurs to me that it might have been better to collect some more powder and some musket balls from my bag. I shall have only one shot at my disposal, then I shall be as defenceless as I would have been with no weapon at all. Other feet are running too, across the rush-covered floor of the parlour below. A door is unbolted and opened. A dark figure steps out into the night and then pauses just beyond the threshold.

When I, too, arrive outside, the moonlight at first reveals nothing, except the landlord, who is standing stock still, an ancient wheel-lock musket in his hands.

'You heard something?' he asks.

'Yes,' I say.

'I didn't dream it, then.'

'There was a shot fired. The question is whether anyone was hit.'

'I thought I heard somebody fall,' he says. 'But there's no sign of a wounded man out there.'

The Plague Road

He and I scan the scene before us. It is a cloudless night. The dirt road leading up to the inn is pure silver—the long grass and bushes on either side are various shades of grey. The moon hangs large above us and the stars are bright. In the distance the trees sway almost imperceptibly and completely silently in a faint breeze. I feel the damp, fresh summer night on my legs and face.

'No sign of the man who fired the shot either,' I say.

The landlord and I look at each other, he clutching his musket and I my pistol. Two shots between us, then. It would be a good plan to hit our targets first time if we can.

'Everyone must have heard the firing,' I say. 'The others will be down in a moment.'

I wonder, however, if Pepys is cowering in his chamber with a blanket over his head. I agree with Aminta: he doesn't look like a man of action. Hopefully Underhill too will have stayed where he is, if he is wise. But where is our taciturn driver—and Pepys's driver, come to that?

Pepys's driver is in fact the next to arrive, from the direction of the stables and, like me, stockingless, though he has donned a doublet against the chill. He is a small, active man with several days' stubble on his chin and a scar on his face—another veteran of the wars, I suspect, who is putting his experience of life as a cavalryman to good use.

'Did one of you just fire?' he asks. 'You'll frighten the horses with that noise.'

'Not us,' says the landlord. 'But there's somebody out there who did.'

I lower my gun and rub my eyes. Here and there a shadow seems to move in the moonlight. In a moment there could be a flash and a small ball of lead could be spinning in my direction.

But Pepys, too, now makes an appearance. He is in a Turkish silk dressing gown, too good for a country inn, which he wraps closely round him. I see a finely engraved pistol in his hand—silver chasing on dull grey steel.

'Where have you been?' I ask.

'In bed,' he replies. 'Alone. Until that shot woke me. I heard the front door opening and came down to investigate.'

'You didn't fire the shot yourself?' I ask.

He holds out the barrel of the gun. 'Feel it,' he says.

I put my hand out carefully. The barrel is stone cold.

'What's happening?' asks Aminta over my shoulder. The noise seems to have woken everyone.

'You should get back inside the inn,' I say. 'It's not safe out here for a woman.'

She pulls her shawl round her. 'I am, with the greatest respect, a smaller target than you are. If the person who fired the shot is going to fire again, he has the choice of a great many large men standing around, lit up by a full moon and making enough noise to wake the dead.'

'Good morning, my Lady,' says Pepys, making a bow. 'Your...*husband*...believes that I may have fired the shot. I am attempting to persuade him otherwise.'

We wait. Still nothing stirs in the moonlight. Nothing at all. The landlord fetches a lantern from the inn and we advance cautiously, like a line of skirmishers, into the long dry grass that separates the inn from the road. But, having gone a short way, we halt again, as if by some unspoken agreement. It isn't clear what we are looking for and none of us wishes to walk into a trap.

Pepys, who has been viewing our efforts with growing contempt, now appears to lose his patience. 'This is ridiculous,' he says. 'We are simply wasting our time. Whoever fired the shot will have long since made their escape. We have no good reason to believe anyone has been hit. I would recommend we all retire to the parlour. I shall certainly do so.'

I watch him go back across the grass, accompanied by his coachman, who for some reason wishes to stay close to him. The coachman looked ill at ease. There is a flash of light as the inn door opens and closes.

'Mr Pepys is right,' says the landlord, still peering into the night. He lifts the lantern higher but it adds little to the moonlight we already have. 'There's nothing moving at all. Most likely the shot missed.'

'But we heard somebody fall,' I say. 'You did and I think I did too.'

Then there is a groan from the long grass just in front of us. A face emerges, contorted with pain.

'Good Lord!' I say.

'I am injured,' Underhill moans. 'I am injured and nobody cares. You could at least try to help me. Give me a hand, Grey.'

'It seems to be your servant,' says the landlord. 'Though he addresses you in a most familiar and impertinent fashion.'

'As your servant I'd hoped you would take greater care of my safety,' says Underhill. 'Not leave me to be shot at by everyone.'

I kneel by him to check how he is wounded.

'Where did the ball strike you?' I ask, for I can see no blood.

For once Underhill appears embarrassed.

'It missed me,' he says. 'I twisted my ankle in this grass as I ran. I cannot stand. I may never walk again.'

I do, however, help him to his feet, and he does stand, albeit carefully and with the weight on his other leg. I feel his ankle. There is perhaps a small amount of swelling.

'Try to take a few steps,' I say.

Underhill hops a little, pulling a face as he does so.

'I may have broken it,' he says.

'I don't think so,' I say.

'It's *my* ankle and I know it better than you do,' he says.

'Why are you out here in the middle of the night?' I ask.

'I couldn't sleep. I left my room for a walk and some fresh air. It stinks in the stables. You should try it. Then there was a shot. It only just missed me. I heard the ball hiss through the air. So I ran for it and fell over in the grass. I must have knocked myself out. When I came to, I could make out voices, but I couldn't tell whose they were, so I kept my head down. I could have cursed you when you all started to walk across the field like that, playing at soldiers, but Pepys at least had the sense to stop. Anyway, it's not just my ankle that's broken. It's my head too.'

I briefly examine his head but can see no sign of bruising. I touch his scalp with my fingertips. 'Where does it hurt?' I ask.

'Everywhere,' he says, noncommittally.

'You will live,' I say. 'You've had a fall, but it could have been much worse.'

I look over my shoulder at the inn. Nobody seems to be observing us but it is difficult to be certain. 'Pepys has retired to the parlour,' I say. 'I would suggest that you make your way back to the stables as quietly as you can with a broken ankle and a cracked skull.'

❊ ❊ ❊

'Did you discover anything?' asks Pepys, when we all (save Underhill) return to the inn. He has taken the opportunity to order himself some canary. This time he does not offer me any.

'A man staying in the stables was shot at,' I say. 'He is unharmed. We don't know who fired the shot.'

'Well, we have at least established that it wasn't me,' says Pepys huffily. He strokes the barrel of his gun.

'Wait,' I say. 'You said, Mr Pepys, that you possessed *pistols*. You have but one there. Where are the others?'

Pepys turns to his coachman. 'Was it found?' he asks.

The coachman, who has not looked happy for some time, now looks properly scared.

'I looked in the coach, truly, but I didn't find it. Perhaps if I look again, now that it is almost daylight...'

'You looked everywhere, as I instructed?'

'Indeed, Mr Pepys. Exactly as you asked me.'

'Then how do you expect to find it now?'

'I don't know, sir, but...'

'You're an idiot,' he says to the coachman.

Pepys turns to the rest of us. 'Last night I realised that I had only one pistol with me in my chamber. I recalled that I had had the other weapon with me in the coach, ready to fend off any highwaymen. So I asked James here to search the coach thoroughly and keep the gun safe.'

'And so I did,' says James, though with no great conviction. 'But maybe I'll find it now. Just give me a moment.'

I catch James's eye and he looks imploringly at me, but I am in no mood to be merely obliging.

'Why don't we all check the coach,' I say.

I lead the group back outside and round to where the yellow carriage stands. Even in this strange light, the colour glows. It is newly built, the wheel spokes are picked out in red, and the dust of the road does not diminish its beauty. This is what a navy clerk can afford to hire—and indeed aspire to owning.

One door is already unfastened. I pull it open and look inside, but there is no gun to be seen.

'Did you leave the door open?' I ask the coachman.

'Indeed not, sir,' he says.

'Then, if it was in the coach last night, a gun has gone missing,' I say.

'If it has been stolen through your carelessness, I shall have you whipped,' says Pepys to the coachman.

'Let's get lanterns from the stables,' I say. 'We'll search the grass. The would-be killer may have taken it with him after firing, or he may have thrown it down—especially if he is still amongst us.'

Pepys scowls at me but says nothing.

We return to the front of the inn and again form a line. Now we know what we are looking for, we discover a pistol quite quickly, in the dry grass, not far from where Underhill emerged from it.

The weapon is beautifully engraved, just like the one Pepys is holding. I pick it up and touch the barrel carefully. It is still slightly warm. The flash pan is blackened with gunpowder. The grass around it is also slightly scorched. The gun has been fired and thrown here, still smoking, only a short time ago.

'This, I think, is our weapon,' I say. 'It would appear to be the brother of the gun in your hand, Mr Pepys.'

Pepys turns to his driver. 'Can you explain this, sir?' he demands. 'Is this not the gun I asked you to look after? Is this not the gun you said you'd looked for? How did it get here?'

'I couldn't say, Mr Pepys,' says the coachman. 'Perhaps it had already been taken when I looked?'

'James,' I say to the coachman, 'there may be a killer amongst us. If we are to discover who it is, then we need you to tell the truth. It may matter a great deal whether the gun was stolen last night or this morning. When did you first look for it?'

'You see, Mr Pepys...' he says. He looks at the rest of us as if for help, then continues: 'When you came up and asked me to hunt for it, I was already in bed,' he says.

'What of it?' says Pepys. 'Do you cease to be in my employ the moment you decide to retire for the night? I think not, sir.'

'Of course not,' says the coachman, 'but, as you were going back down the stairs, I remembered that I'd seen you put the pistol in one of the pockets of the door of the coach. I reckoned it was safe enough there. Anyway, the coach would be dark and I didn't want to take a candle and spill grease over the new leather. So, I decided not to get dressed again but that I would look for it at first light. And I would have done, too, if I'd been allowed to.'

'So, my gun was in the coach all night?'

'Yes, Mr Pepys. Until it was stolen, sir.'

'Idiot.'

'Sorry, Mr Pepys, sir.'

'So,' says Pepys, 'because of your negligence, somebody has taken my pistol and tried to kill this person, who you say resides in the stables. As a result I might have stood accused of the deed myself, if it were not so obvious that I could have done nothing of the sort. I should whip you. Indeed, I shall whip you until you know your business better than you do...'

'Your desire to improve your coachman's efficiency does you credit,' I say. 'You are right that he shouldn't have left it there. But as for it being obvious that you could not have fired the gun... Perhaps you had already taken it last night and your request to the driver was merely for show. You must have guessed he would not look until morning. It would have been easy for you to come downstairs, fire the pistol, then toss the gun aside when you thought you had hit him. When it was found, as it would be, James would have taken the blame for his carelessness. Is that what happened?'

'Why should you think that I would wish to shoot a complete stranger?' asks Pepys. 'Unless...' A look of understanding appears on his face. 'Unless he is the man we spoke of. Is he, Mr Grey?'

'He's Mr Grey's servant,' says the landlord uncertainly. 'And a most impertinent and complaining serving man he is. I would not employ him myself.'

'Indeed?' says Pepys. 'How interesting. I thought you were travelling without a servant, Grey?'

'A clerk,' I say. 'Not a domestic servant.'

'And you are accusing me of trying to kill your *clerk*?'

'Did you try?'

'I came out after you did,' he says. 'You saw me.'

'I saw you out there. I didn't see you leave the inn.'

'And you think I would have thrown away a perfectly good gun, spoiling the set?' Pepys demands. 'Then you do not know me, sir. You do not know me at all.'

'Better lose one of a set than be discovered,' I say.

'Discovered? You are mad, sir.' I think that Pepys may be about to have apoplexy. Then he relaxes and laughs. 'Well, I have my missing pistol back and we now know you are conveying Father Horncastle to Salisbury under the guise of your servant. And he is clearly unharmed by the night's adventures. Good. We can now look at our options in a rational manner. I was, however, in bed when the shot was fired at him and, in any case, I want him alive. But perhaps somebody else wishes to kill him?'

I look round the group: the landlord, Aminta, Pepys's driver—and indeed myself. Exactly where was everyone? Our own driver is still missing, presumed asleep. And didn't somebody arrive on horseback in the middle of the night?

I hear a cough at my shoulder and turn to see Callingham's creased and one-eyed face.

'Why the commotion, good sirs?' he declaims. 'Did I hear a shot a moment ago? Salutations to you, Mr Grey. I hope you still have Mr Underhill safely secured?'

'And now I also know his real name,' says Pepys. '*Underhill.* Excellent. What a useful night we are all having.'

CHAPTER 19

Outside in the world, the dawn is breaking. Here, in the parlour, a gentle half-light prevails. We are all seated about the room in various states of dress. The landlord is serving us ham and beef and bread. Sophia, now wide awake, chews thoughtfully and then takes a sip of my beer.

'I need,' I say, 'to establish exactly where everyone was last night. Until we have done that, nobody may leave.'

'Are you claiming to be a magistrate?' asks James, still unhappy that I have caused him to be admonished by Pepys.

'I am acting with the authority of the Secretary of State,' I say. 'As Mr Pepys has informed you, I am taking Esmond Underhill to Salisbury to give evidence to the King. It is possible that one of you has tried to kill him. As his guard, only I am permitted to do that.'

'This is even more ridiculous than your accusing me,' says Pepys. 'You hold no official position. Let me make it clear, sir, that I do not accept your authority to detain me.'

'I would be happy to send for the nearest justice of the peace,' I say, 'and report an attempted murder, but that may take some hours, since he is almost certainly still asleep.'

'I'm content with that,' says Callingham, observing us one by one with his single eye. 'Send for a magistrate by all means. Let him question us. It wasn't I who fired the shot.'

'Well, *I* am not content,' says Pepys. 'You may believe that your master Arlington gives you some authority, but I report to the Duke, who will not forgive you for delaying his business.'

I turn to the others. 'Perhaps you would each like to tell me where you were?'

'Well, you saw me unbolt the door and go out,' says the landlord. 'So I couldn't have already been out there firing Mr Pepys's gun.'

'But you were out earlier, when Mr Callingham arrived?'

'Of course. I have to be there to receive all visitors to the inn. How could it be otherwise?'

'What happened then?'

'It was about one o'clock when I heard a knocking at the door. Mr Callingham said that he was travelling to Salisbury but had lost his way. He asked if I still had any spare rooms and I said I had. So he put his horse in the stable while I got him some food and prepared a bed in one of the empty chambers.'

'How long was he at the stables?'

'I don't know. Fifteen minutes? Half an hour? The food was on the table when he came in. He ate and went to bed.'

'And then you locked the door?'

'Of course. There are all sorts of people on the road now.'

'And the windows?'

'Yes. On the ground floor. In Guildford they say that travellers, sick with the Plague, threw their dirty bandages in through the windows of houses to infect the healthy. Don't look at me like that—it's what they do. Those Plague people hate us. So, I keep the windows shut.'

'Even in this heat?'

'Yes.'

'But they can all be opened from the inside?'

'Obviously.'

'So anyone could have made their exit by a window at any time. And the stables were not locked, so those in the stable block could also have left whenever they wished.'

'Well,' says Callingham, rubbing his eye, 'I can confirm my arrival time. I was aware of a church clock striking midnight some time before, so around one o'clock must be right. I took about twenty minutes looking after the horse. I would have eaten and been in bed before two o'clock and the door was certainly barred by then.'

'Did you go anywhere near Mr Pepys's coach?'

'I went to the stables. But I didn't look inside the coach. Why should I suspect anyone had left a loaded gun there or want it if they had? I have my own pistols. If somebody took the gun from the coach then they must have already known it was there.'

'But you had good reason to want Underhill dead. He had cost you an eye at the siege of Colchester.'

'And I don't doubt he killed Fincham. I hold that against him too. But I swear to you, I did not use Pepys's gun, and my own guns are still up in my room above us. You may check. They have not been fired tonight.'

'How did you discover we were here? And how did you manage it at such speed? Will hadn't set out for Stepney when we left.'

'I chanced to call half an hour after you left. Will told me you were taking Esmond Underhill, alias Father Horncastle, to Salisbury, and that Lady Pole had gone with you. That seemed unwise—I was fearful for her safety on the road. So I came after you on my horse to act as escort. I was able to ask after you at the various roadblocks, but I still had to try a number of inns and villages. By the time I reached here, my horse could go no further. It was pure good fortune that this was the one you were at. So, I'm here to help you, not to try to kill one of your party. I'd be grateful if you could remember that, Mr Grey. Question those who *did* know the gun was there. James, for example.'

James turns to him resentfully. 'Yes, but if I'd used it, I'd have returned it to the coach. Why would I leave it in the grass for everyone to find?'

'You could hardly just return it having fired it,' I say. 'That is one thing Mr Pepys could not have overlooked. You would have needed to clean it and reload it. Better then to leave it somewhere as if it had been used by somebody else and abandoned.'

'But I'm not the only one who knew it was there. Any of you could have overheard Mr Pepys asking me to look for it, including you, Mr Grey. You could have gone to the stables to see Mr Underhill... Or she could have picked it up, for that matter. Nobody's asked her where she was.'

All eyes turn to Aminta.

'I was in bed,' she says. 'With the child.'

'That is true,' I say. 'When I left the room they were both in bed. I can vouch for Lady Pole.'

And yet, even as I say it, I realise that I only glanced towards the other bed. It had somebody in it for sure, but were both of them there? And Aminta was every bit as much Fincham's friend as Callingham. Nor can I doubt, knowing her ability to scale any tree in her father's garden, that she could climb out of any window that I could.

I look round for our own driver but there is still no sign of him. I can question him later. He at least won't be leaving without us. But this thought is now running through my head: almost anyone could have taken a shot at Underhill, including Aminta. But, even if they could have found the gun, how would they have known where and when to lie in wait for him? Only our (apparently heavily sleeping) driver would have been aware that Underhill was dressing and about to make a run for it. And since he never stirred from the chamber above the stables, he could have overheard Pepys. Perhaps the one person I really need to question isn't here.

'I am going back to my chamber to wash and shave,' I say. 'In the meantime, nobody may leave the inn.'

'Since I am the only one with plans to leave,' says Pepys, 'let me make it clear to you that I do not recognise your authority in any way. I have indulged your fancies for long enough. I'm departing in twenty minutes, Mr Grey, and if you don't like it, you may complain all you wish to Arlington. *La commedia è finita*.'

I return to the stables.

'Pepys knows you are here,' I say to Underhill. 'He knows your real name. Callingham let it slip.'

'Callingham is here?'

'You need have no fears. He came to help escort us. But he saw you and told Pepys before I could stop him.'

'Pepys *and* Callingham? Then I'm leaving at once,' says Underhill.

'Callingham's no threat whatever you do; but, if you run, Pepys will pursue you.'

'I don't think so. He won't recognise me on my own. I've seen Pepys at the Duke's house but we were never introduced; I was just one of the Duke's minions, beneath his notice. He knows you well enough, though. No offence, but I'm safer alone, Grey. That's all there is to it. It's light enough to travel. I can head for the woods first, where Pepys won't follow in his pretty yellow carriage. And I'm going as soon as I can.'

'You'll stay with me if you have any sense. It may not be Pepys you need to worry about. Where's Luke?'

'He's finally awake. He's gone to the yard to wash. He won't be back for a while.'

'Good. So, let me ask you again, what information are you taking to the King? Somebody killed Fincham for it, then somebody strangled the guard trying to find the rest of the letter. Now somebody has tried to kill you. If I'm going to risk my life getting you to the King, and if I'm to work out who shot at you, I want to know what the secret is you are taking to the King.'

'You don't think I'll tell you that, do you?'

'Strangely, I do. Because, if you don't tell me, I shall do exactly as you ask and leave you to make your way to Salisbury alone, as best you can—on foot, unarmed and with no money. How does that sound? Pepys doesn't need to track you through the woods, just to wait for you outside Salisbury with one of the Duke's men who *does* know you. I suspect that's why he's anxious to get away now. So he can arrange a welcome party. Good luck, Mr Underhill.'

Underhill reconsiders his position.

'You wouldn't,' he says.

'I wish you a pleasant journey to Salisbury,' I say. 'You may leave whenever you wish. I won't stop you.'

Underhill laughs. 'Except that you wouldn't go against Arlington's instructions.'

'You don't know what Arlington's instructions are,' I say.

'I know Arlington well enough,' says Underhill. 'Maybe better than you do.'

I turn, without saying a further word, and head back across the yard to the inn.

In our chamber, Aminta is getting ready to leave.

'We're going on to Salisbury now,' I say, 'and without Underhill. We'll find Sophia's people and then travel back to London. If Underhill won't tell me why we're risking our lives then he can do it on his own. I'm not putting you and Sophia in further danger.'

'That is an expensive decision.'

I mentally total the lost fee and the expenses I shall not be able to reclaim.

'I'll need to find a few more clients with disputed wills,' I say.

'And am I not to become Arlington's creature?'

'No,' I say. 'I fear that is a pleasure you will have to forgo.'

'Don't be too hasty. I think we should take Underhill anyway, even if he won't tell us why his life is at risk. Isn't it enough to know that he is planning to tell the King something that isn't to the credit of the Duke? Something that may affect the security of the whole country? We've brought Underhill this far. I think we should finish the job.'

We look at each other.

'Unless you are careful,' I say, 'I shall believe that you have other reasons for wanting to keep Underhill within your reach.'

'As so often, cousin, your precise meaning escapes me.'

'Underhill may have killed your friend Fincham.'

'And you think I am suggesting we keep him with us in the hope of getting my revenge? Perhaps you think I had a premonition last night that Underhill might decide to escape, climbed out of a window in my nightgown, found a pistol that I had no previous knowledge of and then lay in wait, possibly for some hours, until the moment arrived?'

Yes, that's possible.

'No,' I say. 'Of course not.'

'Precisely. I think the person who fired the gun is with us. But it wasn't me. The one thing we do have to do is to trust each other at least. I could accuse you with as much reason, but I haven't.'

'I agree,' I say. 'I'm sorry.'

'Anyway, I don't think Underhill did kill Fincham. Not any more. If I'd killed somebody I'd have the decency to look guilty from time to time. Underhill just looks as if somebody had shoved a rotten herring under his nose. I don't think he would have it in him to murder in cold blood. I am worried about Luke, our driver, however.'

'I agree there's something very odd about him,' I say.

'Nobody sleeps that heavily. He was the one person who would have known Underhill was about to make a run for it—unlike Pepys or Callingham or even Pepys's driver. He'd have heard the moment Underhill slid out of bed. And, unlike the others, he was in the stables all evening—he could have overheard Pepys and the driver talking about it and realised there was a gun there for the taking.'

'But why?' I ask.

'You said Arlington was quite willing to see Underhill dead. Morland found the driver for us.'

'Luke is a hired assassin? It would be a convoluted way of arranging things.'

'Morland's thinking *is* convoluted. Do you trust him in any way at all?'

'I'm going back to the stables,' I say. 'Luke should have completed his ablutions. Perhaps he will have something to say for himself.'

The driver has returned, slightly damp and looking tired in spite of his long rest. Underhill is not there, but I doubt he's gone far.

'I'm sorry, Mr Grey—I must have slept heavily. I heard nothing last night,' he says.

I look at him again. Perhaps this is true, but he doesn't have the air of a man who has slept well. There are dark rings under his eyes. 'Where are your boots?' I ask.

'Over there,' he says, puzzled.

I examine them. They are dry. Not a trace of dew. So maybe he has not stirred.

'How well do you know the road ahead?' I ask.

'I know the way to Salisbury quite well from here. If there is danger, as you say, I can use a still less frequented route, where nobody will find us.'

'Unless they follow us,' I say.

'The driver says we'll be on the road at seven,' I say to Aminta, meeting her in the parlour. 'How is Sophia?'

'Missing her parents, as you might expect. Yesterday was an adventure. Today she's not so sure. She's gone to see the horses. Hopefully that will divert her. I'm going to join her.'

'Have you seen Underhill by any chance?'

'There's no sign of him. Do you want me to look for him?'
'No,' I say.

But when I return to our chamber to collect my own bag, Underhill is already there. Somehow he has managed to make his way upstairs undetected. He backs away slightly from the table the bag is on. I immediately check it. The pistol, the shot, the gunpowder, the pass, Arlington's letter, my clean linen. They are all still there.

'I wasn't trying to steal the gun,' says Underhill. 'That's the truth.'

'What are you here for then?' I ask.

'You're right,' he says. 'I need to tell you just how things are. So you know.'

'Go ahead,' I say.

'It's like this,' he says in a whisper. 'There aren't many, even in the Duke's household who know, but they don't all listen at doors the way I do. I've heard a few things that I wasn't supposed to hear. The Duke of York has long been known to protect the Catholics. But now he is apparently about to turn Papist himself. When he does, as best I could hear what they were saying, the French will finance him to fight against the King or anyone else. James is already Lord High Admiral. He has the fleet in his pocket. The French will send troops over.'

'He means to overthrow the King? That isn't possible.'

'Who else would he use troops against?'

'And you think that is what was in the missing part of the letter?'

'I'm certain of it.'

'Do you think that the King will welcome this news—that his brother is about to stage a rebellion with the help of the French?'

'As long as he pays me, I don't much care whether he likes it or not.'

If Arlington suspects any of this, and Arlington suspects most things, then I can see why he foresaw some danger. And I can see why he would prefer not to be the bearer of this message himself. And after the King's initial rage...the Duke would face exile at least. It would also be the end of Arlington's enemy Clarendon, who could not survive his son-in-law's downfall. Which would complete Arlington's design very well. So, surely he needs Underhill alive to give evidence, not shot by me or captured by a third party?

'Get your things together,' I say. 'We need to be on the road. And if Pepys has really never set eyes on you, don't let him see you now. I do not doubt for a moment that the Duke wants you dead.'

'Neither Pepys nor his coachman has seen me,' says Underhill. 'I've made sure of that.'

'He'll be watching to see who gets into the carriage. There's a way down to the road through the trees. Go that way on foot and wait for us at the crossroads. Hide in the bushes until we can meet you there.'

Callingham is drinking small beer, preparatory to his own departure. Dressed, as he is, in his travelling clothes, he looks much less of an actor and more of a soldier. But there is still something of the footlights about him. He rises to his feet and sweeps off his hat.

'When do we leave, Mr Grey?' he asks. 'As you can see, I am armed to the teeth and at your service. If I can help in taking Underhill to face charges in Salisbury, then I'm your man, sir.'

'I'm taking him to the King,' I say. 'What happens after that, what charges he may face, is out of my hands.'

'I'll trust your judgement, Mr Grey, and Lady Pole's. And I trust His Majesty, though I fought against his father. I'll ride behind the coach. You may find another pistol or two useful, if you are ambushed. I see that Mr Pepys is already preparing to depart, though he was skulking round the stables earlier. If he or his coachman did fire at that rogue last night, then I wouldn't rule out him laying some sort of trap for you in the road ahead.'

'Do you know these roads?'

Callingham nods. 'I have a sister living near Salisbury. I've travelled this way often. I certainly know my way better than Pepys will. Where's Underhill now?'

I wonder how Underhill will react to having Callingham ride with us.

'He's safely concealed,' I say. 'But the best thing may be for you to ride ahead of us and see what Pepys does. And discover who else is on the road. It may not be just the Duke of York's men we have to worry about. Buckingham also seems to be after Underhill. We'll follow on as best we can.'

'Buckingham as well?' says Callingham. 'Do you think so?'

'I'm certain of it.'

Callingham shakes his head sadly. 'Underhill has a lot of enemies then. I think you're lucky I caught up with you.'

'At least we'll be in Salisbury soon,' I say, looking out of the coach window. 'With Callingham keeping an eye on Pepys, I hope we'll have warning of any attempted ambush. You are sure Callingham can be trusted, though?'

Aminta glances sideways at Sophia. She is an attentive listener and is proving to have a looser tongue than some six-year-olds. 'Callingham's appearance here suggests greater loyalty to me than I would have thought I merited. But I do not doubt his good intentions.'

'It's our own driver who concerns me most,' I add in a half-whisper. 'How can he possibly have slept through last night's disturbances? He must have heard the shot, yet he alone failed to appear. And he looks in no way rested after his long repose. He was slow in getting the horses ready this morning. Now we are finally under way, he seems determined to delay us. We make no speed at all, though the roads are as smooth as we could hope for.'

Callingham and Pepys must be many miles ahead of us, but we dawdle along, scarcely raising a puff of dust on the hard, dry road. We have just entered a village and two or three small boys are running alongside us, keeping up our pace with no great effort.

As we approach the inn, the coach slows to a crawl and then stops, neither in the yard nor exactly on the road, but at an angle. I hear the horses snort and toss their heads. Some children who had been playing nearby approach the carriage cautiously. One of them points up at our driver and says something I do not hear. Then they start to back away.

I open the door and jump down to tell the coachman that we must press on. I see that he is holding the reins slackly in his hand. His head is slumped forwards. He looks at me, as if surprised that we have stopped.

'What's the matter, Luke?' I ask. But already I know. I think I have known for some time, but didn't want to believe it.

'I am unwell,' he says. 'Help me down, please, sir.'

I hold up my hand to steady him but he almost falls on me as he descends. His hand is cold and clammy to the touch. As he takes a step back, I notice with horror that his face and throat are covered with small red spots. The tokens of death. Others have noticed too.

'The Plague!' calls out one of the children. 'He's got the Plague.'

Involuntarily I too take a step back. I know that my best course of action would be to run from here as fast as I can, just as the children are running now. I need to grab Aminta and Sophia and run.

'Help me, sir,' the driver repeats.

'What is it?' asks Aminta, sticking her head out of the carriage window.

'Luke's sick,' I say.

'Then we must assist him,' she says.

But Underhill has already jumped down on the other side of the vehicle and is adjusting the strap of his satchel, ready to depart.

'I'm not staying here,' he says. 'I've been shut up once, with a guard at the door. Didn't like it much. Doubt I'll like it next time either, but I'm not planning to hang around and confirm that. We need to get out of here fast. And I'm not travelling in an infected coach. We'll have to do it on foot until we can hire another carriage or find seats on a public coach.'

'We can't just leave him,' I say.

'Are you a physician?' asks Underhill. 'No, I didn't think so. You're not going to cure him with a *habeas corpus*, are you? You're not going to serve Death with a writ of *quo warranto*. Look at him. He'll be dead in an hour or two, whatever we do. If you make us stay, the only difference will be that we'll be dead too, or at the best locked up for a month under strict quarantine. And, when we finally get out, some pack of ruffians hired by Buckingham or the Duke of York will be waiting for us. Are you coming with me or not?'

Underhill is of course right. Why should we die for somebody whose name I learned only yesterday? Logic, if not Christian charity, is on Underhill's side.

But news that the Plague is in the village has spread fast, possibly aided by several children yelling the fact at the top of their voices. The inn door opens and a large red-faced man with white whiskers strides towards us.

'Is this the sick man?' he demands.

'Yes,' I say. 'His name is Luke and he has been driving us to Salisbury. That's all I can tell you about him.'

'He's not coming into my inn.'

'He can't travel any further; you can see that. He can scarce stand.'

'That's his problem. He can crawl if he can't walk. And I don't want him dying in my yard either. Who's going to clear the body away? This isn't London. There are no dead carts here. If he's made up his mind to die, then take him right out of the village and take yourselves with him.'

He holds his neck cloth against his nose to ward off any effluvia emanating from the driver or me.

'We have no way of moving him anywhere,' I say. 'Would you have him die on the road? Is that what this village calls Christian charity?'

A small hard object strikes the coach with some force. One of the village boys has decided to take a firm line with us. 'Plague people!' he yells at us. 'Stone them, lads!'

For the moment nobody takes up his invitation, possibly because they don't want more dead bodies on their hands than is absolutely necessary. But I see one or two other boys looking around for missiles of their own. They don't want to miss out when the action starts properly, and I think it will very soon now. Our unwillingness to abandon Luke straight away may have cost us our chance to escape with our lives. A couple of women appear from a nearby house, brooms in their hands. A group of labourers, on their way to the fields, pause out of curiosity. There is in fact a growing circle round us, close but not too close, and many carry cudgels or pickaxes or whatever they had to hand when they heard the news. Even if Underhill made a break for it now, I'm not sure he'd get very far. They'd close on him like a pack of wolves and beat him senseless. And it would only take one of us to say the wrong thing and the stones would start flying in earnest. In ten minutes' time we could all be dead.

'Is there a doctor in the village?' I ask.

A ripple of mirth passes through the company. I have at least lightened the atmosphere for a moment.

'Doctor, he says! He'd have a pretty poor practice here,' says the bewhiskered landlord. 'Try Winchester, young sir.'

'There's a nurse though,' says one of the women. 'We have a nurse. Mistress Norton.'

'She's a witch,' says the boy who proposed stoning us. 'Should have burnt her long ago.'

There is a general nodding amongst the group. That's something else that they're agreed on then.

'Maybe so. But she cared for my father during the last Plague,' says the woman, 'and he lived to tell the tale.'

'She's no witch,' says the landlord. 'She's not too clean, and she doesn't have as many teeth as some other folk. I wouldn't want to get into a fight with her cat either. But she makes rare potions for all sorts of ills, and some of them don't make you sick. You go and fetch Goody Norton, Jem, and you can leave those stones where they are—they're part of the King's Highway. They don't belong to you, or any of the rest of you boys with stones, come to that.'

Jem disappears on his errand, with some of the King's Highway in his pockets, just in case the general consensus changes while he is away.

For several minutes nothing at all happens. Nobody introduces themselves. If they're going to have to kill us, they don't want to be too well acquainted. Underhill's eyes flick to and fro. He seems to be watching for a gap in their defences. Sophia defiantly clutches Aminta's hand. She looks as if she may be about to tell the crowd what she thinks of them. I really hope she doesn't. Our driver is sitting on the ground, his back to the wheel, breathing heavily. After a while he starts to shiver. There are horse blankets on board the coach. I take one of them and wrap it round him.

Then the boy returns, with an old woman following in his footsteps. It is impossible to say what colour her dress may have been when it was new, ten or twenty years ago, but it is black now, as is her petticoat. Her hair hangs in tangled ropes. Round her neck is her only concession to vanity—a necklace of bright pink coral.

She kneels down in front of the driver, pulls away the blanket and examines his face and chest. She tuts, as if annoyed to discover that he has allowed himself to become infected. She leans closer and smells his breath. It must be a while since she smelt the Plague in this way, but it is no doubt memorable enough, even after forty years. Finally she unbuttons his doublet—to which he makes no protest—and inspects his armpits.

'It's cold,' says the driver.

'Can you do anything for him?' I ask. I am doubtful but willing to be persuaded.

'Spots like that is a bad sign,' she says. 'But there's no buboes. So, that is good. Does he have money in his purse? That's always another promising sign in a patient.'

'You can look,' I say.

She inspects his pockets and removes a small leather pouch. It proves to contain a couple of shillings.

'This won't pay for his cure,' she says. 'He's as good as dead with just four and twenty pence to his name.'

'Lord Arlington will pay,' I say. 'He has slightly more, though not as much as he thinks he deserves.'

'And if my Lord chooses not to pay me?'

'He is Secretary of State,' I say. 'He can hardly vanish with unpaid debts.'

'I'd rather have cash up front.'

I point to the coach and four. It's of no value to us without a driver. And I too wonder if it's wise to travel in it. 'They will guarantee payment,' I say.

She grunts. 'Fetch your dad's wheelbarrow, boy, and we'll get him to my cottage, where I may attend to him the better. If God is willing, he shall live. If not, I'll be the proud owner of a coach and four.' She turns to the landlord. 'You look after them horses until I needs them. You hear? I've got me own coach now. I'm gentry.'

The barrow is fetched and our driver is wheeled away, his arms and legs draped over the sides. He is at least unaware of this indignity, or anything else.

'Witch,' mutters one of the women.

'Well, look how she just got that coach,' says another. 'Are you telling me that's natural? Course it ain't.'

'Hopefully she'll die of the Plague too. That'll be two birds with one stone.'

'No such luck. She caught it in 1625. You can't get it twice. She's a safe woman, as they call it. Safe from the Plague.'

'She's protected because she's a witch. Plague's the devil's work. It won't go near witches. Stands to reason.'

'You never spoke a truer word, neighbour. The Devil looks after his own.'

'So, what are you waiting for?' the landlord asks us. 'Your friend is taken care of. Now you can carry your disease to Salisbury.'

'Are there any other coaches to be hired round here?'

'For a crowd of Londoners with the Plague?'

'If that's how you want to put it.'

'What do you think?'

'What about a cart then?'

'Perfectly good cart? Not for the likes of you.'

I climb on board the coach again. I place Aminta's box on the seat, open it and admire the bounty therein. A lady presumably cannot travel with less, but there is no question of being able to carry it further. After a brief discussion, we transfer some of the contents to my bag, jettisoning my spare shirt, which Aminta feels I can do without. She instructs me to pack her own things in it with more care than I take over mine. I sling the now much-heavier bag over my shoulder. Then I descend for the last time.

'Which way's Salisbury?' I ask.

The landlord nods towards the far end of the village. 'You'll be dead before you get there,' he says. 'Of the Plague or of hunger or of thirst. One of those. But good luck to you all the same and God be with you on your travels. You don't seem like bad people. It's just that, if you come back, we'll shoot you like the vermin you are.'

At first it is pleasant enough on the road. The sun shines down on us and the morning still feels fresh and cool. Nobody troubles us, though men working in the fields stop and eye us in a way that is not altogether friendly.

We try to buy food at the next village, but nobody will sell to us. The inn has been closed and its sign taken down as a precaution. As we approach, children are dragged indoors by their mothers. Only the dogs remain to growl at us as we pass. On the village green there is a pump, and nobody has found a way to prevent us using it. I work the handle while the others drink the ice-cold water that rises from the depths. I take some biscuits from my bag, break each in half and share them out carefully.

'Hopefully Callingham will return and look for us,' says Aminta. 'Once we fail to arrive in Salisbury.'

'Hopefully,' I say.

By midday the sun is blazing down. Trees are fewer here and there is little shade. The streams are all dried up, leaving a few muddy puddles. We are not yet desperate enough to drink from them. Sophia feels it most. She constantly asks for water. Aminta and I take turns to carry her. Underhill refuses all transportation duties, saying that his leg is still painful from his fall last night. We have to make frequent stops.

The day has in some ways been too short and in some ways too long, but eventually, like all days, it ends.

The sun sets slowly, first touching the tops of the trees, then slipping slowly down through the branches. Then, for a moment it hovers on the horizon, spreading itself into a flaming oval, finally shrinking back to a thin red streak. A little light continues in the sky for some time after—just enough to see where the road ends and the fields begin. But we are still far from anywhere. We make our way carefully into the dark woods, where we shall at least have some shelter, and I proceed to gather the paper-dry brushwood and light a fire with my tinderbox. The day may have been hot, but soon the night-time chill will begin to creep over us. First the withered leaves, then the small twigs, then the thin, brittle branches flare up, casting dancing shadows on the great gnarled trunks and the whispering boughs above our heads. It is a shimmering world of orange and black. I produce two more biscuits, divide them between the five of us and we eat our supper by firelight. I am cursing that we brought nothing more with us, but I had hoped to be in Salisbury this evening at the latest and now ensconced in a welcoming hostelry. When we have eaten our fill of dry biscuit, we lie down on heaps of bracken and last year's leaves and prepare to spend a night under the stars.

'What if somebody sees the fire?' asks Underhill, pointing to the smouldering embers.

'We're well inside the wood,' I say.

But I damp down the fire with earth nevertheless. We shall have a cold night as well as an uncomfortable one.

'By tomorrow, we shall most certainly be in Salisbury,' I say. 'The worst of this journey is over.'

From My Lady Pole's Esteemed Poem,

The Puritaniad

A bed of leaves served very well
In days of old, for poets tell
Of lovers fleeing through the glades;
Athenian lads, Athenian maids,
Bewitched by *Puck*, who led them on
At the behest of *Oberon*.
When out of breath in their fond chase
Beneath the trees each took their place,
And while *Titania*'s faeries crept,
Around the woods the lovers slept.
Then *Bottom* too, with ass's head,
Woke fair Titania in her bed
Among the flowers, where she lay,
Lulled by her mignons' roundelay.
All turned out for the very best
And none complained of lack of rest.
'Twas different in those times, I trow,
The forest floor's much harder now.

CHAPTER

21

It is indeed a cold, clear night, but the following day dawns every bit as blue and bright as the one before, the sun quickly warming our stiff limbs, even here under the trees. There is nothing to eat or to drink, so we brush the leaves from our clothes and trace our way back to the road through the arching canopy of trees.

We make even slower progress than the day before. Sophia is now tearful and asking to go home. Aminta is running out of ways to amuse her, and I never knew any. Underhill also seems to wish he were elsewhere.

By ten o'clock the sun is burning our bare faces. I cannot remember such fine, dry weather continuing for so long as it has this year. We shall at least not die of cold on our journey, but again all the streams we cross are just cracked, dry mud, and our hopes of drinking water are disappointed. There is no sign of Callingham returning for us.

It is difficult to know whether Sophia or Underhill sulks more blatantly. I cannot carry both on my shoulders. There are few other travellers about. Two horsemen ride by, but pay us no more attention than we pay them. I notice, however, that they cover their faces as they pass. Nobody wishes to talk to strangers on the road. Nobody wishes to breathe the same air. We continue on our way, Sophia on my shoulders, Aminta ahead of us, lifting up her skirts out of the dust. Underhill lags behind, complaining of his leg whenever we stop to let him catch up.

'Are we there yet?' Sophia asks me.

'Not quite,' I say. 'But maybe we'll find an inn soon and can stop for some food and a drink.'

'Are you even sure we're still on the right road?' asks Underhill.

'We struck off south from the highway,' I say. 'Salisbury must be due west from here.'

'You have a compass?' asks Underhill.

'Of course not. But we can steer by the sun.'

'Sun? Let's face it, you're lost,' says Underhill. 'You should have hailed the horsemen as they went by.'

'Yes,' says Sophia primly. 'The horsemen would have told us.'

'Well, we won't get to Salisbury standing here,' I say.

We press on until a fork in the road ahead makes it clear that we shall have to choose between two equally unpromising routes. Both curve off into the woods, one too far north and one too far south. But fortune favours us. One of the men who overtook us has stopped and is attending to his horse's hoof. Just as we reach him, he appears to extract a stone. He looks up, takes off his hat and mops his brow with a clean red handkerchief. He has the ruddy face of a countryman, but something in his bearing suggests that he was once a soldier—which of course half the men in the country have been during the late wars.

We introduce ourselves (he is Reuben, we are Mr and Mrs Grey and Underhill is obliged to remain Ezekiel-the-serving-man for the moment) and I ask for directions.

'Salisbury?' says Reuben, as if he had never considered going quite that far. 'Both paths will take you there eventually, but I'd choose the left-hand one if I were you. It's quieter and you're less likely to run into trouble, if you see what I mean. You're from London, I take it?'

'How can you tell?'

'You look troubled, and I am sorry for it.'

'I'll try not to look troubled,' I say, 'if it gives us away so much. And I thank you for your sympathy. But I fear that the left-hand path will take us a long way out of our way.'

'Not a bit of it—but you do need to know the road in order not to lose yourselves. I can accompany you for part of the route and show you which way to go.'

He takes out an apple and offers it to Sophia, who accepts with suspicion, but eats it nevertheless.

'She has a good appetite,' he says. 'It's a pity I have only the one apple with me.'

'We haven't eaten for some time,' I say. 'And I doubt we'll find food or a bed to sleep in before we reach Salisbury.'

'Look, I'm bound for a farm just up the road, where I'm sure you'll find a welcome and some dinner. My travelling companion went ahead when my horse went lame. Why not walk with me now to the farm and then go on this afternoon to Salisbury? You'll make much better progress for being fed and rested. Do you have water bottles?'

'No,' I say. 'We weren't planning on travelling on foot.'

'I have a couple of old ones back at the farm that we can fill for you. You shouldn't be on the road without them. Not in this heat. And we can let you have more apples to eat on your journey.'

'That is kind,' I say.

Reuben responds by passing me the horse's reins and hoisting Sophia onto his shoulders, giving her a badly needed fresh mount. He sets off at a trot, leaving me following on behind, leading the horse, which fortunately does not seem too lame. Sophia turns and frowns at me, but since I smile back she makes no further protest at her treatment. Indeed, in a moment or two she is kicking Reuben with her heels, trying to make him break into a canter, which he obligingly does for a few yards.

Only Underhill is unhappy and lags behind even more than usual. 'We need to get to Salisbury,' he says, 'not play horses in the woods. Look where the sun is. This path is taking us south now. That can't be right. I don't trust that man. Either he's a fool or this is a trap.'

'We need to eat,' I say. 'And the main roads have proved unwelcoming. If we can obtain dinner and good directions, perhaps we can still reach Salisbury tonight.'

The farm proves to be large, neatly thatched and half-timbered—an isolated building in a pleasantly wooded, gently rolling country—and possessing a cobbled yard leading to a barn and a pigsty. We are all offered beer after our long walk and told that dinner is being prepared and will not be long. The noises and smells coming from the kitchen are promising and, for the first time since we left the coach behind, I feel at ease.

'Have your family lived here long?' I ask.

'Some time,' he says noncommittally.

'And you live here with your parents...'

'They are away at present,' he says.

'It's a fine house,' I say.

Reuben nods and makes his apologies to 'Mr and Mrs Grey' (as he believes us to be) and to Mr Underhill, and goes to join whoever is in the kitchen. There is a clattering of plates. I stretch out my legs. It is good to be somebody's guest and out of any danger.

Outside the birds sing, and inside the enticing smell of dinner is growing, but something Reuben has said has made me uneasy.

Then Aminta looks around and says: 'Where's Sophia?'

'Gone to look at the farmyard, most likely,' I say. 'She'll be safe enough, but I'll go and find her.'

'Yes, please, John—would you?' Aminta seems strangely concerned, but that can soon be put right.

I screw up my eyes against the sun's glare as I step into the yard, but Sophia is over by the pigs. I walk across to her.

'Why did the man pretend to take a stone out of his horse's hoof?' she asks.

'Did he?'

'Yes. He had a stone in his hand when we were walking along. Then he pretended to use his knife. Then he threw the stone away. Why did he do that?'

As I am considering this, Aminta walks up to us. Though I have found Sophia, she seems no happier than before.

'You needn't have come out yourself,' I say. 'The sun is hot and the yard is not too clean.'

'John,' she whispers. 'Did you hear what Reuben called us?'

'Mr and Mrs Grey,' I reply. 'That is who we told him we were.'

'And *Mr Underhill.*'

Yes, I knew that something had jarred in Reuben's words. That was it. We look at each other.

'If they know who he is...' I say. 'I'm certain I merely called him Ezekiel. And Underhill would never have revealed his true identity, not even to save himself from being my serving man. Sophia says that Reuben was only pretending to take a stone out of his horse's hoof when we came across him.'

'You mean he was simply waiting for us to catch him up?'

'I think so. I fear we have somehow fallen into the hands of our pursuers. Pepys must have gone ahead and arranged for us to be waylaid by men in the pay of the Duke of York.'

'Well, whoever they are, they now have us in a remote farmhouse in a part of the country that we do not know at all...' There is an implication that I have been negligent, but I do not see how they can conversely have been so skilful.

I shake my head. 'But how? Even if they have a spy in Arlington's office and knew our intended route, this is not it. We should have been far from here. How can they have prepared in advance for our arrival somewhere they could not possibly have expected us to be? And to what ends? Perhaps we are worrying unnecessarily. Perhaps one of us did accidentally mention Underhill's name. But I agree it's not worth taking the risk, just for a good dinner. You can fetch Sophia and head for the road. I'll find Underhill and follow. There's nothing of any great value in our bags. We can abandon them... No, my gun is in the bag—I need to get my hands on that at least before we make our escape.'

'Forget the gun. If it comes to a fight, we're hopelessly outnumbered. Anyway, where do Sophia and I run to? We are on foot and they have horses. Sophia is in any case not the fastest of runners and is too large for me to carry far. Nor do I think you will be able to extract Underhill unnoticed, as you seem to imagine. And let's not forget that we are lost, while they clearly know the country well.'

'What do you suggest then?' I say.

'Go back in. Pretend we haven't noticed their slip of the tongue. Eat our dinner. Pray that Sophia says nothing.'

'Once we're inside, we stand no chance at all. They have us trapped. You and Sophia can get away, reach the highway. Callingham must be searching for us by now...'

We look at each other. I cannot say what we might have decided given time, but at this point Reuben emerges from the farmhouse.

'Dinner!' he calls jovially and, sweeping Sophia up, he carries her off into the parlour.

Aminta and I walk back together. 'Eat nothing that they don't,' I say. 'Drink nothing that they don't. And make sure Sophia does the same. After that we'll have to see what happens.'

'That was my plan exactly,' she says. 'Play along until a chance arises. In the meantime, just behave normally, if you know how to do that.'

Reuben has been joined by two companions, both dressed, as he is, in serviceable leather jerkins. Their names are given as Ned and Dick, which may be true, but then we have given ours as Mr and Mrs Grey, so it also may not be. People seem to lie about their names round here. He does not at least try to pass them off as members of his family. Perhaps he thinks the trap is already sprung and further deception is not necessary.

I try to size up the Duke's other men in case it comes to a brawl, though I can find little to comfort me. They are both just above average height, muscular and in possession of the normal number of limbs. In a court of law I do not doubt I could tie them in all sorts of knots, but I am not sure I could overcome one of them face to face in a fair fight—probably not even if I were to take him by surprise in the most underhand manner I could devise.

The three men are friendly enough for the moment, but they carefully seat us away from the door and give little Sophia the place of honour at the top of the table and as far as possible from Aminta and me. I wonder if they intend to keep her close to them as a guard against our escape. If so, a good plan is needed on our part. I hope Aminta has one.

'Reuben says you're travelling from London?' says Ned, pushing the loaf of bread in my direction.

'We are fleeing the Plague, as others are,' I say, breaking off a large chunk. 'But we do not live in one of the affected areas. You have nothing to fear from us.'

'I do not doubt you are an honest man,' says Ned, 'and would not enter our house if you brought the Plague with you.'

'And your servant here...' says Dick.

'Ezekiel,' I say.

'Ezekiel...' Dick makes some show of committing the name to memory. 'Have you been with Mr Grey long, Ezekiel? Is he a good master?'

Underhill looks up from his broth. 'Good enough,' he says, with a look that implies he will pay me back before too long for having to be Ezekiel.

'And you have come all this way on foot?' asks Ned.

'We had hired a carriage,' I say, 'but it was unable to take us further.'

'A problem with...?' Ned's face betrays nothing.

'A broken axle,' I say.

'That was unfortunate.' Ned smiles at us before attending to his own bowl. He drinks noisily, but also reassuringly. If we are to be poisoned, it is not in the broth.

For my own part, I am beginning to wonder how much these men actually know. Do their questions suggest that they are not sure whether they do in fact have Underhill within their grasp? Was the slip of the tongue deliberate and designed to test us?

'These accidents happen on the road,' I say.

'Of course they do. How unfortunate that you and your wife and child and servant must now walk—at least until you can find other transport. What business do you have in Salisbury, Mr Grey?'

'None. We have friends there who we hope will lodge us until it is safe to return home.'

'Do you want to go home, Sophia?' Ned asks.

Sophia opens her mouth as if to discourse at length on the inadvisability of the Lord Mayor's policy of shutting up the homes of the sick and its consequences for the healthy inhabitants thereof, but she then looks at me and thinks better of it.

'Yes, but I like it here with the animals,' she says. Good girl.

'Good,' says Ned. 'Reuben, take the young lady and show her the new piglets in the sty. The next course will be a few minutes longer before Mary can serve it.'

'I'll go too,' I say, rising to my feet.

'Oh, I don't think so, Mr Grey; they are very ordinary piglets. Why don't you sit down? You've walked a long way today. Dick, take Mr Lowerdale to the kitchen to give Mary a hand. You're not too grand to give us a little help with clearing these dishes and bringing the joint? Your master has brought you with him to work, has he not?'

It isn't clear why Ned thinks that Underhill will accede to this with good grace. Perhaps it is a further test. Or perhaps their sole purpose is to split us up so that they can manage us more easily. They probably realise that Aminta will not flee without Sophia and that I cannot leave without all of them.

'I'm not a kitchen servant,' says Underhill.

'No matter. Mary will show you where to find things,' says Ned. 'And will instruct you in what needs doing. Unless of course I have mistaken your position? Unless your position is different from what I have understood it to be? Have I misunderstood, Mr Grey?'

Perhaps I should say, 'I've just remembered; he is in fact a spy who plans to betray the Duke in some way to the King. Sadly, he doesn't clean dishes.' Or maybe not.

'Go with the gentleman, Ezekiel,' I say.

'I see no gentlemen,' Underhill says. 'Merely a pack of...'

I hold up my hand. The one small chance we have of escaping depends on our playing our parts well and convincing these men that they've got the wrong people. 'Just go,' I say.

Underhill scowls at me again and departs in the direction of the kitchen. Whatever revenge he has in mind for me has just been multiplied several times over.

'So, Mr Grey, how long have you had this man of yours?' asks Ned.

'For some time,' I say.

'I am surprised that you keep him, in view of his insolence.'

'I am not offended by it. Ezekiel may have a sour countenance but—'

Ned laughs. 'A sour countenance indeed. But enough. We know who he is, Mr Grey. We know who you all are. But it's Underhill we want, not you and Lady Pole. You have nothing to fear. You just need to let us get on with our job.'

He still can't know for certain.

'I have no idea what you mean,' I say. 'The man you have in the kitchen is Ezekiel Lowerdale. I have a pass to prove it.'

'I also know about your pass,' he says. 'And I know who issued it. Your efforts do you credit and I shall ensure that my master is informed of your diligence. But there is no further need for subterfuge. We have our man.'

On second thoughts, perhaps he is certain of who we all are—and of much else.

'If you know that much,' I say, 'then you know we are travelling on the King's business. You risk your neck if you attempt to delay us.'

I try to remember the exact wording on the document in my pocket. It gives me, as I recall, the right to take any action I consider prudent. That may come in useful, though only if I can get to my gun, which is still in my satchel on the bench. In spite of what Aminta has said, I'd be happier with it than without it. I edge carefully towards the bag.

'I shall detain you no longer than is necessary in order to obtain the information we need,' Ned says. 'You have delivered Underhill to us and we are grateful. You will come to no harm. But if you in any way doubt where your true loyalties lie, just remember that we have the girl whom you are calling your daughter. We know that neither you nor Lady Pole have a daughter, but you do seem to have some affection for her.'

'You will not hurt her?' says Aminta.

'We shall hurt Mr Underhill as much as we need to. I promise that the rest of you need not fear. If you do as we say.'

'I suppose you answer to the Duke of York?'

He shrugs. 'You do not need the gun in your bag—I mean the bag you are edging towards. Would you like to pick the bag up very carefully and give it to me?'

I reach over and drag the bag towards me along the wooden bench. Ned receives it from me, removes the pistol and checks that it is safe. He tosses the bag back onto the table.

'Thank you,' he says. 'The gun will be returned to you, but it is better that I have it for the moment in case there are any misunderstandings.'

'And are you planning to shoot Underhill?' I ask.

'Why should you care what happens to him?'

'I'd rather arrive in Salisbury with all of the people listed on my pass.'

Ned smiles. 'Then you should hope that Mr Underhill decides to cooperate with us. In the meantime Mary has produced an apple pie. I think you will enjoy it. See, Mr Grey, I am taking a slice myself, just so that you know it is wholesome. I have noticed that you eat only what I do. I should do the same if I were ever in the position you are in. Again, I shall report your sagacity to my master. *Bon appétit*, as I'm told they say in France.'

It is the end of our third day on the road. We should be watching the sun setting on the spire of Salisbury Cathedral. But we are still in a farmhouse, somewhere in Hampshire I think. Through the window, we can see Reuben, outside in the yard, standing guard with a musket. Ned and Dick are presumably with Underhill. Sophia, we are told, is with Mary. She is probably the only member of the party who is enjoying her stay.

'We should do something,' says Aminta for the twentieth time. '*You* should do something. It's your job. You were Arlington's creature first. I am merely an assistant-creature.'

'There is nothing to be done,' I say. 'We have to be patient. Things look bad for Underhill but—and I cannot entirely explain this—not for us. Ned seems to feel that I should be aware that his master could give me an unpleasant time if he wished. But he has chosen not to. He would prefer to be my friend. Ned will speak well of me if we cooperate. What he said is remarkably like what Pepys said.'

'So we are prisoners of the Duke of York,' says Aminta.

'Probably,' I say. 'Arlington foresaw this. He said if we were captured we should surrender Underhill and make our escape. Let us hope the Duke also understands that that is the second part of the plan.'

'But why would Arlington be complicit in such a scheme? Unless he has made some new alliance with Clarendon.'

'With Clarendon and against Buckingham? That would make some sense of what has happened. He has used us to hand Underhill to the Duke.'

'And we are merely pawns in this greater game?'

'There's no point in complaining,' I say. 'You chose to be Arlington's creature and this is what Arlington's creatures do. I've been in worse situations. We are being fed, we are not tied up and we do not have a loaded gun pointed at us. In this business that means you are doing well enough.'

Ned enters. He looks at me oddly. I think he has changed his mind about something. I do not think he still wishes to be my friend.

'Well, Mr Grey. Underhill has decided to tell us the truth. It took a while and involved a certain amount of unpleasantness, but now we know.'

'Know what?' I say.

'He says that Arlington has part of the letter. But he tells us that you have the rest of it. I am sorry you have chosen to deceive us in this way.'

'But I haven't deceived you,' I say. 'I have no part of the letter. Underhill is simply lying to you.'

He takes out a gun and points it at me. 'Let's discuss this down in the cellar,' he says, motioning with the barrel in the direction we will go.

I stand and stretch my limbs slowly. It may be a while before I get to do it again without a certain amount of pain. Depending on exactly how I am to be questioned, of course.

'You see what I mean?' I say to Aminta. 'Things really weren't that bad after all, were they?'

CHAPTER 22

U p there somewhere the evening sun is still shining in all its glory. Down here in the cellar, it does not shine at all. Over our heads are the rough-hewn boards of the floor above, supported on massive oak beams. The walls are composed of large blocks of stone—black and yellowy grey in the light of the candles, which are needed down here even in the middle of the day. I think there are no windows. At the far end is a pile of kindling, so the cellar must be dry enough—that may be useful if I am to be here a long time. Along the walls are barrels that must once have contained last year's apples. There is a smell of packed earth and newly chopped logs and slightly sour apple juice. Empty shelves await this year's harvests. I wonder vaguely who really owns the house and where they are now. Have they been bribed or threatened to stay away? Or are they also prisoner somewhere close by? There are two stools available, probably brought from another part of the house, because this is not somewhere that you would normally wish to sit. Ned motions me towards one of them and takes the other for himself. Reuben stands guard by the door.

'So, where's Underhill?' I ask.

'We've locked him away safely,' says Ned. 'There are two cellars here. He's in another that is slightly less pleasant than this one. He's been very helpful. We may not need to keep him there much longer. Perhaps, if you are also helpful, we shall find you somewhere more comfortable to sleep tonight. So, Mr Grey— and think carefully before you answer—where is the rest of the letter?'

'I have no idea,' I say. 'I expect that you know already that Arlington has what Underhill originally thought was all of it. If I had the rest, I'd have already sold it to him. So would Underhill, if he really knew where it was. It would seem you've been taken in by a very poorly constructed lie. If this second letter really exists, it has either been lost or taken by whoever killed Fincham.'

'But Underhill says *you* have it. And I believe him.'

'How could I? I never went near Fincham, dead or alive.'

Is this revenge for my sending Underhill to the kitchens, or has he been tortured until he will say anything to make them stop? Like the good citizens of London praying that they should not be visited by the Plague, has he simply wished his pain on anyone other than himself?

'You see, Mr Grey,' says Ned, 'Underhill genuinely believes you have it, or had it. Let me tell you something. Some people hold out under torture as long as they can, as a matter of principle. Some talk as soon as we inform them what we can do to them. Underhill volunteered his information almost before we were at the bottom of the stairs. We didn't even have to mention thumbscrews. In short he demonstrated remarkable pragmatism without any trace of principle. But after that he stuck to his story through thick and thin. Would you like to see the thumbscrews, Mr Grey?'

'Do you have the ones with or without spikes?'

'Without. They are, I assure you, no less painful.'

'Thank you, that's a kind offer. The spiked ones might have been interesting but I've seen the other sort before. They're not very complicated.'

'They look very different when you are at the wrong end of them, Mr Grey. We'll see how well you jest then.'

He's probably right. I can in fact easily imagine the small device made of dull grey metal with two plates, between which my thumb would be placed, and a delicate screw device that would be used to bring the plates slowly together. I have seen them before. But watching my own thumb forced into it and feeling the coldness of the tightening steel—I agree that would be another matter. Who should I then claim had what they are seeking? Aminta? Sophia? Let us hope that I have more courage than I believe I do.

'Who do you work for?' I ask again. 'The Duke of York? The Duke of Buckingham?'

'We do not need to tell you that.'

'Lay a finger on me and I can promise you that Arlington will have you hunted down and hanged.' I think I can keep up my tone of defiance for a little longer, though my mouth is now very dry indeed.

'But, in the meantime, we're the men with the thumbscrews.'

'Which are illegal.'

'Only officially.'

'I don't even know what it is I'm supposed to have,' I say. 'What exactly did Underhill tell you?'

Reuben and Ned exchange glances. It is Reuben who eventually says: 'Underhill told us that he did not have the letter we wanted, but said that he could obtain it for us.'

'At a price?'

'Of course at a price. A thousand sovereigns and his release from here once we had it.'

'So, why does that mean I have it?'

'Because, Mr Grey, *one* of you must have it, or Underhill would scarcely be able to make that offer.'

'Then search me. If you are employed by the Duke of York, you will at least know what you're looking for.'

'We will search you, if you don't mind. It isn't in your satchel. We've checked.'

Reuben comes over and pats my breeches and doublet, extracting first Morland's pass.

Ned examines it. 'That seems to be in order,' he says. 'At least we can be sure that you don't have the Plague.'

'And there's this,' says Reuben, passing another paper to Ned.

'Signed by my Lord Arlington,' says Ned, 'and authorising you to take whatever action you think prudent. Very useful.'

'Not as useful as I'd hoped,' I say.

Reuben hands it back to me with a patronising smile. 'Get Mary to search Lady Pole and the girl,' he says. 'If he doesn't have it, they must.'

'There's no need. I can promise you they don't have it either.'

'Are you absolutely certain of that?'

'Yes,' I say. 'I'd hardly endanger them by asking them to conceal it.'

'We'll search them anyway. Then we may have further questions for Mr Underhill. Tomorrow, I think. We have plenty of time and we'll let him dream of thumbscrews before we ask him anything more. We may also need to question you again. So for the moment you can stay here.'

'Am I to have a bed?'

'A man who thinks he could stand the pain of thumbscrews does not need a bed,' he replies.

Indeed, I have slept in less comfortable places. The floor is beaten earth but I have been given two blankets. Once the candles have been removed, I cannot see, but there is nothing to draw my attention. I recite psalms to myself to pass the time. Not that I am a Puritan. But there is very little else to do. I wonder briefly how Underhill is faring. But there is nothing I can do for him. And I don't especially care. Eventually I fall asleep.

But I do not sleep long.

The Plague Road

If I could see, I might know what o'clock it was. As it is, I cannot say precisely when the commotion begins. At first, as so often, the noise seems to emerge from a dream I am having. Arlington is reprimanding me for losing Underhill and is thumping repeatedly on the table. 'Idiot,' he is yelling, 'idiot, idiot, idiot!' With each thump, his nose patch leaps into the air and twists like a little black fish before landing again exactly where it was before. I open my eyes and, because I can distinguish nothing at all, for a moment I do not know where I am or why there is no moonlight through my bedroom window and why I cannot hear the call of the watchman in Lincoln's Inn Fields. And none of the noises that do reach me make any sense. In the distance, there is a repeated, rhythmic thudding, then the splintering of wood and the tramp of many feet on the floorboards above me. There are several shots fired, then a voice calls out and there is silence again.

For the moment, none of this seems to concern me greatly in my dark and windowless cellar. But it would appear that our gaolers are themselves under attack. In which case, one of several things may be about to happen. One of Arlington's men may burst in and announce that we are all free. Or one of Arlington's men may fire a shot through the door without checking who is in here. Or, if the others have escaped in the confusion, the intruders may conclude that their work is done and leave, with me still locked behind the heavy oak door, unable to escape. We are a long way from any proper road and it may be some time before the real owners return or anyone ventures this way again. I think that the apple barrels are empty so I cannot remain here long without starving. But if I call out and the intruders are not in fact Arlington's men, then I may be shot anyway.

I feel my way to the door and run my fingers over it until I find a handle. The handle turns but the door is firmly locked from the other side. I took care to inspect the mechanism as I was led into the room: it is a massy old lock, country-made, simple but strong. I push my finger into the large keyhole and feel the end of the key. So it is still in the lock on the other side of the door. That was careless. I walk slowly in the other direction, my hands out in front of me, until my fingers touch the far wall, then I kneel down and inch my way to the pile of kindling. I reject a number of sticks as much too thick, but eventually select three that may be long and thin enough for my task. Then I retrace my steps. Above me, there is now much less noise. A pair of feet run across the boards, heading—I think—for the stairs. I wonder where Aminta and Sophia are. I need to work quickly.

I try the thinnest of the sticks, attempting to push the key out, but the wood snaps and I waste time extracting the broken end. I try another and manage to push the key back a little. I take Arlington's letter from my pocket and slide it under the door, as near as I can directly below the lock. Then I push the key further until it drops onto the floor. I give the paper a gentle tug and am pleased to note that it is heavy. The key has fallen onto it and not bounced away out of reach. Slowly I pull the paper and the key towards me. The end of the key appears under the door and I grasp it between finger and thumb. It is mine.

The key turns in the well-oiled lock, and I try the handle again.

I can make out the walls of the corridor—some light must be filtering down from the candle-lit room above. I walk as silently as I can across the flagstones and place one foot on the wooden stairs. I pause and listen. Whoever has broken into the house has moved on—perhaps upstairs. Or perhaps Ned and his henchmen have overcome them. It is not clear what I shall meet in the sitting room above. I advance a cautious step at a time, emerging slowly from the gloom and towards the candlelight. The room is empty. I see at once that the door is open and that the lock is hanging from it. A chair has been knocked over, but otherwise all is as it was. Have the intruders taken what they want and gone? Two candles, in pewter sticks, burn on the table, casting a warm glow around them, but leaving the corners of the room in shadow. If I am to find Aminta and Sophia, one of those candles may be useful. As I walk across to them I hear a pistol being cocked behind me.

'Just raise your hands and keep them in the air, please.'

I do not recognise the voice. I raise my hands. There are footsteps behind me and a hand pats my pockets on both sides.

'Take a couple of steps forwards and turn round slowly,' says the voice.

I turn. The man with the pistol is of medium height, dressed in black and completely bald. His face is weather-beaten and scarred and he wears capacious sea boots. He has a cutlass strapped to his belt and a second pistol at his waist. There is more than a little smell of tar about him. He eyes me carefully.

'Who are you?' he asks.

'I might ask you the same question,' I say.

'True, but you don't have a gun. So, the answer to my question first, I think, young man.'

'I'm John Grey,' I say, 'and with luck you've come to rescue me.'

He lowers the gun. 'Good to meet you, Mr Grey. You have not been easy to locate. I'm delighted we've caught up with you at last.'

'Where are Aminta and Sophia?'

'Upstairs. We've already found them. They're safe. But Lady Pole was not certain where they had taken you. She thought to the cellars, but it would seem not.'

'I was able to escape.'

'I would have expected no less of you.'

'And where are the men who were holding us prisoner? I heard shots.'

'We have been watching the house for a while. One went away while it was still daylight. Probably to get fresh instructions. Another had been set to guard the road. He fired a couple of balls in our direction but fled when he saw that we came in numbers. We think we shot the one who remained in the house, but there is no sign of him now. So he must have crawled away too. There's a woman who was sleeping in the kitchen, but she seems harmless enough. She says she's the housekeeper and had no idea who the others were, which may or may not be true. She says they arrived a couple of days ago while the owners were away, threatened her and gave her orders that she thought it best to obey. She's preparing some food for us all now. Then we'll think about how we get you to Salisbury. Where's Underhill?'

'In the other cellar, wherever that is. He wasn't with me. There must be stairs going down to it somewhere, but I've seen only the parlour and my own place of imprisonment.'

'Thank you. We'll carry on searching. There's nothing inside the house but there may be a door outside that leads to it. We saw no sign of your carriage.'

'Our coachman was taken sick a few miles back. Morland hired him. Arlington will need to send somebody to pay the bill for his care and reclaim the coach.'

The bald-headed man nods. 'I suppose he will. If he wants them back. In the meantime, we can arrange horses for you. Lady Pole rides?'

'Very competently.'

'Good. It's important we get you to the court as soon as we can. Has Underhill told you what he knows?'

I hesitate. It is for Underhill to inform the King and for the King to know before others do.

'He can speak for himself when you find him,' I say.

Footsteps on the stairs announce Aminta's arrival. She unexpectedly throws herself into my arms.

'I thought they had killed you,' she says, mainly to my shoulder. 'When they took you away and you didn't return, I thought I would never see you again.'

It is not unpleasant being welcomed thus, but after a moment she steps back and adds: 'Sophia will be happy too. She said you were a much better horse than Reuben.'

'You see?' I say to the bald man. 'We are all grateful to you. We perhaps owe you our lives. The Duke of York's men were determined to gain whatever information they could. They threatened me with torture and would certainly have used the thumbscrews on Underhill. It is fortunate you came when you did. And Sam Pepys, the Duke of York's clerk, is on the road. He too was determined to find out Underhill's secrets by whatever means he could. I am pleased we have given him the slip.'

Our rescuer looks puzzled, but before he can enquire further, we hear footsteps outside.

The splintered front door is pushed open. Into the candle-light steps a small, well-dressed, slightly plump young man, who acknowledges Aminta before turning to me with a patronising smile.

'Mr Pepys,' I say.

'Good evening, Mr Grey, or perhaps I mean good morning. The hour is late.'

'But why are you with Arlington's men?' I ask.

'These are the Duke of York's men,' he says, indicating the bald man and two more who have followed him in. 'Arlington's men have been holding you prisoner for the past sixteen hours. Praise be to God, we have seen them off. Now you are in our care. Where's that rogue Underhill?'

'In the other cellar,' says the bald-headed man. 'At least, according to Mr Grey here. You probably gain entrance from the outside.'

'Excellent,' says Pepys. 'I am eager to speak with him. Then, Mr Grey, I think we should have a conversation about your best interests. I think you may now find they are remarkably like my own.'

CHAPTER

23

'At least you are no longer in the cellar,' says Aminta.

'Perhaps it would be better if I were,' I say. 'Pepys would have had to search harder to steal Underhill from us. Arlington will not be very pleased to know that I surrendered him so easily.'

'Those were our instructions, if you remember. To give him up.'

'It would have been helpful if Arlington had explained that he planned to abduct Underhill himself. But can Pepys be right? They did not behave as if they were Arlington's men. There are others out there who want the letter too. Buckingham. The Dutch. The French. Maybe the Spanish, for all I know.'

'From what you say, those men certainly knew a great deal about us. Things that only Arlington would have known.'

'Or Buckingham,' I say. 'Lady Castlemaine knew a great deal about our journey. It wouldn't surprise me if she had procured a spy in Arlington's office. Morland would be suscep- tible, one way or another.'

'Well, we at least know the identity of our present gaolers. How many of the Duke's men are there?'

'Too many for us to hope to overcome them. Even more than before. There's Pepys, the bald man and at least two others. I'm fairly sure I heard another couple outside. I think they are sailors, from one of the ships that the Duke has at his command. The ones I have seen are well armed. And it would be just the two of us against them. Underhill will already be trussed up ready to be taken to Salisbury or wherever the Duke has requested. There's a guard outside the front of the house but, even if we were unguarded, it's too dark to see the road well enough. We're worse off than ever.'

'So, what do we do?'

'Just wait here. If they were Arlington's men before, then at least one of them has escaped unharmed and knows that the Duke has taken us prisoner. So, they should be back, hopefully in greater numbers than Pepys has. Callingham's out there somewhere too, and should be looking for us with his one eye—maybe he'll bring help from Salisbury. So, if we can delay Pepys a little... If he insists on moving at first light, as I fear he will, then we must slow him down as much as we can and hope that our friends catch up with us. The more time we give them, the better.'

'If I claim that Sophia is exhausted by the journey...'

Small footsteps on the stairs announce the arrival of Sophia. We explain to her that it would be advantageous if she said at frequent intervals that she was too tired to carry on.

'But I'm not,' says Sophia helpfully.

'But you could say you were,' I suggest.

'It would not be true. If you lie, you go to Hell.' She sniffs and wipes her nose on her sleeve. She has no doubt where I am going.

'Not immediately,' I say.

'But it would still be wrong. I don't want to go to Hell.'

'Sophia,' says Aminta, 'we would not let you go to Hell.'

'You said you would take me to Salisbury,' she says significantly. 'But we are here.' She rubs her nose on her sleeve again.

She has a point. This isn't Salisbury. It really isn't. I try a different approach.

'Sophia, we had to lie to get you out of the house you were locked up in and then to get you the paper you needed to travel. There are good lies and bad lies. We told some good lies to rescue you. This will be a good lie too. And it will be a very small one. Not big enough to go to Hell for. Just big enough to go to Salisbury. All we are asking is that, when you are a little bit tired, you just say that you want a rest.'

She considers. 'All right,' she says. 'I'll say I want a rest. And it will be true. I *will* want a rest, even if I'm not tired.' She rubs her eyes and yawns.

'I'll take her back to bed,' says Aminta. 'I'm tired, even if she isn't. We've had one night's sleep disturbed by somebody shooting at Underhill, then a second by having to sleep in the woods. Now Pepys has chosen to break the door down. He can't insist we leave before it is light.'

Aminta takes one of the candles and departs. I decide to await Pepys. He is not long returning.

'How many cellars are there?' he asks.

'Two,' I say.

'You are sure Underhill wasn't in the same one as you?'

'I think I would have noticed,' I say. 'There was just the one room and a short passageway leading to it. Can't you find the other cellar?'

'Indeed we can. There's a door at the side of the house leading down to it. But it is unlocked and the cellar is empty, other than some hams and two barrels of beer.'

We look at each other. You wouldn't mistake Underhill for a smoked ham, not even in poor light.

'I think our bird has flown, Mr Grey. The Duke will be most displeased. And I fear he will blame you. Indeed, I shall make sure he does.'

CHAPTER 24

It is dawn. Another long summer's day is about to begin. The light creeps up on us, first as a vague suggestion on the horizon, then as a pink glow across the sky. I have been slumbering at the table rather than return to the chamber and disturb Aminta and Sophia.

Pepys re-enters the room. He too looks tired. His suit is creased, though undeniably expensive.

'I assume there is still no sign of Underhill,' I say.

'The men have searched the outbuildings and the woods nearby,' he says, 'but there is no trace of any fugitive. We must consider our options, Mr Grey.'

'I am your prisoner,' I say. 'I have no options.'

'Perhaps you do. I've been thinking about it. You see, I could take you at once to the Duke and explain that you have aided and abetted the escape of his most disloyal servant, the purported Jesuit, Father Horncastle. Things would go badly for you, both now and for the rest of your life. That's one option.'

'So there are others?' I ask.

'Or we could work together, Mr Grey, as I originally proposed.'

'Now, why should I wish to do that? I've already said that I don't work with people just because they were at the same college as I was.'

'You must realise that Arlington has systematically misled you.' Pepys smiles in a friendly manner that I do not trust at all.

'So when has Arlington misled me?' I enquire politely.

'From the very beginning, I imagine. You were there. I wasn't. But I can assure you that Arlington never wanted Underhill to reach Salisbury alive.'

I think of the paper in my pocket permitting me, albeit in the vaguest possible way, to kill Underhill if I see fit. I think of his willingness to have Underhill captured. 'Go on,' I say.

'But Arlington *does* want the information that Underhill possesses. He dearly wishes that torture had not been outlawed in England and cannot conveniently have Underhill shipped to Scotland to apply the boots or the thumbscrews there. So, he rolls the dice again and sends you off to Salisbury, where torture is also illegal but accidents may happen on the road. And you did not find the journey easy, I think.'

'No. The roads are hazardous in these Plague times.'

'As Arlington knew they would be. So, what would be easier than to provide you with an escort, to cut through the problems you have faced? Most of his Majesty's troops have of course been sent out of London to avoid the Plague, but he could have spared half a dozen dragoons with swords and carbines. That would have been sufficient.'

'Arlington said that Underhill had refused an escort, but Underhill denied it.'

'Precisely. How could Underhill have refused an escort when the offer was never made? You and Underhill have been told very different stories.'

'That could still be a misunderstanding,' I say. 'And perhaps the troops were not available. London is a large city and, as you say, there are few soldiers left to guard it. The King does not keep as many men about him as Cromwell did.'

'Or as many ships,' says Pepys, with some bitterness. 'And there is never money to keep those we have properly supplied. Still, let us consider what happens next. Arlington knows you will make slow progress in your unguarded coach and four, stopped outside every village by some officious constable or self-appointed Captain of the Watch. He sends some ruffians after you.'

'I can see that they would be able to ask after us, but they did well to know where we would be.'

'Who supplied your driver?'

'Morland,' I say. 'He found the coach for us.'

'That was generous of him, when so few are to be found.'

'True.'

'And did your driver say that he knew a way of avoiding the barricades?'

'He said he knew the back roads.'

'While you had little idea which way you were being taken?'

'None of us knows this country.'

'Had he not fallen sick, he would certainly have delivered you here, as Arlington had planned. In the end, there was an unexpected development: the driver contracted the Plague just short of your destination. Arlington could not have foreseen that. It almost spoilt the design. But you were close enough. When you continued on foot, it was only necessary for his men, who had probably been tracking you every step of your journey, to overtake you and guide you the last mile or two.'

'So,' I say. 'The plan was to make Underhill a prisoner here and extract the information however they could?'

'Yes.'

'But the men also locked me up and threatened me with torture. How does that fit with their being in Arlington's pay?'

But I already know the answer.

'Because,' says Pepys, 'when released, probably through the agency of a second party that Arlington has close by, he would have wanted you to testify that you had been taken prisoner by a group of armed men, whose identity was unknown to you, who locked you up and threatened you. You would have speculated that they might have been the Duke of York's or the Duke of Buckingham's men, but would have scoffed at the possibility of their being in Arlington's pay. There was no danger.'

That all rings true. But it was different when they thought that I might genuinely have a paper that I had been concealing from Arlington. Then, for a few minutes, I think the threats were real. But Pepys does not need to know that.

'Having given up his information,' Pepys continues, 'Underhill would, sadly, have been shot during the rescue. If at all possible, you would have been blamed for the fatal shot, but you would have had your letter confirming that it was in order.'

'Arlington would not stoop to that.'

'Arlington is a man of no account and no ancestry.' Pepys sniffs in contempt. He seems to be forgetting that his own father was a tailor, albeit that he is distantly related to his patron, Lord Sandwich. And that he has ambitions of his own. 'The Duke conversely doesn't wish to harm anyone. *He simply wants his letter back*,' says Pepys. 'That is not unreasonable.'

'You still claim you did not shoot at Underhill at the inn?'

'Of course not. Even if the Duke wanted Underhill killed, he would scarcely ask the Clerk of the Acts of the Navy Office to do it.'

'So who did?'

'Your driver was clearly in Arlington's pay. Perhaps he too had instructions not to let Underhill escape alive. When Underhill left, he followed. He had probably heard me speaking to my driver about the missing pistol, so knew where to find a weapon. He shot at him rather than let him go—and thought he'd hit him.'

'And who killed Fincham?'

'Not us,' says Pepys. 'Why on earth would we wish to prevent Fincham delivering the letter? Underhill had the letter. He would have needed to kill Fincham to get it.'

'Underhill denied it.'

'And you do not suspect him of lying? Of all the people involved in this affair, and I include my Lord Arlington, he is the least trustworthy. Did Underhill tell Arlington's men anything under torture?'

'They scarcely needed to torture him. As you say, he does not hesitate to resort to a lie when needed.'

'What lie?'

I pause. It is often useful to bait your hook with a small worm of truth. 'He told them I had it.'

'And you do not?' asks Pepys.

I empty my pockets and show Pepys what I do have. He inspects the papers briefly and returns to me Morland's pass and Arlington's letter. 'You have nothing else? If we are to work together, I have to know.'

'No,' I say.

'What could he have meant then?' asks Pepys.

'As I say, he lied,' I say. 'He suggested there was a second letter. You would know better than I do whether that is true. If we are to work together, then perhaps you should tell me what we are seeking.'

'There is such a thing,' Pepys says. 'But you might not recognise it.'

'Why?' I ask. 'You mean it is not simply another sheet of paper with writing on it? Did the Duke enclose a ring or some other object that would have had some meaning for the Ambassador but not for anyone into whose hands the letter fell? Something that might have been on Fincham's body but the importance of which Underhill could not have known? Something he might have left behind as valueless?'

'Yes, all of those things are possible,' says Pepys. 'However, you clearly don't have it on your person.' He smiles. He enjoys knowing things that other people do not know. 'You are correct in thinking that, unlike me, you or Arlington might see it on the table there and not know its significance. Which brings me to the meat of this discussion, Mr Grey. You really have little choice but to accept my offer. We both want to recapture Underhill, I for my master and you for yours. If he escapes, neither of us will be commended for our actions. But if he is recaptured, one of us will be richly rewarded.'

'You don't know what Underhill looks like, do you?' I say. 'You never saw him at the inn. You never saw him at the Duke's residence. Nor, I think, do your men know him. So without me you are lost. Moreover, only I can easily approach him. He will trust me, whereas he will flee as soon as he catches sight of you. I think you have more to gain from a partnership than I have.'

'As we have established, you do not know what the object is that you are looking for. You think it may be a ring. I have not yet told you if you are right. Nor do you have half a dozen navy men at your disposal, as I have; nor horses to carry you, as again I do. You have a playwright and a little girl, who thinks you are a horse. So, we should work together. I bring a great deal more to the partnership than you do. My offer is a very generous one.'

'Very well. And when we catch him, then what?' I ask.

'We draw lots. If you win, you take him to the King or to Arlington. If I win, I take him to the Duke.'

He says this so frankly and openly that I mistrust him at once.

'Arlington will not forgive my handing him over.'

'Arlington's star is waning. You have nothing to fear from him. I can see, Mr Grey, that you do not trust me as you should. But, think about it, just for a moment: however things turn out, you cannot lose. If you draw the longer straw, then you will be rewarded by Arlington. If you draw the shorter, then you will be rewarded even more richly by the Duke. Conversely, if you turn down my offer, I doubt you will ever see Underhill again, still less the key to the letter he took to Arlington, and all of your efforts will be in vain. Under those circumstances you have no way of winning. I thought you were an intelligent man. Your hesitation now is beginning to make me doubt it.'

'The Duke must want the other half of the letter very much.'

'Returned or destroyed.'

'And he wishes to keep the whole correspondence from the King.'

'That is not something you need to worry about.'

'On the contrary, I do worry. I may not fear Arlington's anger, but I do fear the King's.'

'You have my assurance that no treason is involved in what I ask. I am happy to swear on the Bible or on anything else that you may hold sacred. Anyway, the Duke will protect you. If you wish to find Underhill—or, more to the point, if you wish to prevent me finding him on my own—then you will have to work with me. At least I shall not have you thrown into a cellar for the night, unlike your master. What do you say, Mr Grey?'

And Pepys smilingly holds out the generous and open hand of friendship.

The Plague Road

From My Lady Pole's Esteemed Poem,

The Puritaniad

So is our Puritan set free
And furnished with some cavalry
A troop of guards in seamen's boots
With faces brown as hazelnuts
And overall a stench of tar.
They were most well equipped for war.
With pistols and with sabres drawn,
They rode away out of the dawn,
That they might take, or perchance kill,
The renegado Underhill.
And yet I fear our hero's actual
Fate depends on things contractual,
A deal that stipulates who keeps
Th' said Underhill. John Grey or Pepys?

25

We have shaken hands and are equal partners in the enterprise of recovering Underhill. Two Magdalene men are working together.

Now that it is light enough, Pepys and I have examined the cellar door. The padlock is hanging loose but not broken. Either Arlington's men have been very careless or Underhill has been released by somebody with a key. The latter, I rather think. There is no sign of a struggle, but there are many large drops of blood on the ground by the door.

'You say one of Arlington's guards was wounded in the fight,' I say. 'This blood would suggest he came here for Underhill before he fled. He would have had the keys to the cellar. That would certainly explain to me the unlocked door and the lack of any sort of Underhill.'

'That was my conclusion also, Mr Grey.'

'Then, if he's already in Arlington's hands, my job is done,' I say.

'Do you think Arlington will pay you if you don't deliver him up yourself?' says Pepys. 'Anyway, Underhill will be looking for the first opportunity to run, and if Arlington's man is wounded then it won't be that difficult. I think our partnership agreement is still valid.'

I concede that Pepys has a good point.

'We can send a man on horseback to check the Salisbury road and another to search the London road. A blood-covered man and his prisoner—somebody will have seen them. And we'll check the woods and fields round the house. There can't be more than two or three ways they have gone, and even then not far, especially if one of them is bleeding as much as we think.'

In fact the spots of blood lead clearly one way—across the yard at the back of the house, then into the cover of the trees, then round to the road. We stand, with the sun at our backs, and stare along the route they have taken. The trees cast early morning shadows over the rough and dusty road, pointing the way Underhill and his captor have fled.

'West. They're bound for Salisbury then,' says Pepys. 'A day's journey on foot—but much more for an injured man, unless they can get horses. He bled all the way to here, do you see? Then much less after. I think perhaps he paused to bind his wound. So, hurt but perhaps not too badly. Still, with luck, it is a wound to the leg and a painful one. God willing, the loss of blood will have weakened him. We shall overtake them before long, Mr Grey. That is all most satisfactory. Time for my morning draught, then we must set out.'

Beer is served to us in the parlour. Sophia is sitting at the table drinking milk. Aminta watches over her, frowning. We all have a long journey ahead.

'I'm very tired,' Sophia says to me brightly as we enter. 'I think we must all stay here. For a long time.'

Much though I admire her quick learning, this is no longer helpful.

'We need to go,' I say. 'Maybe you are not as tired as you think.'

'I'm not telling a lie,' she says indignantly.

'Of course not,' I say. 'It's just that we really do need to travel to Salisbury now. So perhaps you are not quite as tired as you thought?'

Sophia is cross. 'I'm *even more* tired than I thought,' she says. 'I think I'm ill. I may have the Plague.'

Under different circumstances this would be an excellent performance. Pepys looks across at me with no little concern. I think he would prefer not to catch the Plague if he can avoid it.

'We've talked about this before, Sophia,' I say. 'You don't have the Plague. You have never had the Plague.'

'Why should she have the Plague?' asks Pepys.

'No more reason than anyone else in these three kingdoms,' I say. 'You don't have the Plague, Sophia.'

'Don't I?' she asks. Then, with no further warning, she vomits up her milk.

There is a quick consultation between Sophia and Aminta, an unlacing of a bodice and an examination of a chest.

'She has a fever and her neck and chest are covered in spots. I noticed that she had a runny nose and cough, but decided she must have taken cold in the woods the night before.'

'I *do* want to go home,' says Sophia. Tears start to run down her cheeks.

Yesterday I had thought that the mobs that blocked the road and sent us on our way were ignorant bumpkins, lacking the most basic charity. I am beginning to see how wise they were. Today we have the Plague amongst us but they do not.

'You go with Mr Pepys, John,' Aminta says to me. 'I'll stay here with Sophia and send for a physician, wherever one is to be found. I still have the ring that Sophia's mother gave me. I am sure that she would not begrudge that being the price of a cure for her daughter.'

Pepys glances at the ring Aminta has produced from her pocket and nods. 'Lady Pole speaks truly. Make haste, Grey. Underhill is effecting his escape, even as we speak. The horses are being readied. Bring your pistol and whatever powder and shot you still have.'

I watch him depart then say to Aminta: 'I can't just leave you here. I'll stay too. The Duke's men can capture Underhill without me.'

'There's nothing you can do here that I can't do alone,' says Aminta. 'Anyway, I'd like my share of the money, whoever pays it. But watch Pepys. I overheard him once explaining to one of my actresses that he could have his way with her without any fear of pregnancy—fear on her part, I mean. When he wants something badly enough, he'll say whatever he needs to say in order to get it.'

'Whatever he wants from me it's not that,' I say.

'The little girl will do well enough without us,' says Pepys, checking his saddlebag and refastening it.

I nod. I do not know what Pepys's medical knowledge may be, but I doubt that it runs to curing the Plague, any more than it runs to the avoidance of gravidity. We have reined in our horses while the men search a copse a few yards away. A passing farm labourer told us that he thought he had seen somebody entering it an hour or so ago, which may be true or may have simply been intended to get him a shilling from the pompous young gentleman in a creased silk suit.

'I should have recognised the signs,' I say, though the early signs of the Plague are much the same as the early signs of many other ailments: a cough, a sneeze, a runny nose, aching limbs.

'Underhill was well enough?' asks Pepys.

I think he is not enquiring whether Underhill has some cold or aching joints, but I pretend to consider all possibilities. 'Difficult to say with somebody like Underhill. He sniffs constantly, winter or summer. He complains of the slightest pain. But he has lodged recently with somebody who is undeniably now in a Plague pit. And he had as much contact with our driver as any one of us, though perhaps less with Sophia. If living honestly or keeping the Commandments were any sort of protection against the pestilence, he would lie open to every arrow in its quiver. In a fair and reasonable world, Underhill would most certainly have the Plague, but things are not appointed in that manner.'

'You jest, Mr Grey.'

'I wish that I did. I wonder how much prayer and good living has been needlessly wasted this summer.'

'Any sign of him?' Pepys calls out to the searching men.

'Nothing, Mr Pepys. He's not here.'

'How much did you pay the yokel?' I ask.

'A shilling,' says Pepys.

'I hope the Duke is refunding your expenses,' I say.

'I have told you he will not be ungenerous,' Pepys replies.

'The King too is not ungenerous, but his generosity is often delayed by the pressing need to reward his favourites and his mistresses.'

'The Duke is nothing like the King,' says Pepys. 'If the Duke were to succeed his brother, we would have an altogether more serious and sober government.'

'And Catholics in every office,' I say, gathering up my horse's reins. 'Where next?'

'There is a village ahead, wherein we may enquire about travellers.' Pepys calls his minions away from further fruitless searching in an empty spinney. We set off again, away from the sun, and ever towards the cathedral spire of Salisbury.

The man on the barricade looks nervous.

'Nobody may enter the village,' he says. 'That's the law.'

I think that this may have worked for him on previous occasions, but he already has a good idea that it isn't going to work this time.

'Don't try to tell me what the law is, sir,' says Pepys. 'I shall instruct you on the law. The law is that no man may obstruct the King's Highway. Where is your warrant? If you have no authority for what you are doing, I'll have you hanged, every one.' The man looks behind him at his companions, who have all taken a step or two backwards in order not to be last when they make a run for it. They have a single musket between them, and no access to legal advice. The musketeer has grounded his weapon so that it is as little noticeable as possible.

The man swallows hard. 'Very well. You may pass through the village as long as you don't stop.'

'We'll be stopping at the inn,' says Pepys. 'For exactly as long as we choose to do so. In the meantime have you seen two men on foot, one of them wounded?'

'We sent them round that way,' says the musketeer, pointing to a footpath across the fields.

'Even though one of them was injured and in sore need of your help?'

'Yes, sir.'

'When?'

'Maybe an hour since?'

'How badly wounded was the man?'

'He had a bandage round his leg. Torn-up shirt, by the look of it—not a proper one. He was limping. He didn't look too clever. Doubt he'll go far without a doctor treating it.'

'Did they say where they were going?'

'Said they were going to Wilton.'

'Did they indeed?'

'But I think they were heading for Salisbury. I followed them to check they didn't try to get into the village. Heard them talking to each other.'

Pepys nods to me. 'Now move that cart,' he instructs the sentry. 'You're blocking our way to the inn.'

The man looks behind him again at his companions. Somehow there don't seem to be as many of them as there were before. He makes one last attempt.

'You haven't touched any Plague people, sir? I can let you in only if you haven't been near any of them. You see, we've had no Plague here yet...'

'I can assure you,' says Pepys, looking down from his horse, 'that we have had no contact whatsoever with sick people. The gentleman on my left has a certificate to prove it.'

'Sorry, sir,' he says. 'It's just that I have to ask.'

'Of course you do,' says Pepys. 'I understand completely. Now get your filthy arse down from that waggon and move it out of the way or I'll have you publicly flogged.'

That we are gaining on Underhill is evident when we find more blood by the side of the road.

'Travelling has opened up the wound again,' says Pepys with relish. 'How right those men were to send them round the village on that rough path. He won't get far now.'

Nor does he. We find Reuben's body, lifeless but still warm, in the long, dry grass on a patch of waste ground. The wound in his leg has bled copiously, and that has been the death of him. He will never act as anyone's horse again. Our quarry, however, has not chosen to remain with him.

'It looks as if Underhill was briefly his prisoner,' I say, 'but that he has now escaped, just as you predicted. Underhill probably waited until Reuben was already fainting from loss of blood before he made his move. Underhill wouldn't have wanted a fair fight if he could avoid it. He doesn't like them.'

We search the body. There is no purse or weapon. So, Underhill is now presumably armed and in funds. He will also be travelling faster than he was before.

'What should we do with Reuben's body?' I ask. 'We don't have a spare horse to carry it.'

'It's no business of ours,' says Pepys. 'He chose to die by the side of the road and must accept the consequences of his actions. The country is full of unburied bodies. One more will make no difference. Say a prayer over him if that makes you feel better.'

I remount my horse. 'We'll need to go slowly and watch on both sides of the road,' I say. 'Underhill could have taken refuge in any of these thickets. Keep your eyes open, all of you.'

But again, we receive helpful intelligence. For tuppence, Pepys solicits the news that a man has recently passed this way, travelling on foot. His appearance and dress are itemised—unprepossessing features, a blue serge suit of clothes and a leather hat. He does not seem to have endeared himself to our informant in any way. That will be Underhill then.

'And he looked mighty tired,' says the informant, pocketing Pepys's coins.

'But not sick?' asks Pepys, concerned.

'He said he needed somewheres to lay up for a spell,' says the man. 'Maybe he was sick. Maybe he was just tired. I think he may have had a chill, which happens even in these hot days.'

'He was well enough when I last saw him,' I say, though I realise this means very little. The Plague can strike a man dead almost before he knows he is sick.

'Did you tell him where he might stay?' asks Pepys.

'Said there was a tavern very close by—well, I say tavern—just a cottage with mud walls and a barrel or two of bad ale. But it's not a place where they'll ask a lot of questions, if you see what I mean. A good place to hide, if you are being pursued...or if you've got the Plague, for that matter. And it is only a short distance away.'

'So did he go there?'

Our informant looks us up and down, as if estimating the size of our purses.

'I watched him enter. And that's where you'll find him if that's what you want. He told me not to tell anyone where he was going, and I swore on my honour I wouldn't, so I think that merits sixpence at least, don't you, good sirs?'

He is right that the building in front of us scarcely deserves to be called a tavern. It scarcely deserves to be called a building. It is a single-storey hovel made of sticks with wattle and daub between them. At some stage this has been painted white, but not recently. At various stages the walls have been patched with whatever materials came to hand. To avoid confusion with a pigsty, the owner has hung by the door a sign, which reads: 'The Royal Oak, beers, ales and fine wine. Gentry catered for.' Some blobs of green and brown paint above these inviting words may be intended to represent the noble tree in which His Majesty hid from Cromwell's troops after the Battle of Worcester. Or it may just be paint.

'So, Mr Grey,' says Pepys, 'you just go in and tell Underhill that he is to accompany you to safety. He'll trust you. We'll wait outside to grab him if he runs.'

'At what point,' I ask, 'do we draw lots to decide whether he goes to the Duke or to Arlington and the King? I am merely curious, you understand.'

'I shall not need to trouble you with that,' says Pepys. 'My offer was contingent on our need for your services to identify Underhill. But we now know he is in that rather small building. However many of the local gentry have been tempted to drink wine there, I doubt that there will be many fugitives dressed in blue serge to choose from. It would be helpful if you could assist us in extracting him, but I think that you are no longer entitled to a full half-share in the venture. For the avoidance of doubt, Underhill is coming with us to the Duke. There is no question of our handing him to Arlington. You shall, of course, receive the Duke's thanks and generous payment. But we shall not allow you to snatch Underhill from under our noses.'

'Were you ever planning to allow me to do that?'

'In reality, the position would have always been that you were outgunned and lacked the horses you required. It would have been difficult for you to enforce the contract. But you always knew that would be the case, so let us not descend into vulgar recrimination. The Duke, as I say, will not be ungenerous to you. Now, if you would be so kind as to dismount and knock on the door, we can perhaps still reach Salisbury this evening.'

I dismount. I knock on the door.

The keeper of the tavern is a sprightly old man; his face, which is all I can see at the moment, is wrinkled like a walnut and brown with the sun or the smoke of his fire, a little of which creeps round the half-open door to greet my nose.

'Do you have a Mr Underhill taking wine within?' I ask. 'I should like to speak to him. In case he's lied about his name, as I'm sure he will have done, he's a weaselly-looking rogue in a shabby blue doublet.'

'He's here, but he's not speaking much to anyone. Not now.'

He smiles as one might when about to reveal a splendid joke.

'Can I come in and see him?'

'You can come in but he still won't speak to you. He is, you might say, past all that, though he may still hope to sing with the choirs eternal.'

The old man giggles. I think I know how this conversation will end.

'Is he sick?' I ask.

'Plague,' says the man. Not even Sophia could inject the same note of certainty into this word. 'Stretched out on my best bed, breathing his last, may God rest his soul.'

I turn to Pepys. 'Do you still wish to claim the goods?' I ask. 'They seem to have deteriorated in transit.'

'The senile old fool could be wrong. Or lying. I won't be duped that easily. You go in and check, Grey.'

I've done worse for Arlington, but for this man Pepys...

'Any reason why I have to check rather than you?' I ask politely.

'You have already dismounted. It is more convenient for you than for me.'

The man opens the door a little more—enough in fact for me to enter, though he is not expecting me to do so.

The Plague Road

'If you are not afeared of the Plague, good sir—the Plague that has carried off so many of our fellow countrymen in their prime—then please come and pay your last respects to your friend.' He is enjoying this.

There is something in his tone that reminds me of the honest serving woman with her employer's valuables in a sack over her shoulder. On that occasion I declined her invitation to rummage in the filthy, shit-covered sheets to see exactly what she was stealing. This time I think I'll try my luck. Without a further word, I push past the landlord of the tavern and pause for a moment on the threshold. The smoke stings my eyes, but when I have blinked once or twice, I see quite clearly that it is Underhill on the heap of filthy rags that passes for a bed.

I approach and kneel down beside him. I take his wrist and feel for a pulse. It is all exactly as I expected. Nothing for it but to tell Pepys. Looking towards the half-opened door, I can just see him out there in the bright, clean sunshine. He is still mounted and is using his hat to fan himself while talking to one of the Duke's men. I hear him laugh, then he looks towards me, though it is too dark inside the hovel for him to be able to make out anything clearly. I stand again and stretch my limbs. It is a while since I rode a horse and today's short journey has caused my muscles to ache in places that I only dimly remembered they could.

'So,' I say to nobody in particular, 'that's how it all ends.'

The dry heat of midday is a relief after the stifling, smoke-filled hut that I have just left. I take in a great lungful of warm but uninfected air.

'You'll get no more out of Underhill. I think we've had a wasted journey.'

Pepys scowls, as if Underhill has died merely to inconvenience him.

'We return to London then,' he says. 'By the shortest route.'

'You wouldn't care to draw lots for the honour of arranging his burial? I think that's the least you could do. The Duke will presumably be content on hearing he is dead.'

'I have no instructions for his burial. He can be interred here at the parish's expense, or yours if that's what you prefer. I think neither of us are under any obligation to him, dead or alive, and the Duke will certainly not refund your costs.'

'I'll make the arrangements nevertheless,' I say. 'I signed for him when Arlington handed him over and I'll take back what evidence I need regarding his eventual fate. I suspect it would take a few hours to prepare a grave and five minutes or so for the priest to conduct a suitably dignified service, with you and I as chief mourners.'

Pepys looks at me as if I were mad. 'That is very dutiful,' he says. 'But I cannot wait here while you oversee the funeral of one such as he. I have wasted enough time already. If you want to waste your own, then you can return the horse to the Navy Office once you are back in London. The cost of its feed and stabling is yours until it is formally signed for by my office.'

I doff my hat to Pepys and watch him and his men ride off eastwards in a cloud of ochre dust.

I re-enter the tavern. Underhill is sitting on his bed, scratching himself.

'Any luck?' he asks.

'Hook, line and sinker,' I say. 'We'll return to the farm and see how Sophia fares. Then we shall proceed as planned to Salisbury.'

'There is the small matter of your friend's bill,' says the tavern owner. 'Tuppence for ale and a shilling for the bed.'

'He's only been in it for an hour,' I say.

'And half a crown for not telling the magistrate that your friend said he had the Plague. I really ought to have reported it the moment he mentioned the word. I've risked the reputation of my establishment, built up over many generations. Let's say four shillings for everything.'

We settle on one and sixpence, inclusive of all services, and lying to the magistrates if and when required. We are bowed out of the tavern with every expression of hope that we might return to grace it again before too long.

'I'll ride behind you, Grey,' says Underhill. 'Your horse can carry both of us.'

'We found your last guardian by the side of the road. You seem to have been remarkably careless of his safety.'

'He died from lack of blood,' says Underhill. 'Saw it a lot during the wars. A wounded man tries to walk too far. Easy to think that you can go a little further, when you simply can't. Just a matter of biding my time.'

'Precisely. You bided your time until you could make a run for it. So, I'll ride and you can walk in front of me, where I can watch your every move. But first I'll relieve you of the gun you stole from him. You can keep the money.'

'I forgot to take any powder or shot anyway,' says Underhill, handing over a cavalry pistol. 'And he only had a few shillings about him. Poor repayment for what he put me through in that cellar, I'm thinking. Are you really insisting I walk after all I've done for you? I thought you'd have been kinder to one who had just returned from the dead. It's a cruel and ungrateful world we live in, Mr Grey.'

CHAPTER

26

'Chickenpox,' says Aminta.

'You're certain?' I ask.

'As certain as I can be. Sophia would be a lot sicker now if it were the Plague. But it might be as well if we didn't travel for a day or two. She's out of bed, but spots of any sort have unfortunate connotations these days. When we reach the next barricade, she may frighten the poor guards.'

'We can stay for another couple of nights,' I say. 'Pepys thinks Underhill is dead—he won't be back. There's plenty of food in the kitchen. We'll live off Arlington's bounty. Then you and Sophia can ride Pepys's horse and Underhill and I will walk. I still don't quite know where we are, but Salisbury can't be far off. I still have some money and you have the ring. We should do well enough.'

'I expect you'd now like my opinion on the matter?' asks Underhill. 'You usually do.'

'Not especially,' I say.

'Then I'll tell you. Pepys may think I'm dead, but he won't have told Arlington that. Two of Arlington's men escaped. Don't you think they'll be back, especially when Reuben fails to join them? And when they were last here they threatened me with torture. They may decide to finish the job.'

'Last time they could do so because we didn't know who they were. Now we do.'

'That will be a great comfort to me as they apply the thumbscrews, or whatever they've brought with them. Anyway, what if you and Pepys are wrong and they were Buckingham's ruffians?'

'We'll leave as soon as we can,' I say. 'You can sleep in the barn if you're worried they'll surprise us here in the house.'

'Thank you. You've made me sleep in the woods and the stables, so why not a barn?'

'What do you propose, Mr Underhill?'

'Leave now. Once I've told the King what I know and been paid what I am entitled to, Esmond Underhill and Father Horncastle can both cease to exist. I've been many men over the years and I think I might become another, slightly richer and less sought-after.'

'It's too late to start out for Salisbury this afternoon,' I say. 'Not if you don't want another night in the woods. Tomorrow will be soon enough. I'm sorry but, unpleasant though it is, you'll have to be Esmond Underhill for another day or two.'

But, that night, the weather finally breaks. Lightning at midnight is followed by torrents of rain. Water streams down the thatch and cascades onto the parched ground. Watching the storm from an open window, the warm scent of newly wet earth rises to greet me.

'There'll be no travelling until this abates,' I say, 'not with one horse and a sick child.'

'Perhaps it will stop soon,' says Aminta.

'Perhaps,' I say.

But the following day is the same. The whole party is restless, Underhill most of all, pacing the parlour and looking out of the window every five minutes to see who might be coming up the road. He's right. Arlington will certainly send men to investigate what has happened. If they are not here today, they will be tomorrow.

I have been up in Aminta's chamber, checking on Sophia's progress. I descend the stairs to discover Underhill going through my bag. Fortunately I have my pistol with me, so there is no danger that I shall suddenly find it pointed in my direction. He is holding the pass, and Arlington's letter, permitting me to kill him.

'Those don't concern you,' I say.

'On the contrary,' he says. 'I think both of them do. Especially this one, that permits you to do whatever you see necessary to prevent my escape. A fine thing to carry around with you.'

'You can put them back anyway,' I say.

Underhill turns the paper over and examines the reverse carefully before reluctantly handing both letters to me. He watches me stuff them back inside my bag.

'So, would you have shot me?' he asks. 'Arlington says you may.'

'My intention is to get you to Salisbury alive,' I say, 'even if you are worth as much dead.'

'Then you don't need that letter authorising my execution, do you?' He extends an open palm towards me. 'I'd trust you a lot more if you just handed it over, Grey. As a sign of friendship. Because we are friends, aren't we?'

'You're not my friend, Mr Underhill,' I say. 'You never were. And I was never at college with you. You are simply a delivery that I need to make to the King.'

Later, when Underhill has gone to his chamber, and realising that he may still have designs on Arlington's letter, I remove it and stuff it inside my doublet. I leave the pass where it is. Then I go to bed.

It is not until the following morning, when we discover that Underhill has fled during the night and left my bag lying open on the table, that I realise that it was in fact the travel pass that Underhill was trying to steal last night. For that is nowhere to be seen.

The morning is well advanced by the time we depart. Underhill has also taken the horse, so the three of us are on foot and with no travel documents. But the fine weather has returned and there is a brightness and freshness to everything. The sun glints off the puddles in the road. The ferns are a richer, darker green.

'Do you think he took the pass to slow us down?' asks Aminta.

'If we are stopped, then we'll just have to repeat the lie that we are from Essex and that it is wholly free of Plague.'

Sophia looks at us significantly when I mention lying, but says nothing. She has already walked a long way for a small child, and I shall soon be carrying her again.

'The pass will not be of much use to him either,' says Aminta. 'Underhill could have lied his way through the last few miles to Salisbury as easily as we can.'

'I wonder if the King will really reward him for informing him that his brother is a traitor in league with the French?'

'The King can hardly ignore what he says,' says Aminta. 'But Mr Pepys and his master will not be pleased when they discover they have been duped. That bodes ill for all of us.'

'Underhill will vanish utterly, immune to anyone's displeasure. As for the Duke, he will probably be imprisoned or exiled and powerless to take his revenge. Pepys may need to find a new job. I suspect that Arlington might find him work. He already has Morland and Williamson, but I am sure Arlington will have a use for him.'

'So, Pepys has suffered a crushing defeat and we are on the winning side. Excellent. How strange it is then that Mr Pepys is riding in his fine yellow coach somewhere, while we trudge along a dusty road.'

'There's an inn ahead,' I say. 'When we get there, we'll need to say that we are from Clavershall West, near Saffron Walden in the county of Essex. Can you remember that, Sophia?'

'I can remember *Essex*,' she says.

'That'll do nicely,' I say.

The landlord is happy to take us at our word. The further we travel from London, the less suspicion there is, at least for the moment. We are served with hot rabbit stew and newly baked bread and apples by the gaunt-looking man who runs the establishment.

'I suppose you haven't seen a man in a blue serge suit travelling this way?' I ask. 'He had a stolen horse and a pass that may have suggested he was called John Grey?'

The thin landlord turns to his wife, a short plump woman, who is clutching several tankards of urgently needed ale in her podgy hands. 'Two gentlemen who rode in earlier—was one of them called Grey?' he asks.

'Yes, the runty one in blue said that was his name. Stolen horse, did you say, sir? I wouldn't have put it past him. He didn't tip, either.'

'He was with somebody else, then?' I ask.

'The skinflint Grey?' asks the woman. 'Yes, my husband said, there were two of them. The runty one and a tall man with one eye. Not bad-looking, the other one. If I wasn't happily married, I might have thought him rather handsome.'

I frown at this news. 'Was the other one called Callingham?' I ask.

The woman shakes her head. 'Didn't hear him called anything, did you, Bob?'

'Not that I recall,' says the thin landlord, though he seems to recall little without his wife's authority. I don't think he found the one-eyed man attractive in any way.

'Was the runty one...Grey...in any sense the other man's prisoner?' I ask.

'Prisoner?' asks the thin landlord, surprised. 'He wasn't a prisoner, was he, Miriam?' He looks to his wife for confirmation.

'They sat there drinking and talking,' says the plump woman. 'If one was the other's prisoner, I couldn't have told you which was which, and which was the other thing. If you were hoping this man Callingham would recover your horse for you, you'll be journeying on foot for some time, I'm thinking.'

'Did they say where they were going?'

'Couldn't rightly tell you that either,' says the woman. She seems resentful that they did not have their conversation at a level she could easily overhear. 'But they left all of two hours ago along the Salisbury Road. Are you going that way yourselves?'

'We're from Essex,' says Sophia brightly. 'There's no Plague there and you don't get shut up in your house. We're not from London.'

'That's nice,' says the woman.

'Yes,' I say. 'We're going to Salisbury.'

'Good,' says the plump woman, looking at Sophia. 'She hasn't got spots on her, has she?'

'A touch of the sun,' says Aminta. 'Nothing to worry about.'

'We'll never catch them,' I say to Aminta, when the couple have left.

'How odd that Underhill and Callingham have paired up,' says Aminta. 'Callingham said that he hated and feared Underhill. And Underhill has no reason to love Callingham.'

'Well, that's who it must be. Unless Underhill has met some other one-eyed man that he knows well. Callingham, searching for us, has located Underhill and is taking him to Salisbury as we intended. I hope he exercises caution. I fear for Callingham even if he doesn't fear for himself. Nothing Underhill says is to be trusted, and those who associate with him seem to die young.'

We have travelled for another hour, for much of it with Sophia on my back.

'Look,' says Sophia, from her vantage point. 'There's our horse!'

I look towards where she is pointing and there indeed, tethered amongst the trees, just off the road, is a horse very much like ours. We go over and examine it. It is in every respect the one I have undertaken to return to the Navy Office when I have no further use for it.

'So, where is Underhill?' I ask.

'And where's Callingham?' says Aminta.

There is a groan from the bushes not far away. A few steps take me to where the wounded man is lying. He looks up at me. It's Underhill. And if he's faking it this time, he's very, very good. The front of his blue doublet is dark red. A pool of congealing blood lies in front of him.

'There's water in the bottle by the saddle,' he gasps. 'Fetch it, please, Grey. There's not much else you can do for me, but I'd be grateful if you can do that.'

'What happened?' I say, uncorking the bottle for him and kneeling down.

He takes several large gulps, the water flowing down off his chin, before he replies.

'Callingham,' he says hoarsely. 'Caught up with me as I reached the inn back there. Said you'd asked him to look out for me and that he'd ride with me to Salisbury and protect me from Arlington or the Duke. And I trusted him! When we reached this spinney, he suggested we stop for a moment—he thinks his horse is going lame. So we get down and he produces a gun and demands the second part of the Duke's letter. Well, I don't want it that much. So, I take the paper out of my doublet to give it to him, but all I've got is this pass. I took the wrong paper from your bag. That's when he shot me.'

'The second part of the letter? It was never in there,' I say. 'I told you the truth. I don't have it, in spite of what you seem to have thought. I just have the two letters I've shown you.'

Underhill shakes his head and tries to speak again, but the words won't come.

'Let me look at your wounds,' I say.

He shakes his head again. I offer him more water, and he drinks.

'Thank you, Grey,' he says.

'Don't try to speak,' I say. 'We'll find you a doctor.'

'I've seen plenty of wounds to the chest,' he says. 'I know which ones you can survive and how much blood a man has in him. Even if you were a surgeon...'

Underhill lapses into silence again. His face is grey.

'We could bandage your wounds,' I say. 'We can get you to a surgeon in the next town.'

Again Underhill shakes his head.

'Was it Callingham who tried to shoot you at the first inn—with Pepys's pistol?'

Underhill starts to laugh, then grimaces with pain. 'I wouldn't have gone with him if I'd thought there was any chance he'd done that. I overheard Pepys talking to his coachman and stole the gun myself...'

I wait until a fit of coughing has passed. Then Underhill continues: 'Thought I'd make my own way to Salisbury. But I tripped as I ran, didn't I? The gun fell and went off. Almost deafened me. I knew that would have everyone in pursuit so I carried on running, but then I tripped again and turned my ankle. But Callingham did kill Fincham. He told me so. That was what Fincham was trying to say to me when I found him.

He wasn't calling me his comrade. He was saying his comrade had killed him.'

Underhill falls back, as if exhausted.

'Why?' I ask. 'Why should he kill his friend?'

For a moment he says nothing then, as if making one last effort, he says: 'Colchester. Callingham blamed us both for what happened there. He hadn't realised that Fincham had given evidence against him when Fairfax wanted to court-martial me. Not until I told him, just to see if I could turn him against Fincham a bit and get him to help me steal the letter. Well, it was worth a try. What I didn't know was that he'd always wanted the Duke's letter for his own paymaster— Buckingham. Only now he was quite happy to kill Fincham for it. Callingham knew I was the one who had disturbed him when he stabbed Fincham, so he must have guessed I now had what he needed. When you kindly told him we were going to Salisbury, he followed on as fast as he could. It was Lady Castlemaine who recruited him to Buckingham's cause. I think Callingham genuinely believed at first that she was only after his body. Ha! Vanity saith the preacher, all is vanity... Can you give me more water, Grey?'

I pass the bottle to him again, but he can scarcely hold it. I lift it to his lips and he drinks. I unbutton his doublet. He has been hit twice. Once in the chest and once in the gut. Either would be enough to kill. My father, or indeed my mother, might have been of some service to him, but his wounds are beyond anything I can do. His only hope is if we can get him to a doctor. His eyes are closed and he is shivering.

'If we could just get you onto a horse...' I say.

'Onto a horse? Don't try to make me laugh,' he says, half opening his eyes. 'I'll be dead before we've jolted more than a hundred yards. I won't be going on a horse again.' He closes his eyes again.

'There must be something we can do,' says Aminta. But we both know that isn't true.

'Shall I pray for you?' I ask him.

Underhill shakes his head. 'I shall be saved only by my own deeds,' he says. 'No requiem masses for me, thank you very much. I had no plans to die, but I'd have been willing to do so fighting for a restored Republic. No chance of that now. At least I've died trying to stop a Popish Duke take the throne. It's not much, but it's something, I suppose. You must tell the King what I would have told him. And you have the proof...'

'What do I have?' I ask.

Underhill makes one last difficult attempt to speak. 'You have the letter...'

His eyes close again.

There is little point in telling him that I do not possess whatever it is he thinks I have. He no longer hears. We wait with him. When the sun has climbed to its highest, he is dead.

'You say you found him by the side of the road?' asks the clergyman.

'Just as you see him,' say. 'He was lying in the spinney a mile or so away. Within this parish certainly.'

'And you carried him here on your horse?'

'As an act of charity in these harsh times.'

'The magistrate will have to be informed.'

'As you wish.'

'That is *your* duty, sir.'

'I have reported it to you. If that is not enough, then by all means let the magistrate try to find me.'

'And somebody will have to pay for the burial.'

'I'll leave money for that,' I say. 'Including your fee.'

'Really? In that case...' says the clergyman. 'And you have no idea of his name?'

'None at all,' I say. 'Not his real name. I never knew that. He bears scars of previous wounds. Just bury him as a soldier of the late wars.'

'Which side was he on?' asks the clergyman.

'Whoever would pay him most,' I reply. 'He was a fair man in that respect.'

'Well,' I say as we walk along, 'we now know who killed Fincham and we know who killed Underhill. What we don't know is what they died for. The thing that they are all searching for—the other half of the message—is probably buried in a Plague pit.'

'Underhill said *you* had the letter.'

'But I don't. You know that. Anyway, Pepys, who searched me and who ought to know what he was looking for, failed to find it. He also said that it wasn't as obvious as a second letter. He said that even if we saw it in front of us, we might not recognise it. It might be anything…a ring, for example.'

'Which we clearly don't have,' says Aminta.

I pick Sophia up. 'Do you want to go back on the horse?' I ask.

'No, I want you to be my horse. You're not so high up and scary. And you don't smell as bad.'

'Fine. Just one thing: you don't need to kick me into a gallop this time.'

But she does.

We are in luck. We have found another inn where travellers are not turned away as a matter of course. And we are back on the King's Highway. Best of all, a coach is about to leave for Salisbury and I have procured seats for Aminta and Sophia. I shall ride behind on the navy horse.

The landlord, a large and jolly countryman with a red face and muscular arms, serves us beer and ham and eggs. We have eaten well today.

'Now we shall make good progress,' I say. 'Tonight we shall sup in Salisbury and, by tomorrow at the latest, Sophia will be with her aunt.'

'We have neither Underhill nor the letter,' says Aminta. 'I had hoped for a more profitable journey.'

'Nor do we have Fincham's killer,' I say. 'Callingham has made good his escape, unless I can obtain intelligence of him on the road. But we are still alive, and that is no small thing in these times. And we shall have done a commendable deed that may stand us in good stead on Judgement Day.'

I call the landlord over to us. He comes, rubbing his hands at the prospect of making more money out of us.

'I'm seeking a man named Patrick Callingham,' I say. 'Tall, one eye. Has the bearing of Julius Caesar or Macbeth, as he chooses. Quite well known as an actor—or he was thirty years ago. Nobody of that description has passed this way, I suppose?'

'What do you want him for?' asks the landlord, disappointed.

'He's murdered two men, at least. The last murder wasn't far from here. There's every chance he's on this road somewhere.'

'Murder? I'd help you if I could, sir, but I do not know the gentleman concerned.'

Our man is not tall, but he is powerfully built. If we do encounter Callingham before we leave, then I might take up that offer of help. The landlord proposes further refreshment as an alternative to Callingham but we decline. The coach will be leaving soon. He bids us a good journey and goes out into the stable yard, behind the inn, perhaps to check whether the horses are ready.

In fact as I look, just outside our window, the coach is now preparing for the road. New horses are being brought out, led in pairs by the ostlers. Those who have booked seats are starting to stand and drift towards the door.

'You'd better board the coach,' I say. 'I wouldn't trust them not to have sold more seats than it strictly has. Once you're safely inside, I'll fetch my horse and follow on after. I'll have caught you up in a few minutes.'

'Good,' says Aminta, 'but if you do happen to see Callingham on the journey, leave him alone. If he can outwit Underhill, he can certainly outwit you.'

As it happens, there are exactly as many places on the coach as there should be. I wait while the driver finally climbs into his seat and cracks his whip. The great wheels start to turn and the coach moves away towards Salisbury. I watch it gain speed, throwing up a cloud of dust behind. I prepare to go to the stables, then I see another cloud of dust further down the road. It is coming this way, from the direction of Salisbury. Soon it resolves itself into a horseman, cantering towards the inn. He dismounts, and glances round with his one good eye, before leading his horse towards the stables at the back. There can be no doubt. It's Callingham. Has he returned to look for us, not realising that we know he's killed Underhill and Fincham? If so, he has walked straight into a trap of his own making. I'll take up the landlord's offer of help, I think. It is fortunate that Aminta has already left and cannot raise any further objections that I may be unequal to the task. I stride towards the back door and out into the yard. She'll be surprised when I turn up in Salisbury with my prisoner.

The landlord has paused just outside the inn and is staring towards the stable door. His muscles bulge beneath his loose linen shirt. He'd be worth two if it came to a fight. And there's only one of Callingham.

'Thank you for your offer of help,' I say. 'The man I spoke of has just arrived. I am therefore about to arrest him in the name of My Lord Arlington, Secretary of State. I shall wait outside and take him as he emerges, but I should like you to watch from here with one of my guns in case he tries to make a break for it.'

'So you just want me to stand here?'

'That is almost certainly all you will need to do.'

He shrugs and accepts the gun awkwardly, as if surprised by its weight. I think he is not familiar with firearms, which is regrettable, but there is no time now to seek other assistance.

'If necessary just point it at him and tell him you'll fire if he moves,' I say.

He nods. 'Just be quick about it,' he says. 'I have customers to serve.'

I approach the stable door softly and peer inside. Callingham is just finishing unsaddling his horse. I wait for some minutes, my back against the stable wall, then I hear his heavy tread. As he emerges into the strong sunshine, I take two steps and press the cold steel of my pistol into the back of his neck.

'Take out your gun and place it carefully on the ground,' I say. 'Don't turn round.'

He does so. I pick it up and stuff it into my belt. Not bad for a fusty old lawyer, I think to myself. Aminta will have to admit that she has sorely underestimated me.

'Mr Grey, I assume?' Callingham says. 'I don't think there's any need for this, sir.'

'I was with Underhill when he died,' I say. 'There's no point in further subterfuge. I'm arresting you for his murder and Charles Fincham's. You're coming with me to Salisbury. Face against that wall, if you don't mind.'

He does so slowly and with some reluctance. I pat down his pockets. There is no sign of a second weapon.

'Now, you may turn,' I say. 'I'm going to tie your hands, and then we're going to get you back onto your horse, and you'll ride in front of me to Salisbury.'

'You are making a big mistake, Grey,' he says.

'Are you telling me you didn't kill Fincham?'

'No, I killed him. I trusted him as a friend. Then Underhill told me the truth about Colchester—that Fincham had given evidence against me to Fairfax. He'd wronged me. But, more to the point, what he was carrying was worth a small fortune and, according to Lady Castlemaine, Buckingham was willing to pay me well to get it for him. If I hadn't been disturbed, I would have had it. But Underhill got hold of it instead. Except that the fool gave half of it to Arlington and then lost the other half.'

He seems strangely talkative. Does he hope to delay me? A few minutes will make no difference.

'And you are not going to claim you didn't kill Underhill?' I ask.

'Of course not.'

'Or the guard at the shut-up house.'

'I knew Underhill must have the letter somewhere. I came after it, but Underhill had already fled. The guard tried to stop me searching the house, then tried to detain me in it. Fool that he was.'

'So, if you killed all three, and you admit it, in what way am I making a big mistake?'

'Because you've just given my brother-in-law one of your pistols.'

'You mean—' I say.

But at that moment I feel something rather like a pistol butt crash into the back of my head, and the ground rushes up to meet me.

28

I am lying on some straw, just inside the door of the stables. My head is throbbing.

'You see,' says the landlord, 'he's still alive.'

'No thanks to you,' says Callingham. 'You could have just pressed the gun into his back.'

'He might have shot you.'

'More likely the gun would have gone off by accident when you hit him and he fell.'

'Well, don't expect me to do that for you again,' says the landlord. 'Not if you're going to show so little gratitude. What are you going to do with him now?'

'I have a couple of questions for him and then, depending on how he answers, I'll decide whether to shoot him or not. How's that, Mr Grey?' he says, looking down at me from a great height.

'You're not shooting him here,' says the landlord. 'The coach has gone, but I still have an inn full of customers, who will hear the shot. Take him down to the river. That's far enough away. If anyone hears, I'll say it must be wild-fowlers. Or poachers. They'll approve of poachers.'

'On your feet, Grey,' says Callingham. 'We're going for a walk. Just stay on the path in front of me. Though it may inconvenience my brother-in-law, I'll still shoot you, wherever you are, if you try to escape. So, let's take a stroll together. Then you can tell me where the letter is, or get shot through the head, whichever takes your fancy.'

We walk through the yard. The sun is hotter than ever, baking the soil beneath our feet and the burnt-out grass by the path. We enter the shade of a patch of woodland and for a few hundred yards it is almost cool. I concentrate on the path ahead, because my legs seem likely to give way. Though Callingham is suggesting that he will not shoot me if I give him the thing that I do not have, we both know that there can be only one end to this journey. If he doesn't want me giving evidence against him, then he'll have to kill me. It's only a matter of where. I need to think clearly, but the pain in the back of my head is stopping any useful thoughts from coming.

Then, ahead, I see green bushes and reeds and willows, and I know we are approaching the river. I turn. Callingham is close behind me, but he is almost stumbling too. This is the hottest day I can ever remember.

'Kneel there,' Callingham orders.

I do as he says, dropping almost with relief onto the hard, dusty ground. The river is somewhere in front of me, and for a moment a fresher breeze blows towards us. Then I feel the pistol barrel pressing into the bruises at the back of my head.

'I don't have it,' I say.

'Underhill says you do.' Callingham's words are strangely indistinct and far away. I mustn't pass out.

'He's tried that trick before,' I say.

'No trick. It's true…' Callingham seems to be whispering, his voice is so faint.

The pressure on the back of my head ceases. Perhaps he has doubts. I need to keep him talking.

'What exactly am I supposed to have?' I ask.

There is no reply. I wait with the sun on the back of my head for a minute or more, expecting any moment to hear a shot.

'Tell me what it is,' I say. 'What does it look like?'

There is still no response.

'Look,' I say, 'maybe there is a deal to be done. Maybe I don't need to say anything to anyone about Fincham's murder. Arlington doesn't care. And nobody will care about Underhill either. As for the guard, we can blame Underhill. Maybe we can both make money here. But I have to know what I am looking for.'

I turn. Callingham is also on his knees, the gun on the path beside him. I stare at him. Then he vomits the foulest, blackest mess I have ever smelt. For a moment I almost retch too at the stink of it. I stand very slowly and back away. I cannot take my eyes off him. He vomits again, copiously and uncontrollably in long spasms, until he is almost too weak to kneel. One hand is flat on the ground, keeping him upright. His face is white. His breath comes in gasps. He looks up at me helplessly. Somehow, I don't think the citizens of Salisbury will thank me if I take him for trial there. His arm buckles and he falls forwards.

I approach close enough so that my toe is against his pistol, then I kick it several yards away from him. I don't think he's in any state to pull a trigger, but it's better to be safe, and I'm not sure I want to handle any gun he's touched.

I walk back along the path as quickly as I can. Once or twice I turn. Callingham has not moved. There are, as I may have observed, two ways of dying of the Plague. In some ways I'd have been happy for him to die slowly but in other ways quick is good too.

I approach the stables with care. Callingham's brother-in-law has gone inside and a summer stillness hangs over everything. Even the birds are silent. My footsteps seem horribly loud, but they will be even louder if I run. Inside the stables I make out Pepys's horse in the gloom, saddled and ready to go. Very slowly, I lead him out into the yard and mount him.

The landlord emerges just as I pass into the front yard and kick the horse into a gallop. He makes a grab for my stirrup, but he is much too slow. I ride flat out, the hot wind in my face, until I feel the horse start to tire. Then I let the pace slacken bit by bit and we fall gradually back to a gentle trot. There is no sign of pursuit.

I catch up with the coach just before it reaches Salisbury.

'I thought we passed Callingham,' says Aminta, leaning out of the window. 'Shortly after we left the inn. Did you see him?'

'Yes,' I say. 'But I didn't manage to arrest him.'

'So you weren't as clever as you imagined?'

'Something like that.'

'You surprise me,' she says.

Having travelled so long and so far, the spire of Salisbury Cathedral, rising above the trees, seems unreal. We are descending onto a flat plain when we catch our first sight of it in the distance, then slowly the other lesser spires and the tiled roofs of houses come into view. A few wisps of pink cloud dot the sky, but it is a fine evening where we are going.

'I never thought that we would get here,' I say, as I lift Sophia from the coach. 'Now all we have to do is to find the King.'

'And say what to him?' Aminta asks.

'I shall tell him that the man I was bringing to him is dead, and that we do not have the letter we sought—or only part of it. I have only Underhill's word for it that there was any plot. Maybe the King will tell me what it is all about. He's no fool. If his brother is playing some game, my guess is that he already knows much more than I do.'

'And then we need to find Sophia's family by the cathedral.'

'Well,' I say, pointing to the fine spire in front of us, 'there it is in all its glory. At last.'

The Plague Road

We find ourselves a room at an inn just inside the city walls, with a stable that can take Pepys's horse. It is growing dark and too late to attempt to look for anyone now. I do, however, venture out into the streets in the very last of the grey daylight. A low mist has come up from the river, and the houses appear as many small ships, floating on a white sea. Candlelight is beginning to emerge from behind the diamond panes of glass. Inside the great gates of some of the larger houses, torches burn with a red glow. A few clergymen, their gowns and surplices flapping behind them, hurry home. The more sedate part of the city is settling down for the night, though in the backstreets the laity, and perhaps a few of the clergy, will be carousing in taverns. For a moment I am tempted to plunge into the nearest lane and seek out some drinking den for old times' sake and to stagger home, drunk and happy, under the stars as I once did. Because I was not shot by the river and I am alive. But I suspect that illicit drinking under a King is less pleasurable than it was under a Lord Protector years ago. It would be a dull game. So, I make enquiries and am told where Mistress Thatcher lives. I am also told, because the porter at the cathedral gate would rather gossip than do whatever he is paid to do, at which houses the King and his court are residing. With this information, I return to the inn, in time to eat supper with Aminta and Sophia.

I plan to sleep long and late. But I am not allowed to.

It is early morning and I am walking swiftly through the still waking streets of Salisbury. The cathedral gates are being opened with a great creaking sound of iron on iron. The morning is fresh and it will be another clear day.

I awoke to find a letter awaiting me. Lady Castlemaine wishes to talk to me in the gardens of a certain house, just outside the west gate. I doubt that she is used to being kept waiting. A clock strikes. I shall be about ten minutes late then. That should do.

'You did well to find me,' I say.

'I had left instructions at all of the inns inside the walls to send to me if anyone called John Grey arrived. A boy found me at ten o'clock last night with the news I had been waiting for.'

Lady Castlemaine looks again at what she has summoned to her side. I am, I have to admit, a little the worse for wear, having been on the road for some days, my spare shirt and stockings abandoned with the coach. Hunting through the bracken for Underhill has not helped the state of my breeches, nor has kneeling on the ground in front of Callingham. She, conversely, is dressed today in watered dusty pink silk, artificially stiffened and made glossy by some method that Aminta might be able to explain. 'Lutestring'—that's what I think the fabric's called. I do not feel it would stand much rain. The sleeves terminate just above her elbows in a mass of Brussels lace. There is also lace at her shoulders and a large diamond and sapphire brooch pinned to the bust. The canons of the cathedral must wonder what sort of exotic bird has landed amidst the dowdy crows that normally wander the close.

'You are residing here?' I ask.

'The house is small but convenient,' she says. 'It was commandeered for me. The owner was not happy, but he has been promised a good rental, which may compensate him a little if it is ever paid. The King and Queen are at another house in the city on similar terms. I think the city is already tiring of the novelty of having the court in its midst. Let's walk a little, John.'

She takes my arm and the soiled wool of my doublet brushes against the delicate lutestring. She does not seem to mind.

'I am told that Mr Underhill did not reach Salisbury after all,' she says. 'Or at least, he is not with you.'

'He met with an accident on the way,' I say.

She nods. 'But it was reported to me that he did not have the rest of the Duke's letter.'

'Who reported it?'

'A man named Callingham. An actor. I think you know him. I sent him back to find you. His brother-in-law owns an inn on the London Road. He was to wait for you there.'

'He's dead,' I say. 'Or very likely to be by now. He has the Plague.'

I see her shudder. She's hoped she'd left that behind. She's already wondering if the court have brought the Plague with them, along with their perfumes and finery, and calculating when they'll need to pack their bags again and fly even deeper into the country. She opens her mouth and I wonder if she is about to express sorrow at Callingham's passing. He was, in his day, an actor of some talent as well as being a ruthless assassin. He deserves to be remembered. I wait to hear what she will say.

'But you do have it, don't you, John?' she says. 'You have the rest of the letter?'

'I don't even know what the rest of the message consists of,' I say. 'Mr Pepys said I wouldn't recognise it if I saw it. Could it be something that is not obviously part of the letter—a ring, for example...?'

'A ring?' she looks at me incredulously. 'Why should it be a ring? What meaning would that have? You really don't know what you're looking for, do you?'

'No, because I've never seen it.'

She releases my arm. 'Let's stop playing games, shall we? You have what we want. Just tell me: what is your price?'

'Somebody is lying,' I say.

'Underhill swore to Callingham that he had the second part of the message in his possession, but he gave it up because he had no idea what it was. He thought it had gone for good, then he saw you with it.'

'Saw me with what?' I ask.

And then, of course, I realise. I've had it. Arlington's had it. Pepys has had it. We've all had it within our grasp. Underhill thought he'd stolen it back, but in the dark he took the wrong paper and it cost him his life.

'I've no idea what you mean, my Lady,' I say. 'Now, if you will excuse me, I'll return to my inn. I wish you a pleasant stroll.'

I arrive back at the inn out of breath, but I bound up to our chamber.

'A candle!' I say to Aminta. 'Do we still have a candle in the room?'

'It's light enough to see without,' says Aminta, 'and has been these last two hours. But there's the remains of last night's candle in the stick over there on the mantelpiece.'

I take Arlington's letter from one pocket and my tinderbox from the other.

'You plan to burn Lord Arlington's letter?' she says.

'No,' I say, trying to get a spark. 'This is what everyone has been searching for.'

'The letter permitting you to kill Underhill? That will no longer be of any use to anyone.'

'I gave Arlington the paper on which it is written,' I say.

'And?'

'And, it was the sheet of paper that was tucked duplicitously inside the doublet of Underhill's landlord when we found him at the pest house.'

'Yes, I remember. It was just a blank sheet of paper with some dark red wax attached.'

'That's all we thought it was,' I say. 'But Underhill didn't just use any old sheet of paper. This was originally *around* the enigmatic letter from the Duke that Arlington showed me. When I looked at the brief coded letter in Arlington's office, there was no trace of sealing wax on it. But Underhill told us that he had *carefully eased the seal away*. So what we were looking at then must have previously been enclosed in something else that *was* sealed. In other words, this paper here. Underhill decided the apparently redundant envelope would make an excellent decoy, and stuffed it in his landlord's doublet. It was only later, when Pepys confirmed there was a second part of the letter, that Underhill realised that the outer cover might possibly have been more than it seemed; but he assumed it must have been long since buried. Then, when he went through my bag, he noticed the distinctive dark red wax on Arlington's letter and started to wonder if the paper hadn't survived after all. Hence his trying to steal it back to confirm his suspicions. *But, in the dark, he took the wrong paper.*'

My flint finally sparks and catches the tinder. I blow on it for all I am worth and soon have a small flame to light the candle. I hold Arlington's letter close to the flame, but not too close. Brown writing starts to appear behind the black of Arlington's authorisation.

'Invisible ink,' says Aminta.

'Lemon juice most likely,' I say.

I work the flame carefully down the page. The slightest slip and the whole thing may go up in smoke. That would be a shame when so many have died for it.

After a couple of passes the writing is as clear as it will ever be. It makes no sense, but I suspect that, like the first part of the letter, it is a simple substitution code that will not be difficult to break.

Nor is it. Fifteen minutes later I am holding the translation in my hand and Aminta and I are rereading it together.

'Well,' I say. 'I was expecting to discover that the Duke was corresponding with the King of France and offering to declare himself a Catholic and hand over the country to France in exchange for cash and military help to overthrow his brother. But that's not it at all.'

'No,' says Aminta. 'It's not the Duke making the offer to the French. It's King Charles himself. The King is engaging himself to betray the whole country in exchange for cash from the French. How fortunate that you didn't blunder in and tell him that you knew all about it. Odds fish, as his Majesty would say. We really haven't been charging anything like enough for this job.'

CHAPTER

29

I have tracked Arlington down. He too has left London and reached Salisbury before me, not having had to spend time in a cellar in Hampshire en route. Like Lady Castlemaine, and unlike me, he brings a touch of urban sophistication to provincial Salisbury. His suit is glossy and dark grey. His linen is clean. His nose patch glistens.

He holds the original letter and the plain English version in front of him, frowning. 'So Underhill abandoned the paper not knowing what it was? Had you told me where this was from when you gave it me...?'

'You might have objected to its having been in the pest house. Did you suspect that these were the true contents of the message?' I ask.

'I knew that the King was fearful he might suffer the same fate as his father—that he might one day face an armed rebellion—especially if he became a Catholic, as he has contemplated doing. I was not aware that he would offer precisely this alliance with King Louis in return for a pension and military help against his own people if needed.'

'But you knew he might offer something like this?'

'It was in his mind, certainly.'

'So, the French King gets an alliance against the Dutch. Our own King gets cash and promises to declare his new faith at once, if the rest is agreed.'

'I was not consulted on the detail,' says Arlington. 'Indeed, what is proposed would precipitate the very crisis that His Majesty seeks to avoid—a bloody revolution. But it is certainly helpful to know that that is what the King wants.'

'It would have been helpful if you had told me more,' I say.

'I told you all you needed to know,' says Arlington. 'Underhill had overheard much of the discussion that preceded this offer— what I could not be sure of was just how much he had heard or understood. So, for the King's sake, I needed to find out what Underhill knew or silence him. Or both, preferably. Morland's plan of transporting him to a distant place, where he could be questioned more privately and then put out of the way, was a good one. Underhill himself proposed you as an escort. Had you followed my instructions to the letter, you would have come to no harm.'

'Perhaps you should have also told the Duke of Buckingham that. His intervention, through Callingham, could have wrecked your plan and had me shot.'

'A small oversight on Morland's part. I shall admonish him on my return to London. However, I am grateful to you, Mr Grey. It has all worked out very well. I have the letter. Underhill cannot reveal what he knew. And I now know something that the Duke of Buckingham and the King's principal mistress do not. The question is, what do I do with that information?'

'You could foil the King's plot against his own people.'

'Yes, I suppose I could, if all else failed.'

'Well, as you say, the information and letter are yours and that is the end of the matter. I think that, even though Underhill is buried in a Hampshire churchyard, I have fulfilled the terms of my contract by preventing his divulging what he knew. I request payment of the two hundred Pounds, plus expenses, for Underhill, and a further hundred Pounds for the inconvenience of being imprisoned in a cellar.'

'That is not unreasonable. You could have asked for more.'

I shake my head. 'I try to give good service for what I charge.'

'You have done well, Mr Grey. You have helped me a great deal. You see, when you are serving princes, you need not only to note carefully what they say, but to anticipate what they may later *think* they have said. That is the art of a courtier. That is how we advance our affairs. And now I know what His Majesty wishes. Exactly what he is offering would not do at all—it is as well that the letter never reached the French Ambassador. But with some variations…in the fullness of time…and perhaps in discussion with the King's sister in Paris… Yes, I can see that something might be done to arrange an alliance on acceptable terms. Something that would conform to his conscience and his purse but not lead to an unnecessary rebellion.'

'Shall I apply to Sir Samuel Morland for payment?' I ask.

Arlington considers. 'Ah yes, *Sir* Samuel. I suppose that you yourself would not like a knighthood?' he asks. 'In lieu of payment? My budget, as I've said, is not large.'

'No,' I say. 'I'll take the cash. I can't give my clerk a shilling in the Pound on a knighthood.'

'That's a pity,' he says. 'Sir John Grey, Knight. Or even, Sir John Grey, Baronet. That has a pleasant ring to it.'

'Three hundred Pounds also sounds sweet to the ear.'

'The lady you were with—Aminta Pole. Would she not like her husband to have a title?'

Well, perhaps, if such a thing were possible. But it isn't. It will never be possible. I have no need of a title.

'I'm sure she'll find such a husband,' I say. 'They are not in short supply.'

'Very well,' he says. 'Tell Morland to pay you.'

Arlington folds the letter and places it in his pocket. It is his. He bows. I bow. The contract is fulfilled.

We find the house by the cathedral without difficulty. The woman looks at me and Aminta and then frowns when she sees the child whose hands we are holding.

'But surely that can't be Sophia?'

'Why not?' asks Sophia. 'It's who I've always been.'

'Praise be to God,' she says. 'She is safe.'

'I cannot promise the same for the rest of her family,' I say. 'Lady Pole left them locked into their house in the City. I pray that they are spared, but...'

The woman shakes her head. 'I had a letter from them yesterday,' she says. 'They escaped, all of them, soon after they gave you Sophia. They are in Essex, where there is no Plague at present. I suppose you wouldn't like to take Sophia to Saffron Walden?'

'That's right,' I say. 'We wouldn't.'

As we return to the inn, Aminta takes my arm and we walk through the streets like the husband and wife our pass claims we are.

'So, we are three hundred Pounds better off,' I say, 'of which three hundred shillings, that is to say fifteen Pounds, is yours.'

'Let's call it twenty Pounds,' says Aminta. 'It's a nicer number.'

'Very well,' I say, making a mental note to pay Will the same, if he is still alive.

'I already miss Sophia,' says Aminta, drawing me closer to her. 'I miss being her mother. Do you miss being her horse?'

'It seems odd being able to walk unencumbered,' I say.

'Wouldn't you like children of your own?'

She is very close to me. Her cheek is almost resting on my shoulder.

'I haven't thought about it,' I say.

She releases my arm. 'So, you intend to remain single? Being Arlington's creature is enough for you? You have no wish to marry? If you found the right girl? Attractive, intelligent and very literate? A widow possibly, of good pedigree? With, say, as much as twenty Pounds of her own money?'

We are standing in the cathedral close. The trees here are a rich dark green against the clear blue sky. The great spire rises majestically in all its ancient glory. The sun caresses my cheek. It is clear to me that now is the moment. I can simply accept my mother's assurances, and indeed her calculations, which may after all be correct. If I ignore my nagging doubts and my mother's final qualifying remarks that it wouldn't matter because nobody would know, if I say the right thing now, I can ensure that my life will never quite be the same again. It will in fact be magnificent. But I need to say it now before I start to speculate again on whether Aminta may after all be my half-sister. Perhaps the thing I want most in the world is actually possible? I open my mouth, but then the bells all over Salisbury start to ring the hour. Aminta laughs. I laugh. We both wait for them to finish.

'Did you want to say something to me?' she asks.

I look at her. She is beautiful, kind and immensely talented. She could have any man in London. She could marry a Duke. Why would she want me, without even a knighthood? A man who is only a hurried calculation away from being her half-brother? Of course I can't marry her. You know that as well as I do.

'We should get some dinner,' I say. 'Then I need to hire a carriage to take us back to London. We can't both travel home on Pepys's horse.'

CHAPTER 30

'It's good to have you back, Mr Grey,' says Will, pocketing twenty of the sovereigns that Morland has paid me.

'It's good to be back, Will,' I say. 'I need to start work on Ruggles's action against his uncles. There are some precedents I'll need to check.'

'No need,' says Will.

'Case settled out of court?'

'Dead of the Plague. It's reached Essex. They didn't pray hard enough. But not to worry, sir. His heirs have taken the matter up. As soon as his will is proved, they'll be along to speak to you. Unless they die too, in which eventuality I think the three bastards may have a good case.'

'There's always work, eh, Will?'

'Indeed, Mr Grey. People die, but their money lives on. There's also a letter from your mother. I took the liberty of reading it in case action was needed. Now that the Plague has reached Essex, she and your stepfather have left for the north of England. She very much hopes you have made Lady Pole's acquaintance again and spoken to her as you should. How is my Lady? Is she pleased to be home?'

'She is well. She didn't return to London with me. Said in the end she'd rather not. She's also travelled north to some cousins up in Westmorland. She'll stay until the Plague abates and the theatres reopen.'

'That's a pity, Mr Grey. I've always thought well of Lady Pole. Charming. Beautiful. Intelligent. And I know she likes you. But she'll be back. Then you'll have your chance.'

I look out of my casement window. A warm breeze is blowing. Down in Lincoln's Inn Fields the grass is a little browner, a little more worn than it was when I last observed it. A Plague doctor scuttles along, a leather hat perched precariously above his beaked face. A naked man, carrying a brazier of burning charcoal on his head, is walking along one of the paths. Nobody pays him any attention. Why would you?

'I lost my chance long ago,' I say.

Will looks at me, puzzled. 'I'll fetch you some wine then, sir?'

'Thank you, Will. I'd like that,' I say.

From My Lady Pole's Esteemed Poem,

The Puritaniad

Envoi—to the Reader

Job, as you know, protested not
When leprosy was made his lot;
He bore all God's afflictions well,
Just as the story books retell
Griselda's patience when her Lord
Had both her children sent abroad
And told her they'd be put to death
(Though in Bologna both drew breath)
Then ordered her to be bridesmaid
To his new wife… No, I'm afraid
That long before his trick's revealed
As just a test, I'd have *him* killed.
You say I fail? But you must see
That type of husband's not for me.
Still less am I a wife who'd wait
For twelve long years to learn my fate.
But you are made of sterner stuff
You'd match Griselda well enough
In trials of patience, for I see
You've stomached this long history.
You've followed us where'er we've travelled
Observed as all our schemes unravelled,
Watched over us in these Plague times
Forgiven us for doubtful rhyme
One thing remains and that is to
Wish you in turn, Godspeed. Adieu!

NOTES AND ACKNOWLEDGEMENTS

A recent reviewer on Amazon (I think), observing the inordinate length of my acknowledgements in a previous volume in this series, wrote that I obviously didn't know much about the period because I'd had to read so many books. I have taken this constructive criticism to heart. I hope it will be clear to all how little research I have done this time.

Those of you who have read up on the 1660s, on the other hand, will be aware that it is the stranger parts of this book that are true and the duller ones that I have invented.

The 1660s were a time of excess. It was not an age that was honest or prudent or in any way moral. It was of course religious in a conventional way—people attended church and acknowledged God and the scriptures in their conversations in a way that we would blush to do now. It was also God-fearing in the most literal sense: people believed that Hell presented a real and present danger and that eventually they would all have to answer for their actions. But at the same time they clearly thought that God allowed them a great deal of latitude on a day-to-day basis. A gold-plated seam of corruption ran from the very top of society to the very bottom.

The murder of Charles Fincham and the loss of the Duke's letter are fictional. But the broad terms of the deal that Charles II was offering in the letter are true, and resulted, a few years later in 1670, in the Secret Treaty of Dover. Under this agreement, largely brokered by Arlington and Charles's sister Minette, the King agreed to declare himself a Catholic in return for cash and military assistance from the French. It was by any standards an extraordinary undertaking, but the most remarkable thing of all about the Secret Treaty was that it remained a secret until the nineteenth century—most of Charles's ministers remained completely unaware of its existence. That Charles took the money but reneged on other parts of the deal does not in any sense represent him in a better light.

It was, however, very much in keeping with the spirit of the age. Arlington was offered a reward of ten thousand crowns by the French for his part in the deception and initially turned it down—his wife later told the French Ambassador that she'd have the money if nobody else wanted it. Pepys records in his diary frequent protestations of his devotion to the King's service and also shamelessly lists the bribes that he accepted from naval contractors. Guards, Searchers of the Dead and parish clerks accepted small sums of money from all and sundry to cover up cases of the Plague. Everyone was at it. It was just that the King could command a higher price than other people.

The factions within government were also much as I describe. Clarendon had been a major force throughout Charles's long exile and during the first years of his reign, strengthened by the marriage of his daughter to James, Duke of York (the future James II). But a younger group of courtiers, including Arlington, Buckingham and Clifford, were ready to oust him. Charles's mistress, Lady Castlemaine (later Duchess of Cleveland) was also an enemy of Clarendon's. Her constant insults prompted one of his most famous retorts: 'Madam, pray remember that if you live, you will also be old'. The military setbacks of the Second Anglo-Dutch War made Clarendon unpopular and allowed his enemies to impeach him. He was eventually forced into exile in 1667. He was succeeded by the infamous Cabal of Arlington, Buckingham, Ashley and Lauderdale, with Clifford as their 'Bribe Master General'. Lady Castlemaine did indeed grow old and was cast aside by the King in 1673, though they were later reconciled and she eventually outlived him by almost twenty-five years. Her interest in good-looking actors continued well into middle age—she had a child by Cardonell Goodman in 1685, to add to five children by the King and one by John Churchill, the future Duke of Marlborough. Her many descendants include Diana, Princess of Wales, Nancy Mitford and Bertrand Russell.

My description of the hardships of travel during the Plague may also seem exaggerated, but they are borne out by, for example, Defoe's *A Journal of the Plague Year* and other contemporary or near-contemporary sources. Towns and villages did resist the flow of refugees from London, turning them back or making them trek through the fields. They did refuse them food. They did padlock wells to prevent them drinking. Many starved before they reached their destinations. But travel was possible. During July and August 1665, Pepys was constantly on the move between London and Hampton Court and Woolwich and Greenwich. He does not complain of any checks or delays, but he did sometimes have to lie about where he was from. He commented that the Plague was making people as cruel as dogs to each other. Strangely I wrote a great deal of this at a time when migrants were streaming across Europe—fleeing war, on this occasion, rather than Plague. But I must leave it to you to draw such parallels as you wish—history, whether opting for farce or tragedy, never quite repeats itself, whatever Marx thought.

I have to confess that Pepys's part in the action is unashamed fiction. His movements are so well recorded day by day that he couldn't possibly have been where I say he was. Unless he lied in his diary, of course. But he was certainly loyal to the Duke of York (and to his immediate superior, Lord Sandwich), energetic enough to undertake such a journey, and not averse to striking a few blows when he could get away with it, as his servants knew.

Some of the odder facts I couldn't have made up if I'd tried—for example, secret documents being filed under the names of Roman emperors, or Arlington's nose patch, or naked men wandering the streets with braziers of burning charcoal on their heads, or people walking from bed to bed in the pest house because there was no space to walk on the floor. These things are true, or at least were recorded as facts in contemporary sources—which I do realise is not necessarily the same thing. But, reviewers please note, I deny researching any of it.

I must as ever thank the many people who helped me write this, including my wife Ann, my editor Krystyna Green (and the whole team at Little, Brown), my energetic and resourceful agent, David Headley (and his team at DHH), Dea Parkin at the CWA (for rescuing me)—and of course the British Library, where I had a coffee from time to time.